THE
VIRGIN SOLDIERS

Leslie Thomas

arrow books

Reissued by Arrow Books in 2005

1 3 5 7 9 10 8 6 4 2

First published in the United Kingdom in 1966 by
Constable and Co. Ltd 1966

Arrow Books
The Random House Group Limited
20 Vauxhall Bridge Road, London, SW1V 2SA

Random House Australia (Pty) Limited
20 Alfred Street, Milsons Point, Sydney,
New South Wales 2061, Australia

Random House New Zealand Limited
18 Poland Road, Glenfield
Auckland 10, New Zealand

Random House (Pty) Limited
Isle of Houghton, Corner Boundary Road & Carse O'Gowrie,
Houghton, 2198, South Africa

The Random House Group Limited Reg. No. 954009

www.randomhouse.co.uk

A CIP catalogue record for this book is available from the British Library

Papers used by Random House are natural, recyclable products
made from wood grown in sustainable forests. The manufacturing
processes conform to the environmental regulations of the country of origin

ISBN 0 09 949003 X

Typeset by SX Composing DTP, Rayleigh, Essex
Printed and bound in Great Britain by
Cox & Wyman Ltd, Reading, Berkshire

Deciated to my wife
Maureen
with the assurance that
hardly any of this happened to me

During the years 1948–1952
the Communist guerrilla war in Malaya
kept a whole British army occupied.
Some of this army were good soldiers;
others were not.

1

About five-thirty enough light had leaked into the guardroom for Brigg to see his boots. They were in their usual place, on his feet, standing up like two bevelled tombstones, leaning slightly inwards, at the bottom of the camp-bed. The sweat had gone cold inside them.

'There's nothing I hate more than cold sweat in my boots,' he remarked to Tasker, the sentry, who was having an underhand drag by the monsoon ditch. 'It makes you feel as though you're dead.' Brigg rolled off the bed and went to the door.

'Warm it up then,' suggested Tasker. 'Get some tea.'

'I was,' said Brigg. He picked up the bucket and went out. It was the half-dark, the time when the dogs in the village were moving about and sounding off with the cockerels, tugging people from dreams and nightmares. The tufts of the two big palms by the top barrack block were becoming clear against the whiter eastern sky like spiders impaled on sticks.

Now there was not so much talking among the crickets; the bullfrogs burped less.

It was getting towards day.

In the early hours it had rained again, and the rain was lying around waiting to be steamed up by the sun. Brigg kicked the solid bucket with the rim of his boot as he went along the road, partly for nothing, he told himself, and partly because they said that the Gurkha at the cookhouse gate was inclined to draw his *kukri* if you went along before daybreak and didn't make a noise. And once he'd got the thing out, the boys said, he had to draw blood. It was all tied up with honour.

When you came to consider it, thought Brigg, kicking the pail again, there was a distinct touch of military insanity in having a full-grown Gurkha with a sharp *kukri*, and an itchy *kukri* finger, guarding a cookhouse on Singapore Island. What was he doing? Stopping the terrorists getting at the apple crumble or the minced beef or the poison pie?

What's a full-grown Gurkha? he asked himself. None of them were full-grown. Small scraps of men, brown and mild. But they reckoned that when the Gurkhas caught a bandit up-country, they chopped him into little cubes about the size of an Oxo.

Once a whole group of them had an orgy right there at Panglin. It was their Christmas – the same sort of thing anyway – and about two hundred of them sat in their dining-hall for three days and got paralytic. They all danced. No women, just the little fellows, and then they started slicing the heads off live animals with their *kukris*. Some of the boys had looked over the fence into the yard and taken pictures. Lantry got the head of a goat flying through the air when one of the Gurkhas had chopped it off. And the goat's body was still standing up, astonished, just as though it still had a head fixed to it. It was about twenty seconds before the goat's body toppled over.

Brigg saw the dented roof of the Gurkha's hut on top of a shadow by the cookhouse gate. The Gurkha came out and Brigg said quickly: 'It's all right, Bongo. It's the guard. Just come for the tea.' He had slowed to a shuffle. 'Okay?' he said.

A fragment of worry flapped around within him for a moment over whether he should have called the Gurkha Bongo. Driscoll always did, but he wasn't Driscoll.

The Gurkha kept silent, but pushed up the pole that hung across the road to the cookhouse. Brigg shuffled in, still kicking the bucket with the side of his boot, to show himself that he had not been doing it because of the Gurkha, but just for nothing.

There was a furtive cookhouse private occupied over the tea boiler. Steam was writhing around him, pushing and squeezing from under his armpits as he stirred like a witch with a ladle. His head was indistinct in the cloud, but when he came out Brigg saw it was the one who never washed. He smiled at Brigg with the special smile of army cooks when they are stirring something. The secret smile that says they know there is a dead rat in it.

Brigg gave him the bucket without a word. He squirted it full of thick tea and Brigg returned down the road.

Now the slow light was strengthening and flooding the lower sky. There was a dip, a grass ravine, by the road, and some mist was crouching in the deepest part. Across it hung a wood bridge leading to the office blocks and the other buildings on the far bank.

At the root of the road were the little mountains that were the roofs of the Chinese village. Lights moved there now. There was scrubby jungle, still indistinct, to his right, and he could see one of the guards who had been at the reservoir and the water pipeline all night, coming down the path with a bucket.

Brigg did not look much of a soldier. But nor did many of the others. The legs of his green slacks ballooned at the tuck into his gaiters, forming two long peapods. Had he felt the necessity to check the number of his ribs he could have done so quite easily by counting them through his jacket. The jacket was a different green to his trousers. His black beret hung over the right side of his head like one ear of a spaniel.

There were times, in England, when he thought he caught women looking at him, but he was unsure whether it was because he was tall and hungry-looking, or whether they fancied him, or both. Once an eager, fleshy girl at a camp dance had told him he had deep eyes, but although he liked occasionally to think about this he did not set much store by it, because she had gone outside with a fat orderly room clerk.

Brigg carried his bucket to the armoury guard-house. Some of the tea panicked and jumped over the side, committing suicide in a dank monsoon ditch as he stepped across it. Driscoll, who was sergeant of the guard, came from the door as Brigg reached it. He had his towel across his shoulder, but he flicked it off when he saw the tea.

'Good. I'll stay,' he said. He turned back into the guardroom. He picked up his enamel mug from the folded blanket on the bunk. On the mug he had painted the badge of his *good* regiment, the one he was in before, so that everybody would know it was Driscoll's.

With some sergeants of the guard they could put out the lights at midnight, after the orderly officer had been around, and everyone could get a good night's sleep. Except Sergeant Wellbeloved, who kept everybody awake with his everlasting grind about what the Japs had done to him. And Driscoll. There was no sleeping with Driscoll either. You had to guard.

Driscoll was five-ten or around that, with a firm face, close fair hair, and a scar high on his cheekbone, which is a good place to have a scar if you've got to have one. His uniform fitted, uniquely in a garrison noted for its baggy shorts. A consignment of garments made by lunatic tailors had predictably found its way to Panglin three months before, and, as old stock was exchanged for new, a circus effect was gradually coming about throughout the ranks. But Driscoll's uniform fitted.

The Sergeant swallowed his tea and blew the steam from his mouth like cigarette smoke. 'Give it to the others,' he said. 'I was going to have a swill, but it's a bit late now. I've got to go and wake the little soldiers.'

No one at Panglin could play the bugle, and it was the job of the guard sergeant to wake each barrack room. Once, when an infantry regiment was in transit there, waiting to move up from Singapore into Malaya, reveille had been sounded by a shining bugler wearing a sash round his chest, red as the morning. Its call was wasted on the permanent Panglin troops because they had roused early and were standing in the warm, damp dawn, on the balconies, witnessing the martial novelty. Brigg had felt like a real soldier that day.

After the others on guard had taken their dippings from the tea bucket, Brigg bore it across the parade ground, around the hockey goalposts, and up the sounding stairs to the middle floor of Barrack Block Two. He trod along the concrete balcony, his boots repeating like double hammers, and through the centre double doors.

It was full morning now, but the daylight was dimmer in there. His bed was by the door. Sometimes at night he had to leap out and batten the door when a raiding wind came in off the South China Sea and howled through the palms and across the square. Two beds were rigged with droopy mosquito nets, green as mildew. The rest slept without them, bare backs, some pimpled and even now beginning the day's sweat, or lying straight out beneath the sheets like corpses.

Sandy Jacobs, a hairy Scots Jew, slept naked, transfixed across his bed like a specimen spider. Corporal Brook, a thin man who was mad, snored, vibrating the prim rimless spectacles pinching his nose.

Brigg clanked the tea bucket to the floor. He always managed to shout 'Gunfire!' as though it meant 'Action Stations!' even if it were only the army name for early tea. But, on this morning, the syllables had not formed before Driscoll came hooting through the door.

The Sergeant stamped up and down the lines of beds. 'Move!' he shouted. 'Mooooooooove! Come on! Hands off cocks and on with socks! Mooooooooove!'

Some rolled, some tumbled, some slithered from their beds with deep loathing. Some lay as though the finger of death were upon them.

Corporal Brook sat stark upright from his sheets, a frightened and frightening figure, white, thin and calling plaintively: 'What's the matter? What's the matter?'

Driscoll halted at his bedrail and inspected him coldly and closely. Brook trembled like Scrooge.

'The matter, Corporal?' Driscoll said. 'The matter is it's daylight. Daylight, Corporal! And you still live and breathe, though God knows how. Anyway you're here. So gettup!'

Dopily the others picked up their mugs and limped and stumbled towards Brigg's tea bucket. There would not be enough to go around. First was first. Mostly they were naked, some white, some off-white, the colour of fat, some iodine yellow with the insipid Singapore tan. Only Patsy Foster and little Sidney Villiers, two strange friends who held fingers because they were in love, wore issue pyjamas. Some of the others had towels

8

around their waists, but most of them did not bother.

Fenwick, who had the end bed of the first row, leaned towards his neighbour, Sinclair.

'Shout at me,' he said eagerly. 'A good shout.'

'Not again,' said Sinclair wrinkling his face behind his glasses.

'I *couldn't* hear you,' said Fenwick triumphantly. 'Hardly, anyway. Try again. Louder. Through the alphabet.'

Sinclair said: 'A-B-C-D-E-F-G – how much more?'

'A few more.'

'H-I-J-K – and that's the lot. Here's Driscoll.'

The Sergeant went by. Fenwick said, 'I'm getting stone deaf, son. Stone bloody deaf. I'll be home to dear old England soon. Medical discharge.'

Sinclair screwed up his face again. He wanted to get home – they all did – but he couldn't see the point of getting yourself dead deaf to do it. Every evening Fenwick went to the swimming pool and kept his ears as much as possible under water, so that the heavy chlorine washed in and out. Every dip ravaged the tunnels of his head more dangerously, and there were nights when he cried with ear-ache. But soon, he was sure, the reward would come with a medical repatriation to England.

The barrack room was moving into its normal primary activity. The showers and the flushes were gushing outside, blankets were folded at the ends of beds and best boots placed one each side in the instructed manner. A table tennis ball plinked metallically against the distant wall, as it did every day, flicked there with monotonous skill by Gravy Browning, a lance-corporal for whom table tennis was meat, drink, work, recreation, the subject of dreams, and sexual fulfilment all in one. He was in that year's Singapore singles final.

Driscoll had stamped his circle, gone to his room, which was on the balcony, and returned to find one bed in the barrack room still silent and undisturbed. Its green mosquito net hung over it, giving it the solemnity of a catafalque. Driscoll leaned daintily, secretly as a mother, over the bed and raised the hem of the green net.

His tone was gently cajoling. Everyone stopped to watch. 'Private Lantry,' he whispered. 'Time for up. Horace, you're oversleeping. All your friends are awake, Horace.'

From the bed came a whimper and a stir. Lantry looked out like a bird from a nest.

'Are you awake, Horace?' breathed Driscoll.

Lantry blinked and looked closely at the Sergeant as though he were a stranger or a segment of a dream.

'GITTOUT!' roared the Sergeant, 'OUT! OUT! OUT!'

He grasped the mattress like one wrestler

grabbing another, and flung it from the iron bedstead with one throw. Lantry, tubby, white, and regularly creased like a ball of string, sat naked on the floor.

'Just getting up, Sergeant,' he protested affably.

'I know, son,' said Driscoll. 'I noticed. What've you got this bleeding thing rigged up for?'

Lantry gazed innocently upwards. 'It's on orders, Sergeant Driscoll,' he said. 'Every man must utilise his mosquito net.'

Impatiently Driscoll moved towards the door. 'Watch it,' he warned predictably. 'You'll be on a charge, son.'

Lantry waited until he was at a safe distance then called after him, but softly: 'Besides, it hides me from these others, and I *do* like to have a little play with myself in the night.'

It was very safe at Panglin. They saw action only with pens and ledgers, with Army Forms One to One Hundred Million. This was entered here, pay and allowances there, absent without leave, killed on active service. It all went down on paper smudged with indoor sweat at Panglin, recording a remote war that was only eight miles away across the Johore Causeway, where the real jungle began.

Across the strait that separated Singapore from

the Malaya mainland the Communist guerrillas occupied the thick jungle, ambushing, killing, keeping an entire British army fighting a war lost in undergrowth and giant trees.

But Panglin, safe on the island, ten miles from Singapore City, was as peaceful as a suburb. The square barrack blocks sat in the sun all day, the army houses occupied the other side of the ravine, and the wooden bridge was between them. Lower down the road was the Chinese and Malay village, a clamorous place of mud and music, stalls, eating-places, stray dogs, blind beggars, and medicine men who would slash their arms in public and heal them immediately with a magic ointment. Between the army houses and the village was the garrison laundry, peopled by busy Chinese men in vests and little shorts, the offices where the Panglin soldiers worked, and the military swimming pool flanking the green sports ground.

It rained a lot, and steamed when the sun shone. It was always hot. But it was safe.

Tasker had composed a song, which they sang in lorries on the way to football matches, all about the Filing Cabinet Cavalry. One of its lines indicated that at Panglin they would rather fornicate than fight, and there was much truth in it, except that most of them never got around to fornicating either.

The military flotsam of half the British army around the world found its way, almost mystically, to Panglin. It was like elephants going home to die. They had limped in, staggered in, come in on eight toes, and in one case eleven; drifted, dragged and drooled in. They had come in shaking but sober, determined but drunk, lost, stolen and strayed. Men arrived at Panglin who had been mislaid by the army. They came with little chits, certificates and notes, from sympathetic medical officers in many places, with transfers from apoplectic commanding officers who couldn't stand the sight of them any more. They came sometimes with hope for themselves, if no one else, to finish their time, or to put the months and years by in dreadful safe boredom marked only by the scratching of pens on ledgers as other men's lives and occasionally deaths went down in military records.

The conscripts, apart from being idle, homesick, afraid, uninterested, hot, sweating, bored, oversexed and undersatisfied, were in better condition. Their complaints did, at least, include some active ones, so they were not in the same state of decay as many of the regular soldiers.

Fighting soldiers from up-country, the Gurkhas and infantrymen arrived at Panglin sometimes in transit, sometimes for rest. The garrison soldiers would examine them with curiosity, at a distance, as though looking for bullet holes, and grin and say among themselves that it took brains to do deskwork; anyone could be a dumb infantryman. There was a dullness about the infantrymen's eyes, a redness about their faces, so that they looked like labourers or country boys.

At Panglin the soldiers had the pale, yellow tan of steamy Singapore Island and days spent in offices where the secure, screaming boredom of hours clicking and clerking under a hot iron roof, with Wednesday afternoons off, was rarely broken by anything more enervating than the hope of pinching the arse of one of the Chinese civilian girl clerks in the mid-morning ritual queue for the tea-wagon.

By eight o'clock the four companies were on the parade ground. It was hard and sharp white, curiously like ice, because the sun had cleared the buildings and was now directly on the concrete. Brigg came out of the shower behind the barrack room, knotted a towel around him, and went to stand in a slice of sunlight on the balcony.

He heard Driscoll laughing and saw that he had come from his room at the end and was leaning on the door-frame, naked except for his beret and socks.

The Sergeant moved forward and leaned on the pipe-rail of the balcony, considering, with disgust, the parade ground and the soldiers.

'The echelons of power,' he breathed. 'See the might of Britain's Army in foreign parts. For King and Country. With men like this, how can we fail?'

Brigg shuffled to the rail and bent over it. Directly below, the mad Corporal Brook was squeaking his wan and sickly section to attention.

Brigg said, 'Well, it's not supposed to be the Coldstream Guards, is it?'

Driscoll turned and suddenly shouted at him: 'It's the Royal Army Crap Corps! Look at it! For God's sake, look! Kids who can't get home to Mum quick enough, and misfits – sick and stupid bastards, hanging on because it's all they have and they haven't got anywhere else to live.

'Go on, look! You don't see an army, do you? They're not soldiers. They're a freak show.'

He calmed quickly and turned his naked belly to the parapet again. Quietly he said: 'Just take a look at the Corporal we all love. Do you know why Corporal Brook is mouthing like that and nothing's coming out? D'you know? Well, I'll tell you why. It's because he's got a blockage. Up here, in his nut.' Driscoll tapped his own head spitefully. 'Yes, no kidding. Up here. The poor sod is incapable of getting the next order out. He knows what it should be – he *knows* all right – but he can't say it. So he's stuck there. Like a bleeding goldfish.'

Deliberately Driscoll leaned over the rail. The wordless, panicked, white Corporal Brook was immediately below. 'Stand aaart ease!' bellowed Driscoll.

The section stood at ease. Brook gave a jump of terror as though the message had come from the sky. He looked and saw Driscoll, and with relief, shame and anger, mumbled: 'Yes, that's right. Stand at ease.'

Brigg, laughing without sound, backed away from the rail so that Brook would not see him.

Once, at night, the Corporal had sidled to his bed like an old aunt and sublimely detailed how he was an illegitimate son of the peerage, but that he did not tell everyone because it was not the sort of thing he wanted to get around.

Driscoll continued his commentary, the complaints drifting towards Briggs, but only casually, as though the Sergeant did not care whether he was getting them or not.

'Now, *who* would do that?' he whispered in disbelief. Then louder: 'Who in God's name would *do* that? Put Cutler behind Forsyth? But they *can't*. Surely even they must realise how it looks. I mean, they know Cutler's got a diseased thigh and he hangs over to the right. But if that's not bad enough, they have to put Forsyth in the rank behind him, and he's got amnesia or dreaded pox or something nasty in his left hip, and he's leaning the other way! It's horrible. Horrible. Don't they know? Can't they see. It's a carnival, not a parade.' He swore viciously but quietly to himself.

Brigg looked up from examining Cutler and Forsyth, their opposite arms hanging limply as they marched, like men fishing from two sides of a boat.

'Observe Sinclair,' said Driscoll. 'See the damp look on his face? He is dreaming about trains. Trains! He's drilling, and his mind's on railway engines. I wouldn't mind, I wouldn't complain a bit, if he had incest or something that mattered on his mind, but it's not. It's bloody engine numbers and which chuff-chuff has the biggest and the littlest wheels.'

Brigg knew the analysis was sound. Sinclair hated the army even more than most of them, and flew away from it often by closing his eyes and arriving at platform nine, Euston, with the steam and the grinding wheels, and the handsome engines. They were the things, the real stuff, he said, that counted. He could also do it with his eyes open, as he was now.

On his own, Brigg began playing Driscoll's game. He counted first the men who wore glasses. There were fifty-two out of one hundred and sixty, including two pairs with yellow lenses. Seven of the N.C.O.s wore them and all of the officers but three. In addition there were minor psychiatric cases, men with fingers or toes missing, men with ruptures, bald men, one of them aged twenty-two, those who were visited by deafness, and many who had curses, the details of which they preferred to keep to themselves. There were also two members of the unit who were each only capable of vision in one eye. One of these was the Commanding officer, Colonel Wilfred Bromley Pickering, and the other a regular lance-corporal called Hackett.

In the dull, hot, everyday life of the garrison, there were few more stimulating experiences than witnessing Hackett march to his commander, each salute, and, in a stretched moment of aching suspense, each try to focus the other with his active eye.

Walking out of the sun, Brigg felt the shadows flow cold across his shoulders and neck. He sat on the side of his bed, by the double door, and began to polish his boots with no enthusiasm. Being on guard meant he was excused the morning muster, but he still had to be in the office at eight-thirty. He could see Driscoll on the balcony rail, and Driscoll could see him cleaning his boots.

'In Private Longley,' said Driscoll, unhurried, like a medical lecturer, 'we have a unique physical oddity. Even for this place. Unique. He is the very opposite to a hunchback. He is a hunchfront! Just see that pigeon chest. It's forcing his head back. And here . . . oh, now this is really it . . . Here they are, top of the circus bill.'

Brigg got up and with his left boot still over his hand walked into the streak of sun again. He saw what Driscoll meant. Rolling along, now directly beneath him, like two benign, green elephants, were Sergeant Organ and Sergeant Fisher.

'At last night's weigh-in,' recited Driscoll, 'it was twenty-two stone to Herbie Fisher, and Fred Organ – he can't help his name, poor bastard – was twenty-one. I know, I'm not kidding, because I was there when they were talking about it like a couple of poncing chorus-girls. "You know, Herbie, I think I'm losing a little bit." "I reckon you are, too, Fred, and I am too, I'm sure of it." God, you should have heard them.

'I mean – look! Look! Great pounding slobs. You'd think the army would have enough pride to pension them off, wouldn't you? But no, they send them abroad where all the bongos can laugh at them too. And they keep providing great bales of cloth for special uniforms for them, and no shorts, because that would be too hilarious, and on top of that size eighteen boots and reinforced beds. Jesus help us! How can men get like that and keep their self-

19

respect? And they quarrel like a pair of fashion models. I heard Fred call Herbie "Fatty" once. Fatty!'

Brigg turned and went back to his bed. He sat down, his towel hung across his knees, and spat on the toecaps of his boots. Driscoll, who somehow did not look ridiculous even if he was wearing only his socks and his beret, half turned.

As he looked down intently at the dull black toecap gradually coming to a reluctant shine, Brigg guessed what was coming next. He did not raise his head, and Driscoll said: 'And then there's your little bunch.'

Still looking down, Brigg said tonelessly: 'We don't want to be here.'

'What sort of an answer is that?' rasped Driscoll. He mimicked: '"We don't want to be here." I don't suppose the poor buggers who built the Burma Railway for the Japs wanted to be there either.'

Nor all the dead men we left lying around outside Caen, he thought, but he didn't say it because he'd killed three of them by mistake with his own bren gun.

Instead he said: 'Pale little ninnies, bleating and moaning and crossing off the dates on your going-home calendars, and getting that Chink in the village to make you swank suits. You can't wait to get home to Mum, can you? You get out here and the first thing you want to do is to go home.'

Brigg thought he had finished, but he hadn't. 'But when you *do* get home,' he said. 'Then it will be different. On Saturdays with the girls. "I was out in Malaya. Murder out there. Stinking hot and those Communist bandits . . ." I can hear all you little bastards now.'

Driscoll was riling him, so he got up and went through the barrack room to the lavatory. He sat down and thought how true it was. When they got home he knew just how it would be. They would go around like proud little fighters, armed to the teeth with lies. Their stories would be as good as the next man's, even if he had spent his National Service with swamps and fear and true death waiting every day and night.

Some of Panglin's clerks, whose conscript years had been scratched and blotted away on wooden desks, had gone to the village tailor and been fitted with splendid uniforms for the day when they arrived home. They were of smooth, lime, slime green, and they had fancy flashes and impressive insignia, and MALAYA in yellow letters across the shoulder. The fragile, sere, rickety virgin soldiers of the hopeless garrison became stern, strong, eye-catching warriors, once they had reached dear old England and safety. The uniforms cost forty dollars and they could only be worn for the two weeks of terminal leave. But what glory.

Driscoll heard him pull the chain and turned and waited for him to come out. But the Sergeant changed his mind about talking and returned to watching the parade. Brigg walked through the rows of beds, got to his own, and began to dress. He put on his socks and boots first and then his drawers cellular. He caught a sudden appearance of himself in the full mirror at the end of the barrack room and confirmed that he looked long, white and ridiculous.

He had never had sex, and one of his most virulent fears was that he might, by some military mischance, get killed before he had known the experience. It was of huge importance, bigger, much bigger, than any of the other things he could think of living for, or, at least, that he would miss if he died. Not to know about it would be the ultimate, awful tragedy, far worse, for instance, than never knowing who your mother was.

Now, at nineteen, he did not know, and could not imagine, although he tried hard enough, what it actually felt like. When you did it, was it hard or easy, inspiring or merely perspiring, comforting or exhausting? Did it drift into boredom, as so many things did with use, or was it new and tremendous every time? Did it hurt first time? How quick or how slow was it? Was it HOT?

Once he had thought this was a private obsession. It seemed unreal and unreasonable that you could miss something so much when you did not even know what it was. Miss it more than you knew you would miss ordinary happiness. But he had come to realise that it was the same with the others.

Sometimes in the evenings, particularly on a Tuesday or a Wednesday when they did not have any money to go out, Tasker and Lantry would lie on their beds and see who could think the dirtiest thoughts and get the biggest and best erection.

They pursued this activity with fetid enthusiasm, sometimes beneath the sheets and sometimes above them, and viewed their finished achievements with academic, even medical, pride.

'That blue vein seems to be getting bigger,' Tasker would announce with concern. 'Perhaps I'd better show it to the medical officer.'

'Well, you've shown it to everyone else,' said Lantry amiably. 'Why miss him out?'

'No birds, though,' grumbled Tasker. 'There's never a woman seen this, except my Mum. I wonder if I'll ever get around to using it at all.' He turned over and regarded Lantry with ashen seriousness. 'I might get killed first. I mean it's possible, isn't it?'

Brigg, sitting on his bed writing to Joan, his girl, glanced up.

Lantry looked drawn, fully sharing the concern. They lay there with their sheets propped up like a small Arctic encampment.

'You could, you know,' said Lantry. 'Get killed, I mean. There's blokes getting killed out here regularly – well, up-country anyway, and it's no distance, is it? Those three last week. I saw their papers today and their numbers were all 2234-something, younger than us. It's a bit worrying.'

Panglin's only casualty of the Malaya Emergency had been a drunken cook-corporal who was decisively struck by a truck while staggering across the garrison road by moonlight and who was buried with solemnity and honours the following day. So the chances of Brigg, Tasker or Lantry being killed, as things were then, were remote. But only as remote, Brigg considered, as his chances of opening his sexual life.

There were the obvious ways, but he was reluctant to pay for it at the very start, because it might spoil it for good and it might become a habit. Besides which, it was expensive and unhealthy.

At Panglin there was a small unselect stable of W.R.A.C. girls, who could have been winners of a whole series of reverse beauty contests. They were the ugliest girls in the world, and even the humidity and the scarcity of the commodity could do nothing to make them un-ugly. Apart from this there was a downright jinx on some of them. A thirsting lance-corporal, a wine steward, was still doing three months after being apprehended while screwing one of them on the top table, at the officers' mess.

A few nights later a harmless mechanic, while quietly furgling another W.R.A.C. in the long elephant grass at the side of the garrison road, was accidently soaked when a passing Hussar paused to relieve himself.

Brigg considered the W.R.A.C.s out of the running for his virginity anyway. There remained the everyday Malay and Chinese girls, some of whom looked very soft and gentle, but these were very hard even to talk to. There were the officers' wives, grey and timid or rosy and exuberant, but all out of the question; and the N.C.O.s' wives, who were not really made for loving, even had they been willing.

There was also Phillipa, the twenty-year-old daughter of Regimental Sergeant-Major Raskin. Brigg did not dare think of her because when he did he had fiery, uncomfortable dreams, and had to take a walk on the balcony in the dark to cool off. Sometimes it took an hour or more.

2

When the Japanese had been in Panglin during the war they had taken some Australians down to the cricket field and murdered them. They had buried them in a flat, wide grave, and about three months after Brigg got to the garrison the grave was found.

First, two small Japanese cannon were dug up when some new drainage for the field was being dug. Colonel Bromley Pickering blinked his eye for joy, because they were the first guns that the unit had ever captured. He ordered all the red mud to be scraped from them; men on punishment fatigues had to do an hour's cleaning and polishing on them every evening.

When they were shining they were pulled along to the guardroom block and positioned ceremoniously outside. It was when the men at the cricket field had dug a few more yards along from where they found the guns that they turned the earth from the bodies.

It was a hot Wednesday. There had been no rain for three days and the earth was shrinking under the raw sun. Brigg, Tasker and Sandy Jacobs went to the swimming pool in the afternoon. It was cool and almost empty, because, although Wednesday was a half-day, most of the others reclined in sweat and sheets.

Some of the W.R.A.C. girls crouched in a coven along the side of the shallow end of the pool. George Fenwick was there too, submerging himself and his worsening ears in the water. Patsy Foster and Sidney Villiers squeaked and splashed each other in the kiddies' paddling pool.

A storm which had been building on top of the heat over the Johore Straits moved across in the late afternoon. The clouds lumbered low over the ragged palms, and on the northern horizon lightning cut the sky as it came to the boil.

They went from the pool across the cricket field because it was quicker. As they ran jerkily they saw Sergeant Wellbeloved on the other side of the field and heard him bawling to them. He was with the fatigue men who had been digging the drains.

'What the hell's he want?' said Jacobs, hesitating in his run. He glanced up at the bruised sky. 'We'll be caught in this.'

But Wellbeloved wanted them. They ran towards him over the coarse grass, close cut but still blowing with the low wind that was running before the storm. Out of habit, Tasker and Brigg avoided the cut wicket turf. Jacobs ran right across it because he was a Scots Jew and he did not play cricket.

Wellbeloved was swinging his arms like an orang-utan. He had a rancid face, and a yellow bald head.

His eyes were wide like eggs and his face was trembling. Around him the four fatigue men stood with their spades by the pit they had made. Three of them were holding their heads away, and the fourth stared at the swimming pool as though he had never noticed it before.

Now the rain was in big, individual bullets, warm, and softly hitting their heads and the grass. Brigg, Tasker and Jacobs ran up. Wellbeloved stood there, the rain running down his angry face. They knew they were meant to look into the pit and they did.

In there were the old bodies. The Australians. It seemed like a bad joke, but there was a decayed bush hat in there, and that is how they knew. The rest was mostly just bone and some bits of cloth. The skulls were separate and piled in one corner like coconuts.

It was hammering rain now. Pounding over their heads and necks, over the grass and the bright new earth, washing the bones in the pit a startling white and pattering on the skulls.

'See that!' Wellbeloved was screaming, as though they had done it. The rain was drumming on his baldness just as it was hitting the foreheads of the skulls. 'See that, you sickly bastards! That's what happened! That's how it was!'

At the first moment he had seen the disgusting thing in the pit, Brigg had jerked his head away and fixed his streaming eyes on a round, single tree at the end of the field and some birds that were arising from out of it as the rain became thick and frightened them.

Deliberately he remembered how the man in the next road in England used to free his racing pigeons early in the day and how they used to curl up into the sky, their silver wings and bellies finely outlined like fleur-de-lis on a shield. Wellbeloved was a shit. All they ever got from him was the war, the war, the bloody war. How the Japs had hung him up by his hair, which would be a hard job today, and all while *they* were guzzling orange juice and cod-liver oil.

He resented that they had not been there to share his war. On guard duty he would expect them to gather at his feet like Christ and the Disciples, and listen while he fought and lived it all again. Single-handed he had harried the Japs from the Singapore Jungle until at last they caught him and threw him into the awful place at Changi and all but murdered him a bit every day. Now, even now, he could not leave it alone, or leave them out of it with their glad memories of orange juice.

Ranting now, he stamped there on the field, with them standing sick and soaked, and the bush hat floating like a sailing boat on the gathering water in the pit.

'Don't you have it easy? Don't you now?' he stammered. 'And *stand to attention* when I speak! Soft, that's how you get it. Bloody cushy! And they're in there with their heads cut off. You should be in there with your heads cut off . . .'

He stopped, panting because of his shouting and the rain. It was so solid they could hardly see him now. 'Get out,' he said. 'Go on, go back and count how long you've got to do. Go on. Piss off!'

They went.

The man who used to fly the pigeons had them in a shed a few gardens down from Mrs. Pern's house in Willesden, London. Brigg's room was at the top of Mrs. Pern's and he could see them from his window, soaring free over the split mess of houses and factories, and thrown up sickeningly by the hot air coming from the cooling towers of the power stations.

In summer, with the air clear and ungritty early on they would rise in a squadron wing on wing, touching heaven and dipping and turning from it again. When the morning sky was dark they flung themselves into it just the same, their undersides as bright as paper.

Brigg had lodged at Mrs. Pern's for two years. His getting-up time was the same as the pigeons' freedom time, so he saw them often. It was a dusty three-floor house, full of stairs and locked cupboards. In the next room was an old, lonely Mick who liked to sing about Sligo at midnight and who threw his empties into the loft through a trap-door over his bed. Brigg had started counting the thuds and he knew that there were at least one hundred and seventy-two bottles lying up there with the darkness and the spiders.

Brigg had only known Joan an autumn and a winter, and the beginning of a spring. Often he had regretted that they had never had a summer together and done any rolling in the grass.

But usually on Sundays they would get a bus out to the beginning of the Chiltern Hills and spend the afternoon there.

In February they had walked up the shoulder of some rising fields, and along a ridge path to an old gate that looked as though it had died during the winter. The top bar was broken, and the next one, but the third held, and they sat on it, holding hands, and looked across the afternoon.

It was spoiled countryside but it had a certain beauty. There was a squat gasworks, but there was a river too, the Chess, flat as a sword, lying between cress beds in the bottom of the valley. There were ugly new houses, but old, strong trees keeping them in disorder, and patiently waiting for the spring that would give them leaves to hide the houses. There were builders' yards, but placid fields; a factory chimney, but a church steeple just as straight; a modern bus station, but seven grazing cows. There was not much colour, just a grey misty wash that darkened as the short afternoon went away. They sat there and watched a train going towards Amersham.

Joan had a bulky red coat and she turned its big collar up around her hair. She had a pale face, conditioned by a town's smoke, steam, and power station fall-out. The smoke had got around her eyes, years before, when she was small, and they were set deep in it. She had noticeable cheek-bones, well-formed, and thick, splendid hair. There was a slim hardness about her body. She was a nice girl. She was beautiful too. Brigg thought: a bit like a hawthorn in a shunting yard.

Brigg kissed her. 'When do you think you'll have to go?' she had said.

'I went to the Labour Exchange today,' he replied without looking at her. 'I asked them if they would hurry it up a bit.'

'Hurry it up?' she said, suddenly looking at him closely. 'What for?'

'Well, the quicker the better, after all,' he said guiltily. 'It's this hanging about gets me. And after all the sooner the army gets me, the sooner I'll be out.'

'Is that all?' she asked.

'Of course it is,' he said. 'And the fact that I'm fed up with work. When I get out I won't be going back there, I know.'

There was another train, its windows lit like a necklace, going along the valley. This time towards Wembley.

Joan said: 'Perhaps you won't be all that far. And it's only eighteen months. Most of them are home every week-end anyway. That Kenny Jones is in a nice little office in Aldershot. He's home more than he is in the army.'

I don't want Aldershot, Brigg thought. Nowhere in this country. Germany or Egypt or Hong Kong, if they liked, somewhere where you could have a good time and have some women.

He got up from the gate and took her hand. They went down the slope of the fields again and to the road and the bus stop. It was dark now and there was nobody there. Before the bus came along they stood and embraced and kissed.

Brigg told himself that they were in love, and one day, after he had lived and had some women, they would get married.

*

Phillipa Raskin, the daughter of Regimental Sergeant-Major Raskin, was a self-contained lunatic asylum, a young and lovely nut, a collection of quirks, paradoxes and agonies, a psychological fireworks display exploding mostly inward.

This was her own analysis, carefully thought out and explored, and terminated with the conclusion that there was nothing she could do to cure herself.

She had to work every day until three in the garrison kindergarten because her father said it was either that or clerking in the orderly room. He wasn't going to have that little cow sitting in front of a mirror all day.

On the other hand, she could have gone home to England to live with her Uncle Gregory, but he was a good deal randier than he ought to be at fifty and had fingers like red sausages. When she was thirteen he had got them around the top of her leg, above her school stocking, and she had spit expertly into his right eye, hitting him full in the ball before he could close his eyelid.

She preferred children to soldiers, although she disliked both, so she took the job in the kindergarten. It was disturbing, though not altogether surprising to her, how even a five-year-old boy managed to get his hands all over the place at once and show every sign of enjoying it.

At three, when she was finished for the day, it was

always an effort to climb the road from the compound with its rocking-horse and see-saw to her house, where her mother would be holding long conversations with the angel fish. The heat then lay heavy along the road, wearying her as she walked.

On this afternoon it was like pushing through a swamp, and uphill at that. She could feel her linen dress, wet and sucking at her backbone, and the sweat rolling down to her backside.

The white houses of the senior non-commissioned officers were strung over the top of the hill like the cockade of a hat. Her father's house was in the middle. She reached its door and gratefully felt the cool shadow of the porch touch her and close over her.

She had only turned her key and opened the door a fraction when she heard her mother's sherbet voice in deep discussion with the angel fish, who were kept in a tank in the sitting-room. Phillipa was glad her mother had them captive because there was an empty sameness about her conversation that was suited to angel fish.

Her mother repeated every sentence she said, with minor variations in key, annotation, content and emphasis with each repetition, so that talking with her was like keeping up with an auctioneer. Phillipa had been ordered by her father to speak to her mother, and she was afraid of her father, so she obeyed: when he was there anyway.

She was at the top of the stairs before her mother detected her, and she got to her room without the necessity of answering her inquiring call.

Inside the room she kicked her shoes adeptly into the cupboard, second shelf up, as she did every afternoon. She stripped and threw her damp clothes into a corner. Then she sat in front of the dressing-table mirror to examine her false eyelashes. They were a bastard in this climate. They collected all sorts of rubbish.

She pulled the black, sticky eyelashes off, brushed her hair and then did her impersonation of what she imagined her mother's face was like on her wedding night: a diversion that never fell short of amusing her. Then she got up from the stool and lay on the bed.

The sky was hard blue outside the window. There was a palm in the garden against the sky, its green tongues still and strong. One afternoon, lying naked like this on the cooling counterpane, she had seen the Malay houseboy sitting in the top of the tree looking at her. He was holding something in his hand, and it wasn't a coconut either. She had slid from the bed, sideways like a log, and the boy knew she had seen him because as she sat weeping on the floor in the corner of the room she heard him panic and scramble down from the tree.

For a week after that, every afternoon, she lay the

same, naked, with the curtains open and the sun streaming in, and her father's service revolver lying beside her on the quilt. It was loaded and the catch was off. If the boy got into the tree again she was going to shoot that thing right out of his hand. But he did not climb up for another view. He must have noticed that the revolver was missing from its place on the sideboard. Which was more than her father did.

Today she had intended to shower, but it was too wearying even to get up again from the opal silk covering, for a while at least. She put another pillow behind her head so that it was propped up and she could look down between her breasts at her body.

It was like viewing a distant country, a place detached from her, with two strong hills, each with a spired temple on its summit, a valley, a plain beyond, and a forest beyond that, a dank little forest in another valley.

The perspiration lay on her like oil. She was finely tanned and the inside slopes of her breasts and the little dome of her pelvis looked as though they had been treated to a light coat of varnish.

Her thoughtful mother, who loved and cared about her, had placed a fresh bunch of scarlet flowers in the vase at her bedside. They could not have been there long because at one o'clock there had been a brief shower and the flowers still had small globules of red rain on their petals.

Phillipa reached for one of the flowers and shook its collection of raindrops out between her breasts. The scraps of rounded water sat there patiently like a small group of fat people waiting for something to happen. There were two major blobs which Phillipa decided were the Mummy and Daddy and three little ones which were the children.

She allowed them to stay there for a while, then with a sly little grin she breathed in sharply. Her breasts stretched out like cheeses and her stomach caved in under her ribs.

The five drops of water scampered down her body in single file; the two big ones and one of the minor ones finally and gratefully rolled into the hole of her navel; the other two children missed the target and tumbled in infant panic down her belly and her groin and were lost between her thighs. She told herself that it was a good attempt for a beginner.

Then she decided to go to the pool for a swim.

No one had ever dared to ask Sergeant Driscoll how he came to be there. Why he was at Panglin with the lazy and the lame, the fat, the indifferent, the leaning and the halt. Why all he had to remind him of his good regiment was the badge painted on his tea-mug.

The reason was that he could not close his left eye. The right lid slid with oiled precision over to butt beautifully on to the lower lash. Both eyes together performed the same mechanical function in perfect and noiseless harmony. But in all his life, with no amount of physical and mental practice could he get the left eye to close on its own.

Sometimes he lay in silent struggle on his bed, attempting by sheer will-power, of which he had plenty, by self-hypnotism, by brute force, to close the eye; but it remained open, tranquil and triumphant and full of sight.

Driscoll was right-handed, and to fire a rifle or automatic weapon from the shoulder with correct aim and accuracy requires the closing of the left eye and the sighting of the right eye through the rear and foresights of the gun. Very early in his life as a regular soldier he had personally made the astonishing discovery of his incapacity. Quickly he had changed the rifle he happened to be firing on the range to the left shoulder. He was in a good regiment and he wanted to stay. Through the years, after that, in both battle and at rehearsal, he had fired from the left shoulder with the right eye closed and the left eye sighting down the barrel.

Then they found out. The Adjutant of the unit, when they were on operations against the bandits in North Malaya, had spotted the right-handed

Sergeant firing left-handed. He didn't like Driscoll and Driscoll didn't like the Adjutant. But the Adjutant was a Major. They gave Driscoll a special test, failed him instantly, and within a week he was heading south for Singapore and Panglin garrison.

'Why did they do it?' he muttered, lying on his bed and wrestling with his eye. 'It stinks! Stinks to hell and back. Can't close his eye – so kick him out!'

Frantically he tried closing them both and opening the right one when the left one wasn't looking. But he had tried it before and he could never catch it out. He had tried waking up from sleep one eye at a time, but that did not work either.

It had never mattered. Only once. He could use anything from a .303 to a bren, firing from that left shoulder. His control of the weapon was perfect, nearly. That early morning before Caen had not been all his fault. He was slipping bursts of bren into a farm outbuilding which the Germans were using when the thing somehow lurched. There was some mortar shelling and some of it close, so it could have been that. But it went wild and slewed sideways, and by the time he had stopped it three of his own platoon were pinned dead against a grey wall.

He had broken cover and run across sobbing: 'Get up, please get up. It was me! It wasn't them! It was me!'

Then he had run away from what he had done

and a stick of mortar bombs had demolished the wall and the men. So there was no inquiry, no suspicion. And after all, Driscoll told himself, they were going to be killed by the mortars anyway. All he had done was to cut their lives by thirty seconds.

When he was tormented by his optical frustrations Driscoll's thoughts would frequently swivel to the other thing in his life which enraged him most: Sergeant Wellbeloved. Conversely, thoughts of Sergeant Wellbeloved sometimes prompted him into despair and agony about his eye.

Occasionally he would give the muscles on his lid mechanisms a respite by concentrating his attention on the Sergeant's white tapes sewn to the arm of his jacket hanging behind the door. He would imagine them vanished from the arm, sacrificed in the excellent cause of beating Wellbeloved into a generous pulp. The vision entranced and amused him, particularly when he imagined the pulping interrupting one of Wellbeloved's stories about what the Japanese did to him. Driscoll often wondered how the Japanese had endured Wellbeloved at all.

But he needed to stay a Sergeant because of the money. So he normally took his anger down to the swimming pool and drowned it. He did this afternoon, being mentally tired of crunching his fellow Sergeant and physically exhausted trying to get his eye shut.

He was there, swimming like a crazed gudgeon for length upon length, when Phillipa came out of the ladies' dressing-room and quietly dropped into the water at the shallow end. She watched him with unusual interest, threshing through the water as though he were attacking it with his fists, and swearing almost continuously, although most of the oaths ended as guileless bubbles.

Driscoll did not see her at all. Eventually he took down a mouthful of chemicalised water, staggered comically out, and capered and spluttered on the side of the pool. Then he slopped towards the dressing-room, passing within a foot of her head without seeing her.

As he went croaking by she heard him say: 'Can't close the left eye! What crap!'

3

Colonel Wilfred Bromley Pickering had lost *his* eye in the savage battle in Normandy in July 1944. It was not a bullet. It was a bee.

The day had been hot and the battle had shattered from horizon to horizon, the explosion of guns brighter than the lovely day and dead men lying in meadows as though peacefully sleeping beneath the sun.

Then the sky bled into the most prolific sunset, mocking the attempts at the spectacular below. Major Bromley Pickering, as he then was, had warred hard all day with the rest of the armies, but towards evening things quietened down and everyone seemed to be going home. He had gained temporary shelter in a former pigsty and was observing from there the movements of a group of German anti-tank gunners, and the manipulations of his own men on the flank.

Heat, generated by the sun and the fighting, still lay thickly and the air was full of little bits of grit. He rested his field-glasses and wondered idly if he could accomplish one of those miraculous oddities of war he had read about, by swapping some prisoners with the Germans for some of their excellent beer.

His attention became focused on a phenomenon, a flowering weed growing unharmed, but dusty, within inches of his quite handsome nose. He looked at it with affection, marvelling at its survival even more than he marvelled at his own after such a day, and feeling almost fatherly towards it as though it were a limping puppy or a needy grasshopper.

Tenderly he projected his little finger from the pigsty and, hardly breathing, brushed some of the grey dust off the lower yellow petal. Some twenty-five-pounders lying in a copse half a mile away threw out a brief salvo and Major Bromley Pickering shuddered with them and urgently cupped the weed in his hands, swearing at the guns over his shoulder.

When everything had stopped shaking, he removed his hands, stretched his little finger once more and returned to cleaning the petal.

The bee, another surprised and surprising survivor of the deathly day, had spotted the lone living colour some time before the major. It was working hopefully, curled in the very kernel of the bloom, when in came the kindly officer's little finger. The bee, who might have considered that humans had caused him enough discomfort for one day, screamed out, hit, and stung Major Bromley Pickering in the eye.

The wound caused him to lose half his vision and virtually terminated a military career that had seemed welling with promise. He had been a shining cadet, and his passage through the lower officer ranks was predictably swift. He was comfortably confident that he would reach staff rank at an early age, and he dreamed of glory to such an extent that, by the time he was twenty-five, he had already composed and perfected the words he would utter on his death-bed. The bee spoiled it all.

For him there had been no further war, and when it was over for everyone else too, although succeeding in remaining in the army, he descended through military life with the same sureness of a waterlogged piece of wood sinking to the muddy floor of a pond.

True, promotion had come twice, but, like the visitations of a midwife, only when it was due. Ambition had been blinded with his eye, and became enfeebled before eventually dying so quietly that its passing was hardly noticed.

He had a nice house on a hill in England, near Basingstoke, with a group of thin trees in the garden that he liked to imagine were peeping through the bedroom window when his grandchildren were sleeping there. His wife said travelling gave her headaches, and sent him off on overseas postings as though he were going to an afternoon cricket match rather than a three-year separation. She greeted him on his return with the same calm as though no summers and winters had gone by, just hours.

He had arrived to take command at Panglin with ambition, militancy and keenness, occupying a soldier's grave within himself. Charity, kindliness and complete ineffectuality had been born and grown instead. He had also a deep concern for the well-being of the young soldiers, which was what the War Office called conscripts. It was a good term, he felt, and as they filtered in to Panglin from the troopships he felt a harvest of fatherly feeling swelling in his heart as though these fine, if indolent, young men compensated in some way for his eye.

He made it clear to his officers, commissioned and non-commissioned, that these youths had not left their mothers to be bullied or shouted at, that they were a delicate generation and needed careful, tactful tending. He never ceased to be grateful that at Panglin no one was ever shot at. Not intentionally anyway.

So on the morning that the order from G.H.Q. promulgating – and orders from G.H.Q. always did promulgate – the arrangements for a jungle training course at Buksing, on the Malaya mainland, Colonel Bromley Pickering became highly agitated.

The instruction said that it had been decided to give static units in Singapore an opportunity ('opportunity' – the Colonel liked that) to undergo jungle training under actual active service conditions. Buksing, on the east coast, had been chosen for the camp. Communist bandits had been operative in the area during the past three months. Colonel W. Bromley Pickering would be in command of the first training course, lasting two weeks, and he would have three infantry instructors from jungle-based units under him. Up to twenty men from each of the base units in Singapore – a total of one hundred and forty – would be posted in each course.

Under this were the names of the men from Panglin who would be going with their considerate commander in the first contingent. Among them was the mountainous Sergeant Fred Organ, selected by someone remote at G.H.Q. who had never seen him.

Colonel Bromley Pickering shuddered and blinked his eye. Then he let out a dry cry to his Adjutant, Major Cusper, who was writing to his mother in the adjoining office.

'God help us, Cusper!' the shocked Colonel called. 'We're going into action!'

That day, in the office, they had brought to Brigg's desk the paybook of an infantry private called Oxley who had been shot dead in an ambush. You were not supposed to carry your paybook with you when you were on operations, but Oxley forgot.

They put the brown book on Brigg's desk because he was filling in a file about how much leave and ration allowance Oxley had enjoyed. The first three pages were stuck together with the young man's blood, dried like thick gravy, and the details Brigg wanted were on the second page.

Oxley's birthday had been a month after Brigg's and, now he was dead, Brigg thought about him all day. He had lived in Dock Street, Hull, and Brigg imagined him growing up there with the fishy smells coming off the docks, and the mist, thin and horizontal, lying like resting ghosts along the street on mid-winter nights.

He had grown and been conscripted and sailed for Malaya, and then died violently at nineteen, with his paybook in his pocket.

When he knew he was on the list for the training camp at Buksing, Brigg lay on his bed, thought of Oxley and imagined what the paybook of Private Brigg would look like gummed up with blood. He was still thinking about it on the Saturday night before they left.

In the end, that night, he rolled off his bed, had a shower and got dressed in the fawn jacket and chocolate trousers he had just bought from the village tailor.

There was a bus at half past every hour from the village to Singapore and he got the one at nine-thirty. The Liberty Club was just off the Padang. It was the place in the town for getting your end in, they said, and it was naturally very crowded.

'I'm only going to look,' Brigg told himself aloud as he left the bus. 'Just a bit of window shopping. But not to buy. No, not buying anything today, thank you very much.'

It was a fat building, standing alone and black. Inside it resembled a desecrated church. There were two lines of stone columns running down the length of the nave. Between the columns were fragile card tables and cane chairs; the space in the middle was for dancing and at the high altar end was the band. Smoke, sweat and perfume hung about like a poison gas.

The girls were Chinese, Malay, Siamese, and some others; the waiters, pallid and sweating under the canopy of their trays, were Chinese; and the rest were British soldiers, sailors, and airmen, lofty, short, pimply, mean, drunk, hysterical, miserable, moping, happy, handy and randy.

Some of them danced with the girls held properly, left arms projecting like jibs, each step, quick-quick or slow, in uncompromising time just as though they had gone there to dance. Others knew why they were there and held their partners tight and close, with the girl's hand stuffed down the front of the trousers.

After pushing through the crowd at the foyer, Brigg strolled around the rim of the activity. The girls were good, most of them, young and showing their busts and bums under their shiny tight satin and silks. He felt excitement stir in him like a cat waking up. But he was only looking, he told himself again, he wasn't going to buy anything. Just in for a beer and a browse.

He stopped by an empty chair. There was a plump youth in a white shirt sitting on the other side of the table.

'Anyone's?' asked Brigg, taking hold of the chair.

'Naw,' said the youth who had a pink cushion face.

'Right, thanks,' said Brigg sitting down. 'Have a drink?'

The young man looked at him with mildly surprised distaste. 'You queer or sommat?' he asked.

'No. Not likely,' said Brigg shocked. 'Why? Just because I asked if you wanted a beer?'

'Well,' said the youth, 'you don't know me, or anything. I mean, we're not mates, are we?'

'All right,' said Brigg. 'Forget it.'

'No, I'll have one,' he said hurriedly. 'As long as you're not after my ring I'll have one. Tiger beer if you don't mind, mate.'

They had two Tigers. Brigg said: 'I just wanted to know how things worked. I haven't been in here before.'

'You mean with the tarts,' said the other, catching on. 'Well you have to buy a little thing of tickets and you give one to a tart when you dance with 'er. Then if you fancy it you get 'er to take you 'ome and give you a rumble.'

Brigg nodded wisely as though he were making a study of international assignation arrangements. 'But it all starts with the tickets, does it?' he said.

'Yeah,' said the youth sucking his beer. 'You buy the tickets. It's like getting on a bleeding bus – and that's what it's like with some of these tarts too.'

He laughed at his joke. Brigg was studying the dancers. 'Are they clean?' he said.

'Rotten some of them,' said the young soldier smugly. 'There's some I wouldn't touch even with mine. Some of 'em are 'ard too. See that one there, the red jumper, well she's Chinese and German mixed, or something and they call 'er Iron Gerda. She nearly killed one of our blokes last week.'

'I'll have another beer,' thought Brigg, 'then I'll get out. I'll go down to the forces club and have a steak and chips. After all, I only came to look the place over.'

He was already fixed on a girl. She was dancing with a stout, florid man with a stoop that suggested he might be in the Catering Corps. She was only as tall as his chin and he had his belly thrust into her as he danced slowly and clumsily.

She was Chinese. Brigg never could understand why they were supposed to be yellow. The peasants were brown, like paper, and the office girls were cream white, like paper. This girl, in the lights that simmered through the smoke, was the palest of them. Her eyes were half closed, gentle and bored, and Brigg watched her work her red tongue along her teeth looking for lipstick pieces to clean.

The band came to a disorganised stop at the far end. The people on the floor broke up, the girls mostly going to their ringside seats and the men returning to the beer on their tables.

Brigg's table companion stood up and went off on some private mission. The waiter came to the table and Brigg bought another beer and a booklet of tickets. Five for two Malay dollars.

He watched the girl anxiously. She was sitting with her back to him and he could see the wet hairs at the nape of her neck. As soon as the band began its grind again he went forward and said: 'Dance, please.'

'Ticket please,' she said automatically and Brigg thought of the bus.

He gave her a ticket which she folded carefully and placed in her brassière. She stood up and held out her arms to him, smiling, and he took hold of her firmly and felt her body suddenly all the way down against his. It was like letting the sea roll over you, but warmer. They moved out on to the floor.

'Didn't you like dancing with the fat man?' asked Brigg.

'Which one?' she said disinterestedly.

'The last one. The one you had the last dance with.'

'Oh, him,' she smiled a little. 'He always come here for me. He wants to buy pussy cat. But I not sell it.'

Brigg experienced a double bite of disappointment and relief.

'You don't sell it then?' he said bravely.

'Not to him,' she smiled.

He was glad and afraid again. She was right with him now. They hardly moved but he could feel her stroking him with her pelvis. Sticky sweat ran down their faces, mingling where their cheeks were pressed, and running free in sweet rivers down their necks.

She moved her left hand, like a snake, down his shirt, outside, and down his trousers. Inside.

'Christ, no!' he whispered.

'Christ, yes,' she said. 'Let us go now. Give me the other tickets and we go.'

'How much?' he said hoping madly it would be too expensive.

'Fifteen dollars,' she said.

'That's all right,' he said, guilty but glad.

They went towards the door like old lovers, hand in hand. She slipped from him with the little smile and went towards the cloakroom. Brigg's chest was heaving with excitement and heat. It was really time to run now. Really.

At his elbow he discovered the ripe pumpkin youth who had been his first adviser. He was eating a sausage roll and staring in the direction of the ladies' cloakroom.

'Very good, that one,' he observed sending out a fine spray of crumbs.

'My one?' said Brigg proudly.

'The best, or one of the best,' said the youth.

'You've been there?' said Brigg, doubtful suddenly, because he had decided he didn't like the look of the pink lad.

'Not meself,' admitted the youth. 'But I've 'eard.'

'What's her name?' asked Brigg hurriedly, thinking that soon it would be too late for formal introductions.

'Lucy,' said his friend blandly. 'Juicy Lucy.'

There was a cab mooning along the street. They got in and Lucy leaned forward and chanted an address at the driver. Then she sat beside Brigg, undid his fly and inserted her slim hand.

'Oh God, don't!' he cried with embarrassment.

Honest surprise filled her nice face. 'Oh,' she whispered, delicately withdrawing. 'You not like?'

'Yes, yes,' he gasped, hurriedly putting her hand back inside his trousers. 'It was a bit of a surprise that's all.'

It felt luxuriously terrible working away in there. Like a velvet spider. Agitated and sweating, he wondered what he ought to do with his hands, which were hanging around uselessly like spare ushers at a wedding. Lucy sensed and solved the problem. She took his wet, trembling fingers and made them undo the three pearly buttons at the neck of her dress. Then she helped and guided them down inside, in the warm, until he had hold of the smooth pudding and little hard button that was her left breast. Half way through the taxi journey he changed hands and breasts.

Brigg was not sure whether he wanted the taxi ride to end or go on for ever, although he imagined that what was to come must be even better. When the cab did stop he staggered out into the close, now drizzling, evening, paid the driver blindly, and hobbled up some wooden stairs after the girl.

She stopped to unlock a scarred green door. There was a small ailing lamp over the stairs and from where he paused, four steps down, waiting for her to complete the unlocking, he could see her good legs, white and shaped, disappearing up her skirt towards darkness. He wished she would hurry up.

A voice like a cough suddenly came up from the pit at the side of the stairs making Brigg jump with fear because he thought it might be a military policeman. He looked over and saw a head like a dim lantern, Chinese shaped, with trenched eyes and a pale glow about it as some hidden light caught it.

The man croaked again and Lucy, half twisting at the door, looked over and rebuked him in Chinese. The light on his old face seemed to go out and Brigg could hear him grumbling in the cave below the stairs.

'He want rent,' shrugged Lucy.

This is the catch, thought Brigg, bitterly disappointed. Now she will want the money for the rent. It's just routine.

But she did not mention it again. She had opened the door and pulled the piece of string to turn on the light. Brigg stared in eagerly, with a sense of excited anticipation he had not experienced since he was ten and had craned forward to get a first look into Santa's cave at Selfridges store.

Weak with suppressed energy and fear, he went in after her, stumbling badly over a large china doll lying in the doorway.

It was not so much a bedroom as a storeroom. Lucy was apparently a collector. Of anything. There were dolls, fans, and three stuffed poodles. Boxes and trinkets, books and comics, gramophone records, lubricant jelly, three sizes of contraceptives, a picture of Mao Tse-tung and a beautifully embroidered plaque saying: 'Happy New Year from the Gordon Highlanders.'

'Nice place,' said Brigg lamely.

'This too nice place,' she joked, stretching backwards over the bed and flinging her legs wide.

'Oooooh, Yes,' said Brigg embarrassed, but feeling he ought to say something.

But that was not the start. He had been standing, an enchanted spectator, and was about to move forward into what he imagined must be the opening hold, when she rose coolly from the bed and began flopping her hair about in front of the mirror. Her blouse buttons were still free and as she raised her hands to her black hair, in that most graceful of all womanly movements, he could see her breasts attempting escape like prisoners trying to climb a wall. She pushed them back again with a pout. Then she smiled at him, a full professional smile in the mirror, all eyes and teeth and simpered: 'You pay now. Then we have nice filthy time. Please fifteen dollars.'

He sorted it out clumsily and gave it to her and she vanished it like a conjuror. He was sorry that she had asked for the money first because it spoiled it a bit.

If the money came afterwards you could at least pretend. It would be nice if she never mentioned it at all. Perhaps have a collecting box at the door so you could put it in on the way out, or even a plate, like in church. Still, he thought, there would be those who would shortchange her.

After he had given her the dollars, he stood around awkwardly wondering what to do next, like a man waiting for casual labour. She looked at him peculiarly then moved away from the mirror and sat on the edge of the bed.

'How you like me?' she inquired sweetly.

'Oh,' he stammered, thinking she was awaiting instructions for the position she should assume. 'Just the usual.'

'The usual?' she asked. 'What's usual? How you like me? I am pretty, yes?'

'Yes, yes,' he hurried, annoyed at his mistake. 'You're very beautiful, Lucy.'

'Then you give me five more dollars,' she suggested. 'We have love all night and half tomorrow. Lots of extras.'

'I can't,' he mumbled doing furious mental arithmetic. He couldn't either. He owed the garrison canteen three dollars and the ice-cream man another three, and he was playing cricket the next day anyway so he couldn't stay with her.

'You just poor soldier,' she mocked.

'I am too,' he replied firmly, angry at her spite-fulness. 'I haven't got much. We only get twenty-three dollars a week.'

'Private soldier, tradesman class two, get twenty-eight dollars,' she recited knowledgeably.

'Yes, but I'm class three,' he explained wretchedly.

'All right,' she said, sweet again, standing up. 'You pull.'

She turned from him and nodded her head over her shoulder towards her zipper. With uncontrolled hands, and immediately on fire again, he stole to it and took it gently, delicately, like a boy manoeuvring with a piece of a jigsaw puzzle.

'It goes down, doesn't it?' he said in his foolishness, and she laughed because she thought he was making a joke.

He unzipped her, an experience in sight, sound and sensation as erotic as anything he had ever dreamed even on one of his bad nights.

She was wearing a white bra, stretched across her pale, brown shoulder blades like a suspension bridge. Her green panties had a hole in the seat, which was unromantic and frankly off-putting, but it was obviously the work of moth or mouse rather than man.

'Undo,' she ordered casually over her shoulder. He managed to unhook the bra and feel, with considerable joy in achievement, the weight at the front pull forward. She remained quite still now, expecting him to do something.

But Brigg was immobile, almost at attention, his eyes fixed on the smooth valley of her back, with the small bulge of the spine travelling down it like a half-buried water pipeline.

Lucy glanced at him suspiciously in the mirror, saw no menace in his face, only a fearful wonder, and put her slim hand behind her to take his. She guided it to her front and he experienced an awful happiness, in spasms, as he found it slipping down her belly and squirming under the elastic of her panties like a boy wriggling beneath a wire fence.

'Oh my God,' he kept whispering. 'Oh my God.'

Down it travelled, further, channelling through her thighs and one adventurous finger getting trapped and tangled in a knot of delicious hair.

'Oh my God. Oh my God.'

'Your God very good to you,' she suggested, wriggling involuntarily as his leading fingers began sliding.

'Oh my God,' said Brigg.

She executed a sharp scissor movement with her legs so that his fingers felt like bait with a carp snapping. The Chinese tailor always skimped his cotton on fly buttons, and now one flew off Brigg's new trousers like a bullet and hit her in the small of the back.

'Sorry,' he said stupidly. 'It came off.'

She turned solicitously and said: 'You break out of your trousers, Johnny. You better take off.'

He did, although it proved more difficult than he could ever remember. Then his shirt, and everything. Last of all he removed his shoes and socks, and hurriedly, because they looked ridiculous.

Lucy surveyed him with professional approval.

'Big boy,' she murmured. 'Very big. Come here.'

As they stumbled towards the bed he noticed her panties on the floor, with the floorboards showing through the hole, and mistily wondered why he had not noticed them come off.

She lay back, looking at him over the tops of her breasts. Her thighs were going like bellows. Beneath her was a blanket and Brigg felt it rough against his knees. He fixed his starving, anxious gaze on her and scrambled forward in the crawl that infantrymen use over broken ground.

When he was near, or thought he was near, he stabbed at her frantically and missed. It was painful. The second time he all but fell from the bed.

She grabbed him and held him with great and genuine concern. 'Jesus, Johnny,' she breathed. 'Don't kill yourself. Plenty of time. Easy, darling, easy.'

Brigg was sweating waterfalls. Where was it? Where in hell was it? Fancy hiding the bloody thing under there. He wiped the perspiration from his eyes so he could see better. Then he made another huge lunge. This time he did a fantastic pole vault, hurting himself, and landed heavily on top of her. She was holding her breath expectantly and he knocked it all out of her.

She started to be angry, but looked and saw he was crying. With a tender, involuntary movement, she brought him close to her with his cheek against her breast and the tears wetting both.

'You cry?' she whispered in wonder. 'Why so rough, then cry?'

'It's the first time,' he sniffed like a schoolboy.

'The very first . . .'

Lucy emitted a round little whoop, sitting stark upright as though she had a spring in the small of her back. Her slant eyes were round and glistening with amazement.

'First time?' she repeated as though it were the Hidden Name of God. 'Never have before?'

'Never,' he mumbled miserably waiting to be tossed with scorn from the bed.

'A virgin,' she breathed unbelievingly. 'A little virgin soldier.'

'All right,' he snapped. 'Don't go on. You had to start sometime, didn't you?'

'Long time ago,' she sighed happily. 'Oh, Johnny, I never have a virgin. Not till now.'

Suddenly he realised he was on a good thing. All his anger, fright and dismay collapsed as she lounged luxuriously back and dreamily pulled him down to her. Then, just as he thought it was all going to begin, she sprang up again.

'I took money first,' she cried, horrified. 'You wait.'

'It's all right,' he gasped, grabbing at her as she leaped from the bed. 'It's all right, really.'

But she had conjured his fifteen dollars back. 'You pay later,' she said climbing back to him. 'And only ten. Only ten dollars for a virgin. And after we have cocoa. Cadbury's.'

She giggled deliciously. He had the notes in his hand now and tried to stuff them in his pocket, only to make contact with his bare backside. Not that he cared any longer. She was working on him with such loving devotion and skill that he could scarcely remember pushing the money under the pillow.

She started from the beginning and went all the way. He felt like a balloon being slowly blown up. When she showed him the big secret, she whispered: 'How the virgin like?'

'Oh, it's lovely, Lucy,' he shivered. 'It's lovely, really it is.'

4

At night the swamp stirred and groaned like a man in dishevelled sleep. It lay about three sides of the camp at Buksing, with the elbow beach and the sea on the other. There was a baked mud road leading north for five miles to a wooden town, and another track wriggling south to a Malay kampong, beside a crocodile river.

Lying beside the ammunition pit in the guard tent, Brigg was putting his hand in the sickly light of a carbide lamp and projecting the shadow on to the brown canvas wall. The image, with fist folded and thumb upright, pleased him.

'There,' he asked himself, because the two Malays and Sinclair who were also in the tent, were prone and sleeping. 'There now, what's that?'

He paused and moved his eyes quickly around, before answering himself.

'That,' he said, 'is the British Army Thumb. See, there it is. The good old British Thumb. Thumbs up lads, we're going off to war! Thumbs up, we'll beat the Germans, or the Bongos, or whoever it happens to be just now. Just keep those thumbs up. You can't go wrong as long as they're up.'

He had thought all this out before, and been sad, mystified and terrified by it. All those thumbs. Tommy's here, don't ever fear. He had seen photographs when he was a little boy of all those dreadful thumbs extended, each bent a little back, as they went to Flanders to be shot off by the Germans or lost in the mud. God knows how many thumbs there were lost in that mud. He could think of them individually, still erect and bravely bent showing that even mass murder, or brave suicide, couldn't stop the British Thumb.

Why did they do it always? Off they went again in the next war, those proud, confident mistaken digits. Thumbs up on the troopships, thumbs up in the tail turret of the bomber, thumbs up on the Arctic convoy. That's right, lads, just show we're not downhearted. Come on now, you on the stretchers, thumbs up all those who've still got 'em. Thumbs up! Thumbs up!

The camp was an old one. When the Japanese had been riding their bicycles down through Malaya there was a little battle there and twenty thumbs were lying in caked mud graves on a prong of land north of the perimeter.

Out to sea, fishermen lived on stilted village

houses that seemed to be wading in the bay. At low tide they threw their nets at fishes who ran in and out of the hulls of the dead battleships – *Prince of Wales* and *Repulse* – lying clearly in the sand of the ocean. They had been there since 1942 and they were full of dead thumbs.

It was not just that Brigg was yellow, which he was, but he had hated the army from the moment he saw them carrying the soldier on to the barrack square in England. He had been in the service a week when this pathetic and futile charade was mimed, and it ground him up inside so that he couldn't sleep all one night just thinking about it.

They carried the soldier on a gruesome little litter of wooden pieces. It was evening and the guard was forming up on the asphalt. Brigg had stood and watched as though it had been a wake or a primitive tribal ceremony. At first he had failed to grasp the enormity of it, or even its significance. Then a pale, grey conscript had come to stand at his side and witness the scene too. But in fermenting enthusiasm and pride.

'What's the matter with him?' asked Brigg without understanding. 'He can get off guard duty if he's hurt his leg or something.'

The grey, pale conscript surveyed him distastefully

as though he had mentioned an unkind word about Jesus.

'They're keeping him clean!' he snorted. 'There's nothing wrong wiv 'im; they're just keeping the bleeding dust off.'

Brigg realised. 'You mean they're carrying him to the guard mounting so he won't get dirty?' he asked. Just to make sure.

'Tha's right,' said the pale private smugly. 'Then 'e'll be stickman and we'll get anuvver twenty points in the platoon competition. We're forty points in front of your lot already.'

'Smashing,' breathed Brigg. 'And you cleaned him all up so you'll get another twenty and get the pennant at the end of the course.'

'Yerse, and don't forget the forty-eight hour passes,' said the young soldier.

'Forty-eight instead of thirty-six like the rest of us will get?' said Brigg. 'Christ, you must have spent twelve hours getting him to look like that.'

Horrified, Brigg watched the khaki waxwork brought to the edge of the square. The litter was laid gently down as though it bore some potent prince. The warrior it had carried, his young face set, he and his uniform burnished, blancoed, blacked and brilliantined, stood deathly still while his friend brushed and bumbled about him.

They were neither sheepish nor laughing, nor

showing any sense of foolishness. Their expressions were set and earnest, as they pursued their useless endeavour, full of restrained joy, like the faces of convinced lunatics attempting to build a wall of water. They licked their fingers and ran down the creases of his trousers and tunic, they checked the lead weights that held his trousers over his gaiters, they looked for any last minute hairs sprouting on his chin and for sly dull patches on his boots, but found neither.

'Why don't they make sure his prick is hanging the right side?' suggested Brigg.

'Just jealous, you are,' said the grey youth, but immediately forgetting his anger in more enthusiasm. 'Look at those boots. I did the right one. I was up till two this morning gobbing on that toecap. Hello, 'ere we go. Keep our fingers crossed.'

The effigy marched on to the square where the dozen other prospective members of the guard were already drawn up.

Brigg prayed painfully, prayed that the glowing guard could please, please, just this once, drop his rifle on the orderly officer's shin. But it did not happen. The officer picked his way along the two ranks, they paced to open order and back again, and there was some smart smacking of rifle butts. The shining soldier's smack sounded better than the rest because he had put two rattling pennies in his magazine.

He was chosen as the choicest on parade and marched off to be girlishly mobbed by his friends. The grey conscript who had stood by Brigg gave a little sobbing whoop and ran to the canteen to buy a comic paper.

There was blood, well dried, on that barrack square, shed and spread one noisy night when an army butcher had taken a meat cleaver to a rival in love and very nearly truncated him. There was one big bloodstain shaped rudely like Africa on the far side of the square, and one morning Brigg had found himself lying on the hard surface with his nose in roughly the position of Dar-es-Salaam.

He had fainted, or half-fainted, because his breakfast had poisoned him, and he fell forward on his face just as the rest of his drill squad were marching away. They were in line abreast across the asphalt and Brigg was in the back rank. He lay quiet and sick, while they disappeared over his low horizon. Nobody in authority noticed him, and no one came back for him. He was there for ten minutes, squinting slyly from side to side along the parade ground. Officers, non-commissioned officers and men passed at intervals quite close to him, but no one made a comment. Eventually he rose unassisted, asked himself what was the use, and went to find the medical officer.

*

Sinclair, at the back of the tent, rolled over on to his rifle which was hard and woke him up. He sprawled on his front, looking across all the ammunition glinting in the pit like uncovered treasure. And then to Brigg.

'What are you sticking your thumb up like that for?' he asked Brigg, who was still doing it.

'That,' said Brigg, prodding his head towards the shadow on the tent wall, 'is the British Thumb.'

'Oh,' said Sinclair without interest. He got up and stepped across one of the Malays and went to have a look at the night. It was blown up very big, full of liquid blue and concise spiked stars. It was a hot night too. Sinclair liked them cold.

'Ever heard a train going through the night-time?' he said over his shoulder to Brigg.

'Not puffers again,' protested Brigg. 'Not now.'

'That's right. Just because you don't understand,' said Sinclair mildly.

'But you're too old to be playing with trains,' said Brigg.

'I've got up at two in the morning to go and see a goods train,' said Sinclair, mostly to himself. Just to see it climbing the gradient, he thought.

And to hear it. On a frosty night was best, with everything frozen still; bird in tree, animal in burrow, and water in pond. Frozen and white, and him crouching on the stump of a tree by the embankment.

You could hear it coming a long way off. That was half the joy of it. Way across the steel air and over the petrified trees and lumpy fields and empty barnyards. Then you could hear it flex its muscles as it reached the long climb, and crackle its steam out into their air. It would pant up the irons, its laden wagons following like a creaking tail.

Then he would see the glow of the fire-box under the phantom steam, and the strong shape of the engine would become slowly formed. Once, when there was a moon, he had seen a fox run along the track before the engine and he had heard sleeping birds stir and complain of the train disturbing them.

No one ever saw him sitting on the embankment. The giant would go by, for him a melody of metal on metal, and fine powerful sounds. It would climb the slope towards Rugby, the obedient wagons grinding the cold rails. He would wait until it had gone beyond the signals two miles away, and the night was settled and quiet again, and then, well pleased, he would go home across the hard fields.

Sinclair was still thinking about it when a burst of red gunfire flew through the trees on the right flank of the camp.

It was a lance-corporal in the Veterinary Corps, given to timidity, but who ought to have known better, who began the shooting. They may have instructed him about mules but he failed to identify a firefly. He failed to recognise it as it wandered through the midnight trees with its exploring companions in the vicinity of the latrine where the lance-corporal was seated.

At first he merely blinked convulsively, then closed his eyes into wrinkles. But when he re-opened them the stubby little lights were still jumping. They winked wantonly, vanished and were there again. Wild-eyed he squatted over the hole, hurriedly and blindly pawing for his trousers and his sten-gun.

The light jerked nearer. And nearer. Bubbling with terror, the lance-corporal tugged on trousers and trigger simultaneously. The gun had become jammed inside the garment and the frightened soldier, in trying to level it out, let off half a magazine through the front of the trousers, shattering them. The fireflies remained unhit. But there was panic among the tents.

Men and shadows rushed and pushed in the jungle dark. There were collisions of hoots, shouts and orders. Few were heeded or clearly heard. Soldiers sprawled over guy ropes and comfortable tree-top creatures woke and looked down in alarm and trepidation at the antics of the men. More firing began on the northern limit of the camp where the boundary guards were shooting into the moving swamp which, they were now convinced, was not moving of its own volition.

Brigg and Sinclair, at least awake when the outburst began, stumbled to the main gate of the camp, which was their duty post, and were there jolted by the appearance of a frightened Malay soldier who would have murdered them in cold blood had he not omitted to release the safety catch of his rifle.

Six of the Panglin contingent had been sleeping, feet to the pole of their bell-tent and innocent as virgin Girl-Guides, when the firing began. At the first burst Tasker, howling like a blind wolf, rushed in the dark towards the patch of diminished light which he believed to be the door.

Through the darkness, the only man with any purpose in his run or his actions, came Driscoll, arriving to find Tasker's head projecting from the wall of the tent like a half-dressed pantomime horse. The shooting had quietened and most of the young soldiers had stopped running and were lying flat on the ground.

'What are you frigging about at?' demanded Driscoll.

'I'm stuck, Sarge,' complained Tasker. 'I thought this was the bloody door.'

'But it's not, is it?'

'No,' admitted Tasker. 'It's the frigging little window. But it was dark.'

Driscoll gave Tasker's head a rough rugby push

and forced it from the tight hole. He stamped around to the front of the tent where the remainder of the occupants were huddled. There were Jacobs, Lantry, the nervous, now petrified, Corporal Brook, and Foster and Villiers who were tightly holding hands.

'Almighty shit!' shouted Driscoll. 'What are you in them for? The pyjamas! You didn't . . . you didn't . . . You're on active service . . . You're not supposed to wear . . .'

His voice staggered.

'Nobody told us,' said Lantry. 'So we put them on.'

'Oh God,' whispered Driscoll. 'Oh dear God.' He looked at Villiers and Foster. 'Stop holding hands!' he roared.

There came a brief movement from the back of the tent and Driscoll quickly cocked his sten and went around like a hunting dog. He returned with the Commanding Officer, Colonel Bromley Pickering.

'It's all right, Sergeant,' the Colonel reassured. 'It's all right, chaps. Nothing to worry about. One of the young soldiers took fright and began to shoot at something he thought he saw. But it wasn't a bandit attack. Understandable mistake. Back to sleep lads. Well done. Well done.'

Driscoll called the pyjama squad to attention

and metallically saluted. He sent them back into the tent.

He had intended to ask them whether they would have liked to have brought their teddy bears and dolls for bedtime. But it was pointless now. God, what had happened to an army where the Colonel turned out in a blue and pink silk dressing gown? With an antelope embroidered on his back.

Dawn would rush up out of the sea in a three minute surge of red, and in the clustered trees beyond the swamp the monkeys would go mad, screaming, and making the branches shudder as they looped through them.

At seven the whole camp would parade on the dusty space at the centre of the tents, and, rank upon rank, would project their tongues so that the medical officer could walk along and place on each an anti-malaria pill as close to the tonsils as possible.

Apart from those assigned to the camp duties the soldiers would then move off in sections for training routines. As they did so the daily benediction of Colonel Bromley Pickering would filter out to them; the incantation: 'Now, keep out of trouble, lads. Keep out of trouble.'

By trouble, he meant danger. His nights and days at Buksing had been riven by a bloody fear that one day a training patrol would return carrying the shattered body of one of the young national servicemen. His eye flapped with apprehension like the wing of a nervous bird as he watched each group of youths, in their undergrowth green, in their jungle boots, long lace-ups like grandmother wore, in their floppy hats, trudge in single file towards the north and south gates.

The track going south was contained on a strip of firm tufty land, with shingle, sand and the sea on one flank and the fingertips of the swamp on the other. Brigg had been in Driscoll's section most mornings, but on the fourth day he found himself walking watchfully in the rear of a string of men led by Wellbeloved. Brigg was the getaway man who was supposed to run back to camp with the warning if they were attacked. He thought he would be good at this.

Driscoll had always been adventurous, striking off on devious ways through the swamp, feeling his way forward in the tangle until Brigg wanted to yell: 'Don't forget the Colonel said keep out of trouble.'

He never did. He just crouched on with the others, deep under the humid tunnel of green, trapped away from the sky, where the sun ran through the brief openings above like sword blades, where every smell, and each shriek or ticking, or no sound at all, was keyed to imagined danger.

Two hundred bandits in this region, Brigg would think, as they waited in the wet undergrowth for Driscoll to move forward. Two hundred. He would watch a fat fly drinking the sweat on the neck of the man in front, or hear the Malay behind him muttering *'Mati, mati'*, which meant 'death', all the time under his breath. But no one ever ambushed them or sprayed them with bullets, or bothered with them at all. The only sounds they heard to alarm them were the huge volume of their own breathing, and once when Tasker accidentally fired a single round within a fifth of an inch of the ear lobe of the man in front. He could have been court martialled. He was reported, in accordance with some section and sub-section of King's Regulations, by Driscoll, but the Ordnance Corps officer before whom the matter came had mislaid a sten gun that day and wasn't disposed to even hear the mention of the term court martial.

With Sergeant Wellbeloved the section kept to a more open route towards the kampong by the green river in the south. They moved cautiously as ever, dropping into the curling jungle fringe at every minute alarm.

Brigg, screwing his head apprehensively, with his short rifle at the trail, half collided with a seven foot ant hill and stuffed the barrel of the weapon with mud, fibre and three thousand ants. He had no time to clear it and he prayed even more seriously than usual that it would not be necessary for him to start shooting.

Wellbeloved had something in mind. Eventually they halted in a plate-shaped clearing. A big round piece of sun came down there like a spotlight and the grass was dry, brittle and booming with insects. From beyond the screening trees they could hear the activity of the Malay village, the crying of children, someone sawing wood, and the airy chanting of a song. Wellbeloved said: 'We're going to turn this place over. Have a good look at what they've got, because they might have arms and supplies and other things for the bandits hidden here. I'll be surprised if they haven't. We'll get 'em all out in the middle first and then we'll have a poke around. Right, come on.'

The ten men went through the last segment of greenery and trunks. They marched straight into the sharp sun across the pedang of the village.

The place dropped silent. The young girls who had been singing as they squatted around a wide-weaving-frame, looked up with brown, bland faces. There was a curve of the river passing the settlement and some men working in boats came to the bank and tied up and walked towards the centre. Three naked boys stopped throwing stones at each other and a gummy old woman smothered a baby's cawing in the doorway of a house. A mongrel wandered up and sniffed around Wellbeloved's knees then, unimpressed, walked away.

Wellbeloved shouted, 'Squad. Halt!' at his most regimental, setting birds squawking in the trees. The patrol halted. More people came out of the houses and from around shadows, and stood dumb, waiting and watching.

Brigg noticed that his Sergeant went first towards the young girls, ordering them to their feet and snapping, 'In the middle. In the middle,' pointing towards the centre of the open space. They shuffled, frightened, in that direction. More men were coming ashore from the boats now, and one of them, square and unaroused, in a white shirt and a sarong, walked slowly to Wellbeloved.

He looked a very good man, Brigg thought. The lines of his face were soft. Wellbeloved's creases were hard and sudden. Brigg watched them both. He wished the Japs had cut Wellbeloved's throat. 'Right,' said the Sergeant, speaking to the Malay as though he were a soldier. 'If you're in charge, get all the lot of them out in the middle. And mind it's quick.'

The man spread his hands and said something to Wellbeloved, who stiffened in rage and bawled at him. The young soldiers stood silently and the people did too.

Then the head man turned a graceful, complete, dusty circle and called all the villagers in. He had a voice like a bell. There were about a hundred of them. They walked in dignified ways to the middle of their settlement. Someone helped an old, fat woman along. Most of the women carried babies.

Tasker, who was next in the rank to Brigg, said: 'He's a Nazi. He's a frigging Nazi.'

Brigg thought Wellbeloved had heard, because he strode aggressively to the back of the patrol. But it was only to detail them off two by two to enter the houses and search them.

Most of the huts were on poles, away from the ground, away from animals and river floods. They were made of thatch and mud and a few pieces of corrugated iron. Inside they were dim and smelly, with rags spread about the floor, some elementary furniture and coloured pictures of film stars, torn from magazines, sticking to the walls.

Brigg and Tasker went into one and out again almost at once. There was nothing to search except the charred cooking pot. They climbed the wooden ladder into the next house. Wellbeloved was there before them. He was standing hunched, bulky, feet planted astride, cheeks puffing out, looking down at a young girl wrapped in a blanket.

'Get up,' said Wellbeloved quite quietly, failing to

hear Brigg and Tasker behind him. Brigg felt dry and ill. Tasker was starch white.

'Come on then, sweet,' said Wellbeloved firmly. He bent down and caught her by the arm or the shoulder and hauled her to her feet. Her face was afraid but calm and she held the blanket in front of her. She was about fifteen.

They could see Wellbeloved couldn't help himself. He shook as he reached forward and caught the blanket and pulled it away from her. She let it fall. She remained unmoved, just standing and letting him see her.

She was slim and shining brown with a young girl's early breasts, a long neck and smooth shoulders, gentle flanks and a dark nest of hair between them at their apex. Brigg heard Tasker make a swift sucking noise.

Brigg wanted to shout out 'You dirty old bugger, leave her alone!' He wanted to run up and catch Wellbeloved a blow behind the ear with his rifle butt, enough to put the bastard down for good.

But instead he said: 'She is sick, Sarge. They said she's got a fever. It might be catching, Sarge.'

Wellbeloved flew around, steaming with rage at seeing them there. He was going to yell 'Get out!' They could tell that. But he stopped himself and turned his back on the girl and went towards the door. 'There might have been something there,' he said awkwardly. 'She could have been hiding something. A gun or something. You can't trust 'em.'

They could see he was shaking as he went down the ladder, clutching each rung until his knuckles were white. He called the squad in. They formed up and marched out of the village by the way they came. On the return Brigg squinted down the blocked-up barrel of his rifle. He thought how much he would like to stuff it up Wellbeloved's arse. Ants and all.

Because Sergeant Fred Organ was twenty-two stone and could not run and could not hide, they kept him busied with camp duties and put him in command of the canteen tent.

He painted 'Fred's Bar' on a plank of cardboard and hung it on the front.

At night, when the guards were out watching, Fred's Bar would be open, two oil lamps hanging, speckled with hot insects, and an amplifier nailed to a pole so everyone could listen to the radio. Fred always turned the sound full up so that the monkeys in the far confused trees, and any other jungle animals, or men, could hear singers like the Andrews Sisters.

All the tents were lit by carbide lamps, dim and

coughing. When it got dark they would all light up with a consumptive light and the men would bend, leave their tents, and walk across the dark and open ground to Fred's Bar.

Around the scrubbed trestle tables they would sit with glasses of yellow beer, and the thick light from the lamps falling on heads, making deep pits of eyes, and caverns of mouths. Hands, red and brown, crouched on the tables. The talk was loud and rough. Occasionally they would sing.

Wellbeloved was bent across the table near to the far-away Sinclair who was trying to remember whether the eight-forty for Euston from Birkenhead changed engines at Rugby on winter Saturdays.

Wellbeloved said: 'There was only one way to get through all that bloody jungle in Singapore in the old days, and that was on the pipeline. You know, the water pipeline that's still there now. Understand?'

'Yes,' said Sinclair. He decided it must be on alternate Saturdays.

'And fast too, I'll say,' said Wellbeloved. 'The Japs could never work it out, how I used to move so fast. I'd be up at the reservoir, picking off one of the guards one minute, and in no time I'd be down on the Buket Timah Road. It never occurred to them that I used to climb up on the pipeline and run along that. They couldn't see how I got through the jungle so fast. I'll tell you this, they were supposed to be smart, the Nips, but they wasn't all that.'

Driscoll was at the extreme of the table, one strong booted foot on the wooden form. He was trying to get his eye closed again, cranking it down with the other one, until the oil lamps had wavered and gone smoky and finally vanished into his personal blackness. Then he would try to unfold his right eye, leaving his left one still dropped. It had never worked and it didn't now. He rested it, summoned Fred for another beer, and studied Wellbeloved, unloved and unlovely, down the trestle.

Wellbeloved said to Sinclair, 'They used to think I was a ghost. What about that then! They *told* me when they caught me in the end and took me to Changi that they used to think I was a ghost!'

Sinclair thought: 'They'll have the new engine sheds all finished at Stonebridge, and the new shunting area at St. Pancras working when I get back home.' And the first big diesels would be on the lines too. And he'd get out of his uniform and hurry down to Royal Oak station to see the strong Western engines and to see Mr. and Mrs. Boot again. They used to go engine-spotting with him in the old days at Wealdstone, where the expresses came howling down full cry for London. They'd spent their honeymoon on platform four at Wealdstone, but Mr. Boot had written to him a few months back and reported that he and his wife had quarrelled.

She had shouted at him that she was weary with spending every week-end at Wealdstone Midland. Things looked very bad for a while, but the change had done them good. The move to the up-line platform at Royal Oak had saved the marriage.

'Mind you,' said Wellbeloved, 'when they put the thumb screws on you in Changi that wasn't funny. God, they got me under the screws a few times. Because they couldn't hold me there, you know. No fear. I used to get out of Changi like some people get out of bed, and they were scared to shoot me when they caught me again because they got the idea that all the prisoners would have rioted. Yeah, that's right, *rioted* because I was sort of a figurehead. You know what I mean?'

'Yes,' said Sinclair.

Brigg came in, ducking under the tent overhang, got a beer and sat at one of the tables across from Wellbeloved. He had a half-written letter to Joan in his back pocket. He had abandoned it because the carbide lamp in the tent was choking and dying in its own agony. Also he kept thinking about the Malay girl and her breasts when Wellbeloved had snatched the blanket from her. The Malay girl and Joan and Phillipa Raskin. And Lucy, dear Juicy Lucy, who had given him such exhausting and athletic happiness for a night and hours of torment in the toilet afterwards searching for signs and portents.

There were thirty soldiers in the big cave of the tent. There were three card schools, thumping the tables, laughing and moaning, clutches of other talking men, and the men from Panglin garrison all apart from each other.

Driscoll was wondering how the Adjutant of his good regiment had noticed his eye. Sinclair was recalling, within himself, Severn Tunnel Junction. Wellbeloved was describing his third escape, and Brigg was mentally lying naked with Phillipa Raskin. Fat Fred Organ was serving beer.

Then they all stopped. The music on the amplifier stopped and the announcer said that the news was beginning. In the tent, with the crickets winding up outside under the fruity moon and the frogs drumming in the swamp, the men hunched lower over their thick glasses, quiet and listening.

Fred moved uneasily, clearing up at his table. The faces around were all hardened and hollowed under the lights. They heard the news from home, as they did each night. And the announcer's suave, considered words flew over the jungle to the monkey who cared nothing. Not for snow in the Pennines, Parliamentary business, nor the draw for the F.A. Cup.

Afterwards they were always left sad. They

moved, haltingly like Communicants, or shadows seeking consolation in other shadows, towards Fred's end of the tent to get more beer.

At Driscoll's end the table was on a rise in the rough ground and sloped easily to the other end, where Wellbeloved sat with his wooden forearms across the wood.

Driscoll poured a slim stream of beer from his glass and watched it slide down the table in a liquid arrow. He increased the amount, thickened the flow, and watched it on its oily journey with satisfaction and huge interest. The yellow advance wriggled around some knots in the wood, was dammed for a moment by a cigarette butt, but then continued, eventually meeting the bare arms of Wellbeloved and trying to nose beneath them.

Wellbeloved picked up his forearms as though he had felt the touch of a snake. The released beer flowed on in a broader stream, dividing at the Sergeant's own resting beer mug, and meeting again the other side. Driscoll was still steadily pouring. Wellbeloved retraced the yellow trail along the table with his eyes until he looked up and met the grinning glance of Driscoll.

'What's going on?' said Wellbeloved.

'Oh, my beer!' snorted Driscoll. 'Sorry, it must have been slipping over the top.'

The talking and the noise in the tent stopped, not

at once but at a descending rate, like a wall falling down. 'The one in Manchester was a raver . . .' said a final single voice. Then that stopped and every face was turned at the two sergeants.

Wellbeloved was staring at Driscoll. They were both still in their seats at opposite ends of the form along one side of the table.

'I heard about the big military operation today,' offered Driscoll evenly. 'The raid on the village.'

Wellbeloved's big face was set like hard, dry mud. He said: 'Just training, that's all. Just to show these kids.'

'Of course,' agreed Driscoll. 'I was told you had a good time down there.' Brigg wondered what Driscoll meant. So did Wellbeloved, because he turned a quick glance at Brigg who looked away.

'What are you getting at?' said Wellbeloved.

'Nothing, but they've never caused trouble. Always helped us from what I've been told. Until today.'

'Oh shit,' said Wellbeloved. Brigg, out of one acute side of his eye, could see Fred Organ flapping his white hands like frantic fans and making fat little agitated runs up and down behind his bar.

It was a schoolboy trick Driscoll did. He stood up. Suddenly, and from his extreme end of the form. It went up like a crocodile opening its jaw and Wellbeloved fell on the floor at the other end.

He clawed at the table, and then at Sinclair's arm opposite. With embarrassment he pulled himself up and went around the table at Driscoll who was now standing in the open middle space.

There was an urgent move by those nearest to get out of the way. One of the forms toppled and all the beer on the table tipped as the men on one side got up in a hurry.

But Driscoll and Wellbeloved never collided. Swiftly, like bouncing, disorganised rubber, Fred Organ came between them, more massive than either, no muscle, just fat, pound on pound and mound on mound. He placed one padded hand on Driscoll's chest and the other on Wellbeloved's: two blubber cushions keeping them apart. Driscoll had remained still, but Wellbeloved was moving hard. Fred's hand stopped him.

'None of it!' shouted Fred in a booming but frightened voice. 'None of it in 'ere.' He continued to stand like a nervous policeman directing traffic. He repeated. 'No scrapping in 'ere.' He looked at them sternly and descended to a womanish whisper. 'You're sergeants, you know.'

Driscoll, who had just said goodbye to his stripes in a good cause, laughed and said: 'All right, Fred. I wasn't fighting.' He turned and went out of the tent into the dark and they could hear him singing as he went away. Fred took his hand off Wellbeloved's chest and put it on his shoulder. 'Have a drink,' he said.

Wellbeloved made a face, but followed him obediently enough, took his free yellow pint, and sat at the end of the far table, next to the opening, drinking it. Brigg looked at him sideways and saw his blind fingers fumbling around the glass.

Fred retired behind his trestle, wiping his beer glasses with little anxious actions, the fat of his forearms and the jowls of it on his face and neck bubbling with the quick movement. There still wasn't much talking. No one but Driscoll had gone and they all sat there like lumps under the lamplight.

'Free pint to anyone who starts a song,' said Fred like a mother's circle leader. 'Worth it, isn't it?' Fred wanted his bar to be happy.

Tasker came in through the flap as he made the offer. 'That's me, Sarge,' he said. 'Let's have the pint.' He marched up to the table and Fred poured it willingly and gave it to him.

'Miserable bunch in here,' said Tasker to Brigg as he went over and sat on the table with his feet on the form. He lifted the glass and let some of the beer slip down his throat. Then he placed the glass on the table beside him, licked his mouth and sang violently:

> 'She's a big fat cow.
> Twice the size of me,
> She's got hairs on her belly,
> Like the branches on a tree.'

'None of that, Sonny!' called Fred sternly. 'Proper songs. Don't you know any proper songs?'

'That is a proper song, Fred,' complained Tasker. 'What d'you want, hymns or something?'

Fred came around his bar. 'I'll have the pint back then,' he said. 'No,' said Tasker hurriedly. 'I'll sing, Fred. Just a tick. I'll think of one.'

'You sing, Fred,' said one of the others. 'Go on.'

'Yes, go on, Sarge,' they all chorused foolishly like children. 'Give us a song, Fred.'

Before the disturbance had died Fred was singing. He held his hands across the great bow of his stomach and launched himself into an oily chorus:

> 'There she goes, my old gal.
> There he goes, my old pal,
> And here am I, b-r-o-k-e-n hearted.'

The last line he yawned with a great stretch of real and felt emotion, descended into a sorrowful verse, and sobbed on into the refrain once more. The song went on and Brigg looked at Fred's face and saw the sweat coursing down to where his Adam's apple, under its load of fat, was bounding.

Dear old fat Fred Organ. What in God's name was he doing there in the awful jungle, singing his song of homeland under the mosquitoed lamps, and being laughed and called at by these youths, thought

Brigg. He should have been in the Mile End Road in a four ale bar where someone would have listened and cheered him.

'And here am I, b-r-o-k-e-n hearted,' wept Fred, his face rolling with the sentiment of it. He stopped and wiped his chin and his cheeks with a dirty handkerchief, gulped briefly and lumbered back, embarrassed, behind his counter. All the young soldiers cheered.

As commander of the Buksing training camp. Colonel Wilfred Bromley Pickering was anxious not to exhaust the young soldiers entrusted to him. In the afternoons he ordered that guards be placed and everyone else lie for an hour's rest in their tents before swimming and games on the sands.

Brigg lifted the flap of the bell tent at three o'clock and walked across the camp and down to the opening by the beach. He was in his swimming trunks, and the sun jumped on his back as soon as he left the shadow of the tent and the trees. The dust burned the soles of his feet in the open space at the centre of the tents, and the loose sand burned them all over when he reached the beach.

He was first out. There was nobody about. The beach curved to his left and right in a white boomerang. The sea came in indolently, merely reaching for the beach and then slipping away again. The sky was polished blue and the palms did not move.

All it needed was a few naked women, thought Brigg. He had a furtive look down the front of his trunks to see if any news had arrived from Juicy Lucy.

He walked into the sea until it got to his waist, then swam awkwardly out to the middle of the small lagoon. They had come in this far in the landing craft that had brought them from Singapore. The Colonel had insisted that they come by sea in case a land convoy was ambushed. He had demanded it for his young soldiers with tears in his old eye. The landing craft could not come right in because of some reefs of coral, so they had to wade ashore in the warm water. Up to their middles, like real invading soldiers. When they got ashore some of them went back into the sea and came through the waves a second time so that Tasker could take some photographs for them to boast about afterwards.

Brigg rolled on to his back and considered the stainless sky. There came a firm bump on his shoulders and he turned anxiously. It was a log split from a palm, flat and broad as a big fish, and broken a yard from the end. The fibrous strands of the wood still held the two parts together. Brigg swam to it and lifted himself on to its back. With his feet he caught the tail piece and moved it like a rudder. He slowly moved back towards the beach.

Some of the others had come down to swim now and Brigg could see Tasker playing soccer with the Malay boys on the sand. Tasker was a good, rowdy footballer and he was always in the middle calling for the ball and thumping the centred kick towards the goal with his head. The Malays ran, and dived, and scrambled through the sand, sometimes dribbling the ball along the wing, feathering the shallow water, and always shouting and shrieking.

Brigg watched them idly, lying on his log and gently voyaging in. He saw Fred Organ come down to the beach, wearing only a pair of green shorts; so fat and white and red, rumbling along slowly towards the sea and a soothing paddle.

He reminded Brigg of a gigantic granny perspiring under seaside sun. Fred Organ, sergeant with thirty years' service, father of two, half-a-husband, barman, fatman, singer. He walked down to the little waves. Each side of him was the lovely beach and the bowing palms. The lovely beach was sown with twenty-eight landmines which had been buried there since the British left Buksing in a hurry in 1942.

One of the excited Malays took a mad swing at the football and it pranced off his bare foot and rolled towards Sergeant Organ.

Tasker, jumping up and down in front of the goal, called: 'Come on, Sarge, bang it in.'

Fred lumbered towards the ball and swung mightily at it. Brigg heard a wail of laughter start from the Malays. Then Fred Organ was blown up in a fountain of sand and smoke. The bang came afterwards, blasting across the sea in a wave that hit Brigg in the face and threw him off the log.

When Brigg reached him, Fred was lying in the sand, his face sideways. He had no legs and his green shorts were wet and crimson.

Tasker, stammering with tears, bent over him and tenderly lifted his huge face. The side that had been down was thick with sand and blood.

'Christ, Sarge,' whimpered Tasker. 'There was no need to kick it that hard.'

But Fred Organ, heavyweight kicker of anti-personnel mines, wasn't listening.

5

To Brigg all the carcass horror of it could not be compared with the final fact and act. Because, although Fred Organ in life had been twenty-two stone, they buried only about nineteen stone of him.

Months after, when he was in his bed in the barrack room, back at Panglin, he would wonder in agony where old Fred's legs had gone.

Winds or dogs used to wake him up some nights, and he would remain in a sleepless hollow with the thought coming back to him like a vice he couldn't leave alone. They could not find anything of Fred's fat legs at all. They didn't even have any shreds of boot to guide them, because he'd gone for his last wander in his bare feet. No shreds of Fred's.

So they had blown the final bugle over nineteen-twentyseconds of him, with Driscoll upright and sick pale beside the grave in the sweaty jungle earth. Wellbeloved wiping the drinking flies off his nose, and the Panglin conscripts, all of them, unable to stem their tears and their personal terror. A croucher monkey had sat in the tree above Brigg's head for the whole of the service, covering its eyes with its hands, in its natural habit, because it was afraid to move and it thought if it couldn't see the men, they couldn't see it.

Some sappers came down to the beach and found the other twenty-seven mines which someone had forgotten since 1942. They were all hidden in the sand, but half a mile away from where the soldiers from the training camp played.

Because Brigg had horrors about Fred Organ's vanished legs, and blamed the night-time's baying dogs, he used to turn over in bed and hiss at Sandy Jacobs.

'Sandy,' he would say. 'Those dogs are on the go again and I keep thinking about Fred's legs.'

Sandy was a good one to rouse, never upset at being disturbed and always glad to talk away the early, bleak hours with Brigg. He talked of his home and the persecution which his Jewish father had known among the Scots. He had for years played the euphonium in the silver band at Airdrie until some baiter at a football ground had tossed a lighted firework into the bright gaping horn. It had exploded deep in the bowl filling his father's lungs with smoke and fire, so that he never took up the beloved instrument again.

Once they were discussing circumcision and

Sandy said that one of the cookhouse men had been circumcised for reasons of hygiene and had just returned after ten days' sick leave.

Brigg got out of bed and woke Tasker and Lantry. It was not really dark because there was a moon looking daggers through the doors.

'If you get yourself circumcised,' said Brigg, 'you get ten days' sick leave.'

'Get stuffed,' said Tasker grabbing the sheet and pulling it over his head. Lantry was sitting up in his bed, but his head had dropped on to his chest, and he was full asleep again.

Brigg shook them again. 'Listen,' he said close to Tasker's face. 'Listen, you nut! I just said if you get circumcised you get sick leave. Ten days.'

'Oh *come* on,' grumbled Tasker. 'Lay off, will you? So if I get circumcised . . . If I get myself WHAT?'

'Circumcised,' said Brigg. 'You know, like Sandy here when he was a little boy.'

'Aw, go AWAY,' said Tasker. 'For Christ's sake go AWAY.'

Brigg looked at Lantry who continued to sleep sitting up, then dramatically fell back on to his pillow like a man invisibly attacked. Brigg returned to his bed. The dogs had stopped now, and he had temporarily forgotten Fred's legs, because his mind was full of what he was going to do with ten days' sick leave.

When he slept, he slept deeply, and for about ten minutes before Tasker woke him up, shaking him by the ear.

'How much sick leave do you get?' asked Tasker.

'What for?' said Brigg.

'For being circumcised. You know, like you said.'

Brigg said: 'Oh. Ten days.'

'We'd better go sick in the morning then.'

'Not all at once though,' said Brigg. 'Spread it out a bit. Do you think it hurts?'

'Hurts? No. You're better off without it, mate.'

One week from then six members of the barrack room were in one ward at the British Military Hospital in Singapore. They included Private George Fenwick, whose ears were bad, but no worse than they had been when he had been submerging them in the swimming pool. They had built up a form of resistance against chlorine. But being in the water so much had resulted in Fenwick developing a rheumatic shoulder which was being treated in the hospital's physiotherapy department.

Fenwick was already in the ward when Brigg and Tasker were admitted for circumcision for reasons of hygiene.

'I've had a lousy time,' he grumbled. 'Every morning and afternoon they take me down to a freezing cold room with a funny smell about it, and they make me turn a great big wheel four hundred times.'

'Twice a day?' said Tasker.

'Twice,' confirmed Fenwick. 'And they have a little clock on the side which tells them how many times I've turned the wheel around. There's an old brass of a sister there, and she won't let me out until I've clocked up the four hundred either. It's murder.'

'Is it doing anything for your ears?' asked Brigg.

'It's not *for* my ears,' said Fenwick. 'I'm *trying* to get them bad, but while I'm in here I can't get near the swimming pool and they're getting better all the damn time. I've got rheumatics in my shoulder, that's why they make me turn the wheel.'

Brigg said: 'Maybe they'll give you a medical discharge because of the rheumatics.'

Fenwick stared at him. 'I never thought of that,' he said in a smiling whisper. 'Jesus! Fancy never thinking of that! If I told them it was spreading all over my body, down in my knees and all that, I reckon I could work it, don't you?'

'What's the nurses like?' asked Tasker.

'Terrible,' said Fenwick.

'None of them any good at all?' pleaded Tasker. 'None that's not *too* bad?'

'Well,' admitted Fenwick, 'there's a night nurse that's got a nice voice and she's not got a bad figure either. I keep sticking my hand out when she comes past and she gets a bit shirty and says that she thought I had rheumatics in the shoulder.'

'What's she look like? Her face?' said Tasker.

'Nothing special,' shrugged Fenwick who was fatigued with it. 'But her voice is all right.'

The day after Brigg and Tasker arrived at the hospital Lantry, Longley, who had the hunchfront, and Sinclair were admitted. The Panglin medical officer had been drinking because of the heat and sent them all in for hygienic circumcisions.

Sinclair brought with him the *World Book of Railways,* which had 593 pages, and Longley said he hoped that they might be able to do something about his hunchfront while he was in there for the operation.

They were all done in the same afternoon, including Fenwick, who, in the end, went along for the ride, and by evening were laid out cosily in the ward with little white bandages wrapped around their operational wounds.

'I'm sore,' confessed Tasker to Brigg who was in the next bed.

'So am I,' said Brigg. 'It doesn't seem worth it. Never mind, we've got the leave to come now.'

'I'm sore,' said Fenwick to Lantry who was in the next bed.

'So am I,' said Lantry. 'Fancy them doing that to little babies.'

Nurse Blessington, the one with the figure and the voice, came into the ward. Tasker looked over the top of his sheet. So did Brigg. So did Lantry.

She was all in pure virgin white with, as Fenwick said, not much of a face, but she had legs that looked cool and tempting.

'Good evening,' she hummed at Tasker from the bottom of his bed. 'And how are we now?' Tasker, devouring her over the top of his sheet, nodded enthusiastically. She began to talk quietly to him, at the same time caressing his toes which were sticking up clearly under the sheet.

'Ooooooooh,' gasped Tasker suddenly. 'Don't! No more nurse. It hurts.'

'Oh come on,' she smiled. 'Now we *are* making a fuss. I was only touching your toes like this.'

'Ooooooooooh,' moaned Tasker. 'It's not my toes. It's my . . . It's my . . . operation. Ooooo. Ooooch.'

She went from one to the other.

'Ooooooh,' said Brigg. 'Oooooh.'

Fenwick said, 'Ooooooooh.'

Lantry said, 'Ooooooooh.'

And Langley, who had the hunchfront and wasn't very interested in women, said, 'Oh.'

Jacobs had been told a lie by the man in the

cookhouse. There was no sick leave. In three days they were returned to Panglin, but still with their flowery little white bandages.

The dogs started the first night they were back, and Brigg began to think about Fred's legs again. The next day he constructed a lethal catapult made from the back of a chair and two bicycle inner-tubes and set it up ready for firing from the balcony. It could sling a quarter brick for a hundred yards with enough velocity to kill any howling dog. When the dogs began to bay in the midnight dark some of Brigg's companions went on to the balcony to see him fire the first shot. The brick went speedily and strongly hitting Sergeant Wellbeloved, who was crossing the square on his way from the mess, on the left kneecap.

Crying with pain, amazement and bitterness, he went at a hobbling run towards the barrack block where he could see congregated figures on the balcony.

'I'll have you all!' he boiled as he stumbled to them. 'You'll be on it now! Just see! Just see!'

Their frozen inaction at his shout was transformed into cowardly juvenile scamper for their beds as they heard him dragging his leg up the concrete stairs.

He fell in the doorway against the post, got up and switched all the lights on. 'Up!' he bellowed. 'Up you lot! Stand by your beds!'

They moaned and shivered as though they had each been sleeping in a deep, warm hole.

'What's happened? Oh, what's happened?' faltered the nervous Corporal Brook who had really been asleep, creeping white from his sheets like a bloodless wire worm.

Wellbeloved was wearing shorts and his knee showed a puffing bruise, with a red eye of open wound in its centre. He went between the rows of bed like a medieval crippled beggar, clutching the injured place, as he half dragged the leg along. He reached and pulled at Lantry's mosquito net, then gathered it in both arms and wrestled with it until the cord snapped and it fell on the young soldier feigning sleep beneath.

'By your beds!' Wellbeloved ordered once more. 'Get out all of you! I'll have someone on a charge for this. I'll get the bastard.'

They were all out eventually, those who had been genuinely sleeping staring stupidly into the yellow lights. Only Patsy Foster and Sidney Villiers were arrayed in pyjamas and they were wearing each other's trousers, both having emerged from under one mosquito net.

Everyone else was naked. They stood straight but shivering on the stony floor, the walking wounded from the British Military Hospital, having their doctored parts still bandaged, hanging out like white flags along a processional route.

Sergeant Driscoll had been in his room playing darts. It was a new idea for trying to get his eye closed. He had fixed a dart board behind his door and had sat up in bed, with a clutch of thirty-eight darts, variously feathered, on his side locker. He threw them clumsily at the board, right-handed, trying to squeeze his eye at least halfway down with each aim and delivery.

He had thrown two consignments of thirty-eight with no great success, had got out of bed to retrieve them from the board, and was just redressing his aim when he heard Wellbeloved blowing like a moose from the barrack room. He got up, wrapped a towel around his waist, and went to see what was happening.

Wellbeloved was crawling down the middle of the room, between the ranks of naked and bandaged recruits, groaning and grasping his leg with both hands. As Driscoll arrived in the doorway the other sergeant stopped and sagged over to one side.

Driscoll said: 'What's going on, Sergeant?'

Wellbeloved swivelled around on his haunches like a performing animal.

'They've hurt me,' he accused in a unusually high, plaintive voice. 'They threw a brick and hit me. Look, take a look at this then.'

Driscoll advanced and examined the sergeant's knee.

'You'd better see the doctor. Sergeant,' he said formally. 'I'm in charge of this barrack room. I'll deal with the situation here.'

Wellbeloved glared. 'Well I want somebody for this,' he threatened. 'There's going to be a court martial about it, you take it from me.' He groped off in the direction of the stairway. They could hear him giving off small complaints which echoed from the concrete walls and were repeated outside the barrack room as he made his faltering way to the sleeping medical officer.

When he had gone, Driscoll's cold eyes went through his barrack room. His face neutral. He went on to the balcony and returned immediately.

'Fine lot,' he snorted, reviewing them. 'Get back to bed. We'll sort this out tomorrow.' They returned to their sheets. Patsy and Sidney glanced regretfully at each other and climbed into their separate beds.

Driscoll went through the door and switched the main light out. He half-returned and commented: 'And whoever put that bloody great catapult on the balcony had better get rid of it.'

He slammed his door, picked up a fistful of darts and flung them joyously at the board, then collapsed across the bed, trying to contain the gale of hot mirth that blew up within him. But the memory was too rich. Wellbeloved, wounded and wanting vengeance, dragging his leg down the ranks of nude,

106

nipped conscripts. The laughter burst from him like an explosion of gas.

The barrack room heard it through Driscoll's closed door and gurgled and guffawed itself: individual riverlets from the beds in the dark that soon flowed and bubbled unchecked. Great hoots and hollering, huge rolling roars, with writhing under the sheets and hanging heads down to the floor.

On the square the dogs sat and listened in fear. Wellbeloved, trying to get the medical officer out of bed, caught the sound with suspicion and anger. And under the cover of the hilarity and the darkness Sidney Villiers slipped from his own bed and returned gratefully under the hem of Patsy Foster's mosquito net.

6

All the day was hot, the clouds close and sluggish with rain, and the palms standing motionless under them like men with lowered heads.

It was Saturday, and in the morning Phillipa watched from her bedroom as the soldiers of the Panglin garrison attempted military training. The valley, which the wooden bridge spanned, flattened out into a broad red field of shale below her house, with the opposite bank sharp green again and above that the tops of the flat yellow barrack blocks like thick slices of cheese.

The soldiers were split into sections distributed over the hard, red field. They wore green shorts, with boots and gaiters, and berets over their right ears, but no shirts. Phillipa observed them without interest but because it was Saturday and she did not have to go to work at the kindergarten.

It was like this every Saturday morning. There was no office duty so the garrison was split into two, one half embarking hopefully for the rifle range two miles away to discharge bullets at the harmless targets, and the other half attending instruction on the red field.

Phillipa was wearing only the bottom of her pyjamas. It had been a night of compressed heat and she had thrown the jacket away in the early hours. She lay on her breasts on the bed, flat and out of sight of the soldiers below. There were a dozen sections in various parts of the field, and she watched her father moving from group to group using his thick cane to point to things, or tucking it tightly under his arm as he marched a few paces to the next soldiers.

She remembered that cane. Her father had carried it ever since she could recall, and one day when they were in England and she was about sixteen he had caned her with it because he had said she was bow-legged.

She had sobbed while she tried to force her thighs, knees and the inside of her calves together to hold the cold pennies that her father had placed between them. The pennies kept falling and he hit her again and told her she was slovenly and couldn't stand properly. And all the time her mother had been talking to the tortoise which had been her pet before she got the angel fish.

'Try again,' Regimental Sergeant-Major Raskin had ordered through his teeth. 'Go on, girl.' Again he lost patience. 'Here, I'll do it,' he stammered.

She felt his fingers trembling as he put one penny half-way up the fatty tops of her legs, one between her knees and the other at the innermost curve of her calves, all the time with the ginger-brown cane hovering in his other hand. She had shivered and dropped them again, the lower two first, but frantically trying to stop the top one slipping out by thrusting her legs together. She was shaking when he beat her with the cane again, but she suddenly went wild and flew around and caught him in his sergeant-major's face with the nails of her right hand. In terror and fury she tore down his cheek until he had five fingers of blood running towards his mouth. Then she had screamed out and run from the room, tripping over her mother's tortoise on the way, and her mother had called, 'Do be careful, Phillipa, darling.'

Her father had never since said anything about her being bow-legged. But sometimes now, just for fun, she would put pennies in the proper positions inside her legs and never dropped them.

On the shale field lines of soldiers were running at sacks suspended from a horizontal pole, thrusting their bayonets into the sacks and shouting 'Aaaah! Aaaah!' Then they ran to the other side and stabbed again, just to finish off the sacks, and cried 'Aaaah! Aaaah!' again very fiercely. One Saturday a ledger clerk from the orderly room had scampered around the wrong way and been nicked by the point of a bayonet wielded by a warrior from the ration allowance section of the pay office. Training had been suspended and the wounded penman had been carried off with some excitement and commotion to have a piece of plaster stuck over the damaged place.

Another gathering was dismembering a bren gun, and another packing bullets into a sten magazine, while two sections were practising riot drill with Corporal Brook. They had formed up before an imagined mob of disturbed natives to whom Corporal Brook was supposed to address an order which said: 'Go away.' But he had experienced one of his blockages and was unable to force the words to his tongue.

Phillipa noticed Brigg for the first time when Driscoll knocked him to the ground with his elbow. Driscoll had been instructing his squad in camouflage and cover when Brigg swore quietly.

Driscoll stopped. 'Come out here, son,' he said.

Brigg went out.

'What did you say?' Driscoll asked.

'Nothing, Sarge.'

'I heard you, sonny. You called me a something. What was it?'

Brigg said: 'No, Sarge. It was Tasker I said that to.'

The squad laughed and Driscoll told them to shut up.

He said to Brigg: 'Ever done any unarmed combat, Brigg?'

'No,' said Brigg.

Driscoll said: 'There's one trick where you get a bit of the loose flesh which everybody's got around their gut, even you, like this, and you twist it like this.'

He had two ounces of Brigg between his fingers when he turned his wrist. Brigg shouted out and did a somersault, landing hunched to the shale on the side of his face, with his bottom sticking into the air. Everybody was laughing except Brigg and Driscoll.

'Come on then, son,' said Driscoll watching his expression, 'Come on, hit me.'

'I will too,' snorted Brigg springing up and rushing at him. He went straight into Driscoll's elbow and fell down again on his back. His head felt like a tunnel with a running train. 'Had enough?' said Driscoll in his normal voice. 'Right then. Up you get, lad.' Brigg got up and rubbed his cheek.

'Let's have a look,' said Driscoll. He examined Brigg's face. 'Nothing there. No damage, boy. It'll be tea-break soon. I'll buy you a cream bun.'

Regimental Sergeant-Major Rasking went stiffly off the red field at noon, exactly, and walked up the steps to the road and his house. He had a puffy face, with a slice of moustache under his nose, eyes as blue as a doll's, and undernourished sandy hair. His green uniform was the usual Panglin misfit and he wore his web belt right so that the bottom of his jacket, outside the trousers, pirouetted like a small untidy ballet skirt.

He let himself into the cool house. His wife was in the sitting-room asking the angel fish if they knew the time. He went in, hung his belt over the baluster pillar and took off his boots. There was still some red shale from the field on them. He put them carefully in the shallow tray under the hallstand and picked up three particles of shale from the wooden floor. His wife was telling the angel fish that it was gone twelve o'clock. She heard him and called shrilly, but he ignored her and went upstairs in his socks.

He knocked and went immediately into Phillipa's room. She was still wearing only her pyjama trousers. She was sitting at the mirror putting grease on her face. When she saw him in the mirror she crossed her arms across her breasts and shouted violently at him: 'Why don't you knock before you come in here?'

He stood clumsily, as scarlet faced as she was. She ran to the wardrobe and pulled on a housecoat.

'I knocked,' he said. 'I did. I knocked.'

'And came straight bloody-well in!' she screamed back.

'Phillipa, shut up!' he said, his voice in a squeak. 'Shut up, d'you hear!'

They stood on opposite sides of the bed, immediately silent and facing each other.

'Why do we have to row?' he said quietly. 'Every time.'

'Because we hate each other,' she replied logically, turning away and sitting down at the dressing table again. She went on putting grease on her face.

'We don't,' he said sadly. 'We don't really. We used to be all right. It's you're so difficult, and you know it.'

'And you come in here without knocking,' she answered.

'I *did* knock,' he said awkwardly. 'I'm sorry.'

He just stood there watching her and she said nothing more.

'I've said I'm sorry,' he said. 'It's not often you hear that from me, is it?'

'That's true enough,' she said. 'All right then. What was it? What did you want?'

'It's the garrison dance tonight.'

'Oh, Christ,' she said. 'Not another of those. Well if you think I'm going along to let every beery corporal around here belch into my face, then I'm not.'

His voice had solidified when he spoke again. 'You are coming,' he said slowly. 'I am telling you

114

that you *are* coming. It's only once every three or four months.'

She looked at him in the mirror. 'No,' she said, her tone unsteady because she was afraid of him. 'I don't want to come.'

'The Colonel . . .' he began.

'Not him again,' she said sharply this time. 'You'd think I was some sort of camp entertainer or something. He says that you *ought* to bring me along and you jump up and salute and say "Yes, sir. I'll see she comes, sir." I had enough the last time.'

'Don't be funny, Phillipa,' he said nastily, putting his face near her shoulder and staring at her in the mirror. 'You didn't come the last time.'

'Well, the time before,' she said. 'It was terrible. You'd think I was one of those W.R.A.C. whores. Well, I'm not.'

He turned away from her, going towards the door. 'You're going to be ready for that dance,' he said. 'Sharp at eight o'clock.'

She turned from the mirror. 'I'm not,' she said trembling. 'I can't stand them. You can't force me.'

Then he lost his temper, which was what she was afraid of. He strode to her and threw her completely around to him. She was still on the stool and she gripped the housecoat around her. He shook her by the shoulders. 'I *can* force you!' he roared into her face so close she could feel his spit. 'And I will.' He stopped shaking her and brought his face right up to her eyes. 'Do you know what they say about you around here? D'you know? They say you're a bloody lesbian! *They say you like women!* Do you understand what I'm saying? Do you?'

She was crying violently, the tears sliding over the grease on her cheeks, under her chin and down her neck. The grease stopped them from spreading out and each tear kept its shape and symmetry as it travelled down.

'It's wrong,' she protested. 'How can they say that? It's cruel, it's so cruel. None of them know me.'

'It's what is going around,' he said quietly, all the heat suddenly gone from him. 'I've heard it myself.' He stooped down before her and put his hand on her face, on the grease. 'That's why I want you to come. I know you don't want it, but you must. I'm *telling* you, Phillipa dear, I'm not asking you. You're my little girl.'

In lines of eight they showered, shampooed and shaved, singing in the steam because it was the night of the garrison dance and each was joyously certain that, this time, there would be sufficient women to go around.

No one knew from where the women were going to appear. Rumours had seeped like gas around the office blocks all the perspiring day that the Colonel had ordered three buses to go off to the Changi air base to be loaded up with sacrificial WAAFs and obliging NAAFI canteen girls and that they would be arriving, smelling sweetly of promise, on the moment of eight o'clock.

Another story was that the buses were raising dust towards the British Military Hospital where devoted nurses, inwardly convulsed with pent passion, would immediately abandon the sick and dying, and scramble for the seats that would bear them to the hungry young soldiers of Panglin.

A third, and more practical, though still untrue tale, was that the buses had been commissioned, with military policemen, to round up a hundred presentable whores from Singapore and would soon speed back with their erotic loads bursting for a charity night.

The illusion that there would be plenty of women at the garrison dance was perpetual, only outdistanced in unlikelihood by the illusion that whatever women *were* there would be only too glad to oblige behind any neighbouring screen of dewy elephant grass.

The preparations for this imagined feast occupied the conscripts in an orgy of cleaning, brushing, wiping and washing, for two hours before it was due to start. One of the few who knew the truth, and knew that the truth would be the same truth now as it ever was, was Tasker, who watched the fleshy queue for the showers with resigned sadness.

'Scrub yourselves then,' he said morosely. 'It can't do any harm. But what's it going to get you? Not a woman. No fear, not even a decent, wholesome, religious, middle-aged woman. It will get you *nothing* boys; only clean.'

Not many listened. Their exuberance and optimism hummed through the steam, sizzled along the line.

'Go on, scrub,' moaned Tasker. 'It won't hurt. But it will be the same as the last one, and the one before that. Fifteen women, two hundred and fifty of you. And what happens? You end up drunk and singing, or playing tombola. There's no women, I tell you. There's none for nobody.'

He was right. Shining celestially as they did, in civvies tailored in the village at the mortgage of months of pay, they would troop from the barracks over the wooden bridge to the recreation hall for the dance. They set off in jovial groups, with many loud-spoken intentions of having a drink in the canteen first, only to decide against it, and to quicken their pace as they clattered over the bridge, saw the yellow lights of the recreation hut, and heard the tortuous tuning of the Marines' dance band from the naval base.

Just as inevitably they fell into a great black hole as

they entered the hall and found it peopled by no strange and champing women, but a sedate assembly from the married family houses, trestle tables covered with cloths and platoons of bottled beer, and the labouring band. Only the floor was naked, only the starched table cloths were virgin, and the only grind came from the musicians.

There was always, of course, the hope that the mythical buses, ordered by the Colonel, would suddenly skid outside and discharge their cargoes of joy. But the hope eroded with time and beer and dumb foxtrots, until it avalanched completely into despair and most got maudlin drunk and cried over old, faraway loves, to whom they were being continually faithful, and sang songs of the better times.

It was the same this time. Brigg waited for Tasker and Tasker took his time. There was, he pointed out, no point in hurrying to shave and sweeten yourself just to fall drunkenly on your face in a monsoon drain.

Brigg said: 'If it's no use, if there's nothing at all but the usual, I'm going to get a taxi down to Singapore.'

Tasker said: 'I'll come too. We might as well now we've got all done up.'

They combed their hair in the barrack room, empty now save for Gravy Browning, batting his table-tennis ball against the hard wall and the harder floor. He was playing in the All-Malaya championships on the following night.

Brigg and Tasker went over the bridge, idly at first, but then quickened by some inherent, malignant optimism that this time there would be some. They sensed it in each other although they did not mention it. But they began to pace out smartly on the other side of the bridge, and eventually, as they saw the bright windows of the hall, and heard the baying of the band, and the machinery sound of gathered people, they jogged and then trotted quite briskly and with growing expectation.

The door was open and there was a mass just inside. All soldiers. Brigg and Tasker burrowed through as though it were a riot crowd. They burst out of the other side and stopped, cruelly drenched with disillusionment. All around the floor were the hungry orphan faces of their comrades. A great circle of them, wearing the forlornness of lost boys. Defiantly, the band played. Grotesquely, in the centre of the barren floor, exhibiting an over-deft fishtail step was Sergeant Wellbeloved and the prematurely-aged wife of a transport pool lance-corporal. Wellbeloved jolted, jerked and jazzed her around, grinning despicably with his shark's teeth, and enjoying every minute of music and the famous attention he was achieving.

Some of the watchers began to turn away from the

hideous pair and make for the bar and the first serious indulgence of a night they already knew would be, at first reluctantly, consigned to getting disgustingly and immaturely drunk.

'Every time,' said Tasker abhorrently. 'Every crappy time. I told you, didn't I? I told them all.'

'Well, have one then,' said Brigg sadly, 'then we'll go down to Singapore.'

He was, inside, doubly ashamed that he should want Lucy so much, and conversely, that he should feel so guilty about her that he should steel himself to keep away. His desire, when he returned from Buksing, had been like a hot shovel and he had intended to go down to her that urgent first night. But he had stopped himself and gone instead over to a desk in the quiet garrison writing-room and had composed a loving letter to Joan. The more he wrote the worse his depression curdled in him. He had reached the end like a man reaching firm ground after trudging through a morass, and he had looked up to see a mean green cricket, six inches long, sitting on the inkwell and staring at him with a black accusing eye.

Tasker bought the beer. 'They'll end up maudlin at the moon. D'you remember that last time, that halfwit Taffy from the armoury sitting on the bridge and singing about Wales and all that crap, and crying all over the steps. That's how they'll be in a couple of hours and I don't want to be here to see it.'

'I've got a girl in Singapore,' said Brigg abruptly, looking straight down into the yellow pond of his beer.

Tasker stopped halfway through a mouthful and let it slip back down into the glass. 'You've got *what?*' he said.

'A girl,' said Brigg stonily. 'A Chinese girl . . .'

'You bleeding twister!' said Tasker enthusiastically. 'Why didn't you say. Maybe she's got a friend . . .'

Brigg stopped him. 'She's on the game,' he said.

Tasker's smile skidded from his face. 'A pro?' he said.

'That's right,' said Brigg, glad and sorry that he had told someone at last.

'How d'you mean *you've* got her, then?' argued Tasker, strangely bitter. 'You and half the army, and half the dockyard, and every dirty sailor who gets in here. I bet she's got a collection of everything.'

'This one's a bit different,' said Brigg foolishly.

'Oh, no,' groaned Tasker. 'You mean she's *your* pro. She waits for you, banging her legs back and fore, just to be ready when you turn up.'

'I've only seen her once,' said Brigg lamely. 'Before we went to Buksing.'

Tasker laughed, relieved. He said: 'I reckon they ought to send you home . . .'

He did not finish because the door of the hall opened

and the women walked in. They were only W.R.A.C. girls, it was true, and three rough nurses from the garrison sickbay, but there were twenty of them. The soldiers rushed like older people rush to see royalty.

Tasker left Brigg's side like a stag. Brigg saw him go through the funnel of the converging hopefuls, and emerge only seconds later with a quarry-faced young woman with a tight bust and thick legs. They began to dance a functional foxtrot. Tasker had a look of reptile contentment.

Phillipa Raskin went into the recreation hall with her parents. They went in first and she followed closely, almost hiding behind her father. She was wearing a dusty pink dress, her father was in his formal uniform with his medals and her mother was swathed with roses on a yellow background. Phillipa's brown arms and neck looked soft with the pink; her father, she thought, always appeared grand in his finery; her mother's grey hair and grey face topping her hothouse dress achieved a hideous effect.

Phillipa's father, unasked, passed his daughter a gin and orange and whispered: 'Now let's see you try to enjoy yourself. Be natural. Don't let them think you're a duchess.'

'Or a Lesbian?' she suggested.

His face angered sharply. 'No more of that,' he said glancing about him unsurely. 'You don't want to take that too much to heart. It was nothing really.'

'It was to me,' she said.

A bombadier with blue pimples, who was master of ceremonies, hugely relieved that after the grim start the gathering had now formed itself into occupational groups, wining and wenching, announced a ladies' invitation dance.

Phillipa moved forward at once, shakily but with determination. Her father, thinking she was hurrying for the door, made to hold her, but stopped when he saw she was walking towards a tall, thin private standing unhappily ten yards away.

Sergeant-Major Raskin was surprised, but not so surprised as Brigg. At first, stupidly, he thought she was looking for the toilet.

'Yes,' he quivered when Phillipa asked him. 'Yes. Sure. Of course.'

'You'd better put your beer down first,' she suggested. That's what she hated about them.

'Oh, yes,' said Brigg. He wheeled and thrust his glass into the surprised hands of Lantry who happened to be standing behind him. Brigg did not want her to get away. Lantry saw Brigg and Phillipa move off on to the floor and drank Brigg's beer.

Brigg could scarcely believe that she had her

hands gently locked in his. That her dark hair was no distance from his cheek. That his subtle glance could see the shaded stab down inside the front of her dress. He moved casually towards the corner of the floor which was more crowded in the hope that their bodies might get pressed closer together. There was a long glow all down him like a hot poker. He saw Tasker dancing with his stone woman and smiled with huge satisfaction.

But Phillipa was hard. She made an insipid face as she stumbled on his right foot for the second time. 'You make that one up, don't you!' she said.

Brigg was a good dancer and he knew it wasn't his mistake. 'Lack of practice,' he said. 'Sorry.'

She carped a couple more times about him leading so strongly. 'You're not supposed to push like that,' she sulked. He felt his foot go over hers like a dog jumping on another dog. He was confused. He mumbled another apology. She complained about the band, and the crowd and the beery air.

He agreed with her each time. When the dance was over he begged for the next one and they made three silent circuits of the floor, before she abruptly asked to be excused and left him standing alone, circled by half a dozen wide and knowing grins.

Brigg walked, stumbled almost, towards Lantry. 'Where's mine?' he said.

'I finished it for you,' shrugged Lantry. 'I thought

you wouldn't be back. And I didn't think you'd be bothered about half a pint of beer.'

Brigg said: 'Well I am. How about buying me one.'

Lantry faced him sharply. Then 'All right,' he said. They pushed through to the bar. 'What was she like?' asked Lantry.

'Who?' said Brigg.

'Oh, *come* on,' urged Lantry. 'The place isn't overflowing with them.'

'She's a real cow,' said Brigg, swallowing the beer.

Phillipa was like a morsel in a fish tank now. They nibbled at her one after another and she kept shaking her head, although when she saw her father's glance, twice, she accepted an invitation to dance. After an hour she was sick of it all. Then she saw Driscoll leaning against the wall ten yards away, caught his look, and remembered him from the swimming pool.

In another hour Brigg was poetically, unhappily drunk. He was as alone as a broom in a corner. Tasker had taken his woman out to a clump of elephant grass. Driscoll was standing where he had stood the whole evening drinking soberly. Phillipa was sitting sulkily watching her mother scream around the floor, a floral flier, in the Gay Gordons.

Her father, sickly with drink, was talking too loudly to the fat Sergeant Herbie Fisher.

Phillipa got up, mumbled, and walked towards the Ladies at the far end. Her father stopped talking and watched her go.

Raskin said: 'She's no good, Herbie. No bloody good. But she's going to stay here 'till the end. You watch, Herbie, I'll make sure she doesn't get near that door.'

First Brigg went to the toilet. Then he went back and bought Lantry a last beer. Raskin and Herbie Fisher were giggling, their big sweaty heads together. Mrs. Raskin was dashing the White Sergeant with a pale private. Brigg went out.

Phillipa was stepping alone and quickly down the sloping road to her house. There had been a shower and the air was hollow and cool for a while. Brigg was full drunk and he remembered how she had treated him. He walked after her and she heard him coming, because, although she continued without turning, he saw she was afraid. Her back stiffened. She had a woollen jacket around her shoulders and she pulled it to her throat. Her feet began to race each other, but still walking.

Brigg, when he was nearly beside her, said: 'Your old man said he wasn't going to let you escape.'

She turned her dark head sharply to see, then she said: 'I got through the toilet window.'

'Yes, it was lousy,' he said. 'But it always is. You didn't do much to help, did you?'

'I hate soldiers,' she said.

'So do I,' said Brigg. 'I hate them all.'

She did not say anything. Brigg said extravagantly: 'I hate them because they're like your old man and because they're like me. Forlorn bastards all of us.'

Phillipa glanced at him. He was striding out a couple of yards from her. They went past the Army Laundry. He looked up at the sky, bereft of earlier rainclouds now, and felt the beer inside him making him feel good and confident and with plenty to say.

'I hate soldiers!' he shouted. 'I hate them because they *carry* them on to guard mountings so they keep clean. I hate them because they're always sticking up their bleeding thumbs – there, like that!' He thrust his thumb triumphantly at the Southern Cross. 'And I hate them because they bury them without legs.'

'You're mad,' she laughed.

He called at her. 'I'm not mad! I'm just a soldier. It's the same. They're all mad. They still teach you to stick bayonets in sacks and shoot little bullets, because they don't believe in the atom bomb. They think it was cheating and that some men in white coats let it off who weren't soldiers, so that it doesn't really count. They still talk about it as though nothing has happened. They want to fight again – their way!

128

They're fireproof, that's what they think. Drunk and fireproof and useless and unwanted and mad!'

She pointed at him. 'I saw you this morning,' she said. 'You were the one who got knocked down.'

'Driscoll, the bastard,' he said. 'Unarmed combat! What good's that going to be with the bomb! Unarmed! That's what they'll be all right, unarmed, and unheaded, and unbodied. Unlegged. That's it! Unlegged, like old Fred Organ. He got killed, you know, in unlegged combat.'

They got to the wooden bridge. He felt fumbling drunk. She helped him on to the top rail and he sat balanced there. She sat opposite on the other rail. Her legs were hooked under the middle slat and her oval knees projected from her dress like two brown eggs. She was laughing at him.

'They'll all be along here soon,' said Brigg trying to focus her knees. 'Sitting along here singing about Wales, or Scotland or the Old Kent Bloody Road. And telling each other what gorgeous girls they've got waiting for them at home. That's except Tasker and some of the others who've got something tonight. Nothing much – but something.'

'How long have you been here?' she said.

'Years, I think. About ten months. I've seen you though. I've seen you in the distance. I couldn't believe it when you asked me to dance. I thought you wanted the bog.'

She sniggered. 'No, really I did,' said Brigg. 'I couldn't think of anything else.'

She said thoughtlessly, 'You were the nearest.'

'Thanks,' he said. He was trying to stalk and pin down his thoughts now, behind the beer. It was like moving about in the dark at the back of a yellow screen. If he could keep her here for a bit, so that he could get an opening, he could ask her to see him again. Go swimming in the reservoir or go for a walk along the pipeline.

'How about going for a walk on the pipeline,' he heard himself saying blatantly before he was nearly ready. 'You know, the big one. You can stand on it and walk along it.'

'It's too dark,' she said without fuss.

'Not now,' he explained, picking the words so he would remember when he was sober. 'Tomorrow afternoon. It's Sunday and it's good walking along the pipeline because you don't get all caught up with the jungle. I'm not saying now. I mean when I can stand up.'

She said she would see him there. She got down from the rail, and helped him descend like an invalid. Then she pushed him along the wooden planks of the bridge in the direction of the barracks. He went, propelled, reasonably straight, and he didn't turn around.

Phillipa walked to her house. She went straight to her father's cocktail cabinet and poured and quickly drank three gins, a beer, and two whiskies. Holding the table, she began to cry.

'Here's to unlegged combat,' she croaked, lifting the empty glass. 'I'll see who's a bloody Lesbian and who isn't.'

She went sobbing in a staggering run to the door. Then she returned and poured a stiff Scotch in the tank of the angel fish and rushed again crying to the door. She looked out, intending to call to Brigg if he was still on the bridge. She saw someone there and shouted: 'Soldier! Soldier!' because she didn't even know Brigg's name.

The soldier stopped and walked up the road to her. She thought there was something wrong because he was broader than he had been. When he got to the gate she saw it was not Brigg. It was Driscoll.

Phillipa giggled stupidly. 'Not you,' she said. 'The other one. You're the one who can't close his eye.'

When Driscoll had killed his own men outside Caen he had spent the night walking and loudly singing to himself along the broken lanes and prostrate woods behind the battlefield. It was a night of recurring horror for him as he kept feeling the bren swivel in his hands again and seeing its bullets stick them like pigs to the low wall. Twice he was all but shot by jumpy sentries, and in the end the military police picked him up because they thought he was wandering drunk. He wasn't. He had not drunk anything all night, or for days before, but he was just walking and singing and they didn't like it because there was a battle going on. They asked him if he realised there was a battle going on and he laughed at that and said he did.

He reckoned, on the just balance of things, that he ought to have a whole lifetime of luck after that. Just to compensate him. But then they found out about his eye and made him leave his good regiment; and that was more debit. And there were other things. Very little of it had ever been made up to him. Really, ending up lying on Phillipa's bed with the light, his shoes, and his trousers all off, was the luckiest thing that had happened to him in all the time since he killed his own men at Caen.

He stretched on his stomach on her quilt, still wearing his shirt. She was still in her dusky pink dress and she was lying beside him but they were not touching. It was sixteen years since Caen, and Driscoll could wait a few more minutes.

'How did you know about me not being able to close my eye?' he said. She was raving drunk and she had been sick in the wash basin. But after all he didn't get her drunk. She had got herself drunk, alone, downstairs. He knew because he had put the bottles and the glass away. There was old Raskin to consider, or course. He would arrive home at some time. But Driscoll doubted if he would manage the stairs.

'Your eye?' she said, trying to remember. 'You had hardly nothing – I mean hardly *anything* – on then either. It was at the pool. I was in it and you were out of it, walking along the edge and swearing about your eye, and I heard you but you didn't see me.'

Driscoll turned his face from her and looked at the dark fan of the palm tree in the garden, shadowed against the sleeping sky. He stretched out his right hand behind him until it left the silk quilt and touched the rough softness of her dress. He let it travel further until his four fingers were lying flat across her leg, on the fatty thigh part where her father used to make her put the pennies.

She thought she felt her stiffen, but she softened again at once. She lay still, looking up through her hair, which had fallen across her face, and she did not touch him.

'What are you?' she said.

'What am I what?' he mumbled, his head in the quilt, his groin throbbing like a factory because of the feel on the remote outpost of his finger tips.

'What are you?' she repeated. 'Like a general or a corporal, I mean.'

'I'm halfway between the two,' he said. 'I'm a sergeant.'

'Sergeant Driscoll,' she said drunkenly. 'It's a nice name, it suits you.'

They were quiet for a minute or more. Driscoll could hear the first maudlin drunk conscripts singing from the bridge.

'You're a sergeant,' she recited. 'And I'm a Lesbian.'

Driscoll thought his luck had run out. But he turned around quietly and gently to her. 'What did you say?' he said.

'I'm a Lesbian,' she said, parting the lace strands of her hair and looking through the curtains at him. 'Didn't my father tell you?'

'No,' said Driscoll slowly. 'He didn't mention it.'

She said quietly, 'I thought he told everyone. He told me.'

Relief blew through him like a friendly wind. 'You're not, then?' he suggested.

'I don't know. My father says I am, and he's my father. I don't really know if I am or not. That's why you're here.'

Driscoll was going to say: 'If you want to find out you should really have another girl.' But he thought it wasn't the right time.

'Sergeant Driscoll,' she said, beginning to cry. 'Show me I'm not.'

Her hands reached out to him like ghosts, and her fingers went to his hard neck. He pushed his hand beneath her, slipping it fluently along the quilt, caught her with both his hands behind her cool legs and rushed them up to her buttocks. Then he levered her towards him, kissing her through her wild, falling hair, all over her face and then her lips. Her hair got in the way too much and they pushed it away, both of them, before returning their hands to the places they had been. Driscoll felt a giant tenderness towards her, suddenly, inexplicably, because he was a hard man and it had never happened before with any woman except his dear wife.

'Never have I felt like this with anyone but my dear wife,' he murmured.

'You have a dear wife?' she said, still kissing his chin.

'Not now,' he said. 'She is someone else's now.'

'I've never had *one* man,' she said. 'But I'm the *second* woman you've had.'

Driscoll did not argue.

'You're a real virgin?' he said.

'Of course. A real Lesbian virgin.'

'We'll soon alter that.'

'I hope so,' she said anxiously. 'Oh, Sergeant Driscoll, I *do* hope so.'

There was a delay while he tried to find how her dress came off.

He cursed himself while he searched. There had been a day when he would have noted every button, every zip, every hidden hook and tiny eye, long before the light went out.

'It's just got a little zip,' she said helpfully. 'A little toy zipper just at the side. Then you have to pull it off over my head.'

He took it off while she lay quiet, lifting each of her lovely arms individually, and separating the rough rustling dress away from her calm body.

Driscoll had never seen anything like her. He was kneeling across her, all his flippancy gone now because this was much too serious. He put his hands beneath her on one side and turned her on to her front. He undid her bra and then slid his palms along the quilt underneath to feel her freed breasts. He rolled her luxuriously in his hands and kissed her buried backbone. Then he slid his palms down the whole length of her trunk and continued down her hips and legs, deftly hooking her panties with his thumb as he went by.

Then he turned her again, naked, and he knew that all the bad luck of killing his own men, and not being able to close his eye, and losing his dear wife, was being repaid.

Her eyes were considering him through the cage of her fallen hair, watching the full wonder on his soldier's face. He met them and pulled the stare away from her face and released it to run like an excited riverlet down the moulds of her body.

He pressed his dry mouth to her and followed the path his eyes had taken with his thirsty tongue. All the way down, on slope and shadowed valley, along the narrow burrow of her navel, in and out the little middle hole, and then into the humid places. He ran his tongue down the inside of her left leg leaving a trail like a snail, and then went back for the right. He kneeled up and she caught him with her wildly seeking hands and all but tore the rest of his clothes away. He knelt there in the dark light and she looked up and saw him.

'Jesus Christ, Sergeant,' she whispered. 'I'll be too small.'

She cried a hollow cry and began to weep. 'I knew I would,' she sniffed. 'Oh, I knew I'd be too small! I always knew it. I'll have to marry a gnome or a midget or something.'

He bent across her. She felt him hot, branding her stomach. He pushed her hair off her face and kissed her again. Almost as an afterthought she reached out and picked up his shirt and pushed it beneath her bottom.

Driscoll levered himself away from her face, retreated a little way down her body, and slowly began to advance again.

'Oh, Sergeant,' she gasped. 'It hurts. Like God it hurts.'

'Not very much,' he assured. 'Hardly anything.'

'But it does. But it does.'

He couldn't think of an answer. He bit her on the shoulder and ran his teeth down to her breast.

'Gentle, Sergeant,' she whimpered. 'Be gentle. I really need a gnome. Oh, how I need a gnome, Sergeant.'

He got closer inside her ear and whispered with cunning: 'But you don't want a Lesbian gnome, do you? You know *that* now, anyway.'

Phillipa flung her arms around the band of his head and hugged him as though trying to break it. 'Now, Sergeant, now. *Please now!*' she choked.

Then it was. The pain made her leap, but then suddenly they were over the reef, and then the warm tide flowed and ebbed, and they lay beautifully, moving clean like swimmers side by side.

'Oh, Sergeant, you bastard,' Phillipa said.

There was a turquoise and violet dawn spilling over the sky when Driscoll went back with his shirt rolled under his arm. The air was cool damp and he could feel it taking the heat out of his bare chest, arms and shoulders. He ran across the wooden bridge like a carefree ape, charged the steps in threes, and spat at, and miraculously hit, a moon-eyed bullfrog squatting on the monsoon drain.

He ran up the stairs on to the middle floor of the barrack block. The boys had enjoyed a good night.

Corporal Brook's bed, unbeknown to Corporal Brook, who was in it, was hung five feet from the ground on ropes looped over one of the main roof beams. Young soldiers lay everywhere as though slain, some on beds, some on the floor, and some shipwrecked between. Most still had their clothes on. Some had been nastily sick. Others held loving bottles and Tasker snored clutching a captured salmon pink bra. Brigg, never to know what he had missed, slept a pure drunken sleep.

Driscoll went into his own room, stripped, and strode to the shower. A queasy lance-corporal was asleep on the dank floor of one of the cubicles. Driscoll went to the next. He let the stream of cold water hit him sharply like a dropping sword, jumping at its first strike, but then tackling it and mixing into it. He soaped himself and let the shower take away the froth. Then he soaped his thick loins again, thoroughly, and looking down at the refreshed region he remarked: 'You're a miracle, you are. You've done very well for your age. And you saved that innocent girl from going queer.

'Saved her. You ought to get the bloody Nobel Prize for Medicine, you did, son.'

It was a delicious memory. Not just Phillipa and all she had given and he taken, not just the way they lay after the third time, resting and listening to the maudlin drunks singing songs of home on the bridge, but the other thing.

7

Rosalind had been Driscoll's dear wife. She had married him in the last six months of the war – and of her pregnancy. They loved each other dearly, like children, but in the end she could stand him no longer and divorced him and went and married someone else.

The first night she knew Driscoll she had supported him home from a party because he had taken too much to drink, and had begun to cry about God not letting him close his eyes properly, and about how it affected his shooting. He had been spoiling the party for everyone else, so Rosalind took him to her house and kept him there for several days until his leave was up.

He was tired from the war, and they did not send him back to it because they had begun to wonder in the army as to whether he was a nut or not, especially after he had been arrested for walking about and singing when there was a battle going on at Caen.

But he was kept in the army, and when peace came they went to the fighting in Palestine. After two weeks their baby girl was killed by an R.A.F. jeep which was chasing Irgun Zwei Leumi terrorists who had hanged some airmen in a lovely orange grove.

Rosalind went back to England. He followed, and, except when he was away, or was drunk, they had days of sweet understanding and happiness together. She was a girl four years younger than Driscoll, with soft careful looks, a great but quiet charm, and an inherent happiness that gradually died every time he hurt her.

Once, after Palestine, when they were trying to forget their little girl, and trying to make another to take her place, they had gone back to Derbyshire, near where she had first met him.

One Sunday they had gone out to a place where some rocks grew suddenly from the countryside – tall rocks, standing like a group of bald-headed singers all in a circle. They had climbed them and by the time they had reached the flat pate of the tallest they were hot with the sun.

It was early summer, about June, as Driscoll remembered – and he did often – and from there it looked like the whole of the many coloured earth was laid out for them to see. They stretched and examined everything in detail, playing at where they would like to live and be happy with their new little girl when they got her. Clouds were big but far between that day, and their elephant shadows flowed over the fields occasionally, extinguishing the glinting of ponds and greenhouses, and cooling cattle. They hung sometimes across the married lovers lying on the hard top of the rock.

'It's going to be good from now on,' she said with her dark head lying on his stomach. 'This is going to be our best summer.'

Driscoll loved her. Loved her then when she was there, and loved her ever after when she wasn't and never would be again.

'You don't have to stay in the army, do you?' she said suddenly. 'They can do without one soldier.'

He took it she was joking. He sat up and her head slid down on to his lap. He said: 'I can see them letting me go now. I've just signed for another five.'

'I mean it,' she said, looking up at his face and his fair bristly hair against a loitering cloud. 'If you come out we can be properly together. I'm sick of counting our lives away, while you're somewhere else and I'm waiting for you to come back or to get there with you. I'm sick of the places the army gives us to live. I'm sick of the army.'

He saw she meant it. She was lying in his lap, her face now turned tight into his legs. 'Ros, darling,' he said. 'I've told you. I've sold myself for another five. There's nothing else I know I can do for a living. I'm a soldier like other men are bakers or bank managers.'

'But the bakers and bank managers used to be soldiers too,' she argued. 'And they got out. I love you, and I want you all the year, and all the years, not a few days at a time.' She looked pathetic. 'You get drunk, and they're all the same in the army.'

He grinned at her: 'Bad company I've been keeping,' he said.

She was going to buy him out, she announced, and he rolled her over on the rock and laughed so loud that it bounced about for two minutes in echoes from the sunny rocks. But she said she was, and Driscoll, to humour her, said she could, but he would be expensive. They made love then, up on the bald head of the rock, because they did not have to be in bed to do it. And no one was about anyway.

The trouble was she did save up. It took her a sacrificial year from that summer's day, but eventually she dumbfounded Driscoll by showing him the two hundred pounds and joyfully telling him that she was buying him out. Because he loved her he let her do it, but two days after he was released he ran away from her, got drunk and dazed, and while he was still in the aftermath of it went and signed on in the army again for seven years. With five in the reserves.

Even then he or she could have got him out. He

was drunk, or just after being drunk, when he did it, and the army would not have kept him. But he knew he was in for good now, for always. It was not the army which was keeping him.

They were divorced in eighteen months, still loving each other with such dearness that they went and had a cup of tea after their court hearing, and then kissed each other outside on the pavement, and went away for ever.

So many times the thought of her lay restless on him after that. Her good sense, her giving and her forgiving, her sweetness and her love for him. He loved her too, a huge needy love that made him reach out from his remote bed and catch only darkness.

He tried to find her again. Before he went to Malaya. He went to Derby and asked around the town for her. In the places where she had worked, in the pubs they had gone together, and the people living around the house where her mother had lived. But her mother was dead. It was winter and it rained cold rain all the time, and he went from street to street and place to place all through the streaming town.

Someone said they had seen her. But they couldn't recall where. Someone said she had gone away, abroad. But they couldn't be sure. He walked, heavy and tired with remembering, down the street behind the market square where they had once lived in two rooms. It was the same house, the weeds in the diagonal front garden patch were the descendants of the old weeds, even the curtains were the same. Some things never changed. But there was no one in, and rain was cutting and there was no porch for him to shelter.

He knew he would never see her again. And then he saw her. It was so simple that it might have been arranged. He got on to a bus, and sat on the end, longways, seat. He looked up and she was sitting directly opposite. She was with a man and the man was holding a shawled baby. Rosalind and her husband were looking into the hidden face. Driscoll saw that she was happy. When she looked up she looked directly into Driscoll's eyes.

They sat transfixed. The narrow gangway between them like a chasm. Driscoll knew she did not want him to say or do anything. So he didn't. He was simply looking at her, feeding on her for the last time. The family got off the bus at the next stop and Driscoll saw her lift her face up to the rain so that it would wash away her tears, which was just like her.

Driscoll remained there, in the wet steamy downstairs of the bus, until it stopped and the conductor said to him: 'This is as far as we go, Sarge.'

'Yes,' agreed Driscoll. 'I suppose it is.'

*

Brigg had walked the pipeline with Phillipa. They had gone along it like circus tightrope walkers, their bare feet to its warm, black, rounded back. They had held hands like a playing boy and girl. That was the trouble. Brigg was not in the market for holding hands. They had been to dances, and swimming, and walks, and had held each other close and enjoyable near her front door afterwards. He was familiar with her feel and her kiss and he was the envy of every man at Panglin except Driscoll. Brigg knew nothing about Driscoll and his girl, although Driscoll knew about him and was not worried.

But it was all wrong for Brigg. It was like buying a packet of dirty pictures and unwrapping them to find views of the Eiffel Tower. He wanted, desperately needed, sex, good unwholesome sex, and Phillipa, he explained to his inward desire, was not that kind of girl.

He pretended to the boys, of course, that it was all they imagined. When he returned from her at night he always stopped deliberately outside the barrack room, pulled his tie awry, and assembled his face into a casually smug, knowing-all, faintly smacking-the-lips smile, and they would catch it as he strolled in. He had seen Tasker roll on his sheets in a sheer agony of jealousy, and even the erection contests with Lantry were discontinued through the pale inadequacy of them.

It had not been easy for Brigg to return to Lucy. But in the end, in the same humble, excited manner as he had gone to her in the first place, he had abruptly stopped fighting, flung his qualms, postponements and indecisions aside, and hurried to her on the bus.

He doubted if she would remember him. She not only did, she welcomed him, her virgin soldier, her pupil, her private Bo-peep, who did not know where to find it. She called him Bigg instead of Brigg, an unintentional compliment born of her pronunciation difficulties. Brigg had from then, been visiting her as often as he could be away from Phillipa and the army, including Wednesday afternoons which were the permitted recreation periods.

That night he lay feeling the wooden deck boards pressing against the small fat of his backside, the bones of his shoulder blades and the tufty hair at the tail of his scalp. It was beyond midnight, lucid and warm, and he stretched naked on the flat prow of the sampan. Lucy lay naked too, at right angles to Brigg, facing the sky, head in his groin, her free black hair exploding over his pale loins.

They had swum from the harbour wall and emerged over the low side of the bouyed sampan. They had made real and primitive love while they were still streaming wet, with bits of harbour refuse sticking to them, rolling like puppies and making the shallow boat pitch in its own storm.

Then they rested, half-drugged by their love making, and began to feel the bruises from the deck, unnoticed before, while the air dried them and comforted them. There were lights ashore, sweeping car beams on the harbour road, and all the still lights that hung to the framework of the rising city, with neon signs flashing desperate signals, and the advertisement on top of the Cathay skyscraper out-gleaming them all. There were lights on other boats too, dipping near the water like people exchanging courtesies. But their sampan was quietly dark.

Lucy said: 'Tell me again, about the meeny miney.'

Brigg grunted a laugh: 'You'll learn it yet,' he whispered, feeling out for her face and running his fingertips fractionally along the slants of her eyes.

'I try,' she said earnestly. 'This time, I very try.'

'Right,' he said:

'Eeny Meeny, miney mo,
Catch a feller by his toe . . .'

She repeated it, singing it, saying it, in her clear tinkling voice. Catch a feller by his toe. Catch a *feller* – no nigger – by his toe. When he was teaching it to her, when they were fooling on the yellow Changi beach that afternoon, he had stopped at 'nigger' and called it 'feller' instead. She was Chinese and her skin was cream white, whiter than his, but he made it 'feller' instead of 'nigger'.

He knew it should have been Phillipa lying there on the flat chest of the boat. But it was Lucy, infant, happy, generous Lucy, who loved him, he knew, and gave to him with love, unlocking the secret store cupboard of special things which all professional lovers keep alone for the ones they want, and who never have to pay.

He stretched until his joints yawned. He thought back across the day and what a full day it had been, splashing in the sand with the bald sun and the wavy sea.

They had swum long off Changi beach, holding hands and sometimes bodies in the opaque water, and they had eaten Chinese crab, and he had heard her laughing like chimes while he flew from the water after doing his comic dive.

If it were not for his guilt about her, lying beneath his surface like a layer of fat. If it were not for that, it would have been all right. It was like having a carefree day, pretending, with someone you secretly knew was dying. The voice was there that she was Lucy, and not just a young girl.

Brigg thrust his closed fist behind his head, pushing his chin up on to his chest, and looked down at her along the thin plank of his body. She screwed

150

her head in his groin, so that her hair gently roughened his skin. She looked young and unused. Her eyes were rounded almond and set in clear, clean places behind her fine cheekbones.

'Bigg,' she said, 'tell me more sayings, more rhymes, like eeney meeny.'

Brigg said softly: 'That's for little children.'

'Well for old people then. The sayings of old people.'

Brigg groped for something. Something simple for her.

'I have one,' he said, moving his eyes from the sky.

'Is it easy?' she asked anxiously. 'It must be small words, so I understand. Little and easy like the stars.'

He told it to her.

> 'Oh, but this world's a funny place,
> And yet it's hard to beat.
> With every rose you get a thorn,
> But ain't the roses sweet?'

She liked it; she thought it was beautiful and wise, and they lay as she stumbled over it and tried to learn it. Then a puff of late wind, on its way home, came over the water and touched their skins. They looked up from their sampan and saw that the town was quiet now. It was time for them to go.

*

Brigg did not see her for three days, but he wrote it out for her. So she would learn and remember it. When he had written three lines he went to the top of the barrack room to collect his mail and returned to find Tasker had completed the verse.

> 'Oh, but this world's a funny place,
> And yet it's hard to beat.
> With every rose you get a thorn,
> Don't it get on your tits?'

Phillipa, who before that one busy night had never had a man, now had two. 'One for *one* thing,' she told herself logically, 'and the other for the *other* thing.'

It did not occur to her that Brigg wanted more than young love, or that Driscoll wanted more than ancient sex, wondrous though it remained.

There were only two cards and Phillipa, to whom nothing simple ever happened, had mis-shuffled.

8

Every first Monday of the month they would go out killing dogs. Wellbeloved and Driscoll were both very good at killing dogs, shooting them with murderous talent right in some special spot in their dirty white, yellow, or brown fur.

Each sergeant had a detail of three men. They would go through the garrison roads and then down to the village and along the white road out towards the city, hurrying around in squat, fifteen hundredweight trucks, shooting dogs all over the place. They were only supposed to kill the waif dogs, the ones without collars who fornicated and multiplied, smelled on hot days, and yowled at night on the barrack square. There were not many dogs without collars, so they shot at every dog they saw. If they found it had a collar when they went up to it after killing it, then they took the collar off and hid it somewhere.

Driscoll took one truck and Wellbeloved the other. They were always in charge of the dog hunters, but Brigg, who hated the dogs more than anyone because of waking up and thinking about Fred's legs, did not like shooting at them because he was sickened by the way they slithered along on their soft bellies when the bullets burst in them. He had only been on the dog patrol once and had kept out of the way after that.

It was the only time that Driscoll and Wellbeloved felt anything in common, any knowledge of contact: when they were skidding in rivalry along the hot roads in pursuit of a screaming mongrel.

'Mine! Mine!' Wellbeloved would call, standing upright like a chariot rider, and giving the driver a stiff push with his knee.

'Mine!' shouted Driscoll, off with a frantic swerve after the fuzz of running yellow. The dogs knew what day it was and they always ran.

The little trucks would roar, the two sergeants cry, hoarse and exultant, and the dog would zig-zag and panic and roll and jump, hide and cover, then run again, always to death. The conscripts hardly ever killed them. They were loaders for the sergeants.

Driscoll was superb at hitting them on the run, sometimes straight up the backside, firing left-handed from the careering truck. If the bullet did not get the dog completely then sometimes the driver would run over it on his follow up.

Wellbeloved had his driver trained to an edge so

that they hunted the animal breathless, and then cornered it, shooting it as it cowered and the truck threw up its final fling of red dust, dancing like a picador's horse.

The first morning of the July killing had been fevered and successful. Driscoll had got three dogs and Wellbeloved two. Tasker, who was one of Driscoll's detail, had also shot dead a small miserable goat which he failed to recognise in time.

Sergeant Driscoll had been in an encouraging mood, giving all his men a chance to kill a dog. Tasker had claimed the goat, Lantry, always inclined to hurry, loosed a whole magazine at a maddened mongrel and caused it no injury at all, and Corporal Brook had a small acorn-coloured dog at his mercy, but was psychologically incapable of pulling the trigger when the moment was complete.

The trucks and the men were covered in red and white dust. At mid-day they stopped in front of the garrison canteen sweetshop.

'One more?' suggested Driscoll, shouting across to Wellbeloved.

'All right,' panted Wellbeloved, the sweat cutting the raw dust on his face. 'Once more around. I'll get that bastard with a limp. The one I missed.'

'That's all you'll get,' taunted Driscoll. 'I'll get a fast one. A real goer.'

The vehicles growled, jolted forward and tore

away again, along the big loop of the garrison road, up towards the reservoir.

Across the road, in stripes, the sun lay, segregated by the shadows of the thickening trees and scrub. Driscoll saw his dog first.

'Tally-ho!' he called, and the truck heaved forward, throwing the men in the back about, except Driscoll who was gripping on and keeping his eyes on the putty-coloured dog haring along the road, spasms of shadow flicking over it as it ran.

Wellbeloved was after it too. From somewhere his driver got an extra kick out of his engine and they tore dangerously alongside Driscoll's truck, each going like a rhino, straining to get ahead to the kill.

'He's mine!' howled Driscoll, pulling his snubbed rifle up.

'No! mine!' Wellbeloved snorted. 'I'll get him. *Run* doggy *run!*'

It suddenly occurred to the dog to get off the road. It skidded and rolled, and flew off at right angles to a wide patch of red ground, punctuated with midget trees.

Wellbeloved, recognising the manoeuvre and relishing his speciality, whooped freely. But Driscoll was not being shaken off. Both trucks left the road, waltzed through the little trees, churning the crusty earth. The dog cartwheeled and went over in a blurr of white behind a bank of scrub.

'Got you!' shrieked Wellbeloved. His truck and Driscoll's flung their heads up as they braked. Both sergeants fired rapidly into the bush.

Someone fired back. From the bush came one, two, three shots. A bullet seared across Lantry's cheek, throwing blood on to his shoulder. They all stood in solid astonishment. For a horrifying second Driscoll thought his gun had slipped again. It was Wellbeloved who realised.

'Ambush!' he howled. 'Somebody's shooting. Run! Run!'

They ran.

By late afternoon tall black trees of smoke grew over the city. There were fires in many places, and in the north of the island a rubber factory burned hungrily and with a huge stench. Rioting and shooting had started in the streets and spread outwards to the villages.

The authorities suspected that it might happen at some time. Because there was no room, and no thick concealment for guerrilla operations on Singapore Island it was safe from the sudden, deathly bandit raids of the Malaya mainland. But there were in the city and in the villages pockets of sympathisers, agitators and Chinese who had filtered in from Communist China, who waited for the moment and then rioted.

It spread, as riots swiftly spread. The years of grievance, and the years of secret scorn, because many had never forgotten how the invincible British were squashed into submission by a Japanese army on bicycles, were remembered in quick anger. Cars burned, Europeans were killed, and the streets were full of savagery. On the first evening the sun went down behind piled smoke from a city whose charred pavements ran with blood and mobs. The neon signs from the tower of the Cathay cinema flashed in red *The Wicked City* and *Panic in the Streets*.

At Panglin the garrison, roused first by the urgent return of the dog-killers, paraded in full battle order, including water bottles and spare socks. Colonel Bromley Pickering rolled up in his jeep and inspected them. It was arranged that the more sickly soldiers should remain behind and guard the garrison and that the doubting, redoubtable remainder should become true soldiers and move into the city to help quell the riot. The office work would have to wait for a few days.

They clattered into metal lorries and the lorries rolled down the road to where the distant fires murmured red. Regimental Sergeant-Major Raskin had suggested a bren crew on the cabin roof of each lorry to fight off possible ambush on the jungle-cut road. But the two men detailed to give this a brief trial run slid off suddenly at the first sharp corner.

Instead the guns and their crews were positioned on the saggy canvas roof of each lorry. The convoy moved off towards the rioting city, three miles from which Sinclair, in one bren crew, straining upwards to get a better view of the fires, forced his leg through the inadequate material. It hung down, booted, gaitered, green-trousered and unfunny, among the anxious young men inside for the rest of the journey.

On the rim of the city military police, at a road block, pushed them off the highway. It was night now. The Panglin convoy rattled down into the Golden World amusement park and sports centre where on normal nights there was boxing or wrestling or, even better, Chinese schoolgirls stretching themselves at basketball. Among the amusement stalls and jumping lights outside could be met the cheapest women in Singapore. On normal nights. The soldiers clambered down and walked in single line into the doorway of the sports arena, lying in the dark like a large humped whale.

They trooped under the ribs, the tiers of seats, set down their weapons and their packs, and sat on the concrete and waited. Brigg leaned back on his pack, felt its crude material rubbing across the bridge of his neck and smelt the blanco powder on it. He listened for sounds of the rioting but could hear only the vehicles moving on the road outside. He began to feel quite strong lying there, resting, with the warm wood of the rifle stock touching his fingers. Fighting rioters was not, after all, like fighting jungle bandits or another army. The others, he guessed, might feel the same. There was no substantial danger, although Lantry had been proudly wounded already, something which made everyone feel an inward heat, as though they had, at last, known battle.

Brigg had been writing one of his careful letters to Joan, when they had been called. He always answered her letters within a day. Joan and Phillipa and Lucy. It was like having three separate girls in three separate rooms. And, in their various ways, even if they were not the right ways, they were his. All of them. And he was a soldier, a fighting soldier, in the middle of a battle. He would write the rest of the letter there, lying there, resting before going into action, and heroic it would read.

Tasker was glorying in retelling the adventure of the ambush when they were hunting dogs. Everyone had heard it to the last syllable before, but gathered there under the skeleton of the sports arena seats, with their forms and faces shadowed in the scarce light, it seemed fitting to narrate it again. Battles were ever told, like this, and warriors ever ready to listen to them.

Lantry had been borne by stretcher to the garrison medical officer, who had been drinking because of the heat again and was under the impression that the young man had injured himself while shaving.

Driscoll, who had been honestly unable to prevent his driver careering off when Wellbeloved shouted, had gone back to the ambush spot, angry and ashamed, with four men, but they found nothing but a dead putty-coloured dog.

The Panglin contingent were two hours under the seats of The Golden World before anything happened. They lay confident and prepared, when a swift and thunderous tattoo hit the asbestos walls and roof of the building around them. They jumped in abrupt alarm, but it was rain.

Another hour and a pack of shapes came in from the dark carrying a long box. Brigg and some of the others sat up thinking with a thrill that it might be a coffin. But it was some signallers, with their equipment. They set up an establishment at the far end of the ribbed section, made some tea, and began bleeping signals and messages in an exciting way that added even more atmosphere.

All the days and nights they were down in the city, Driscoll kept talking about rusty nails. He muttered it, talked it, and shouted it. He laughed about it, sniggered and smiled on it. He would introduce it at any time. 'Sinclair, Brook, and rusty nails,' he would chortle as they went along the gutters, shuffling through the curfew. Or he would observe that the breakfast was like rusty nails, or his mail was full of rusty nails. He believed he was hugging the funniest joke ever. They thought he was trying to work his repatriation by showing he was going mad.

On the third day ten of them from Panglin, five in each gutter, trudged around a corner from a sideway full of Chinese washing and into Sarangoon Road where they were confronted by a wall of rioters.

Brigg felt as though it were starting to rain inside his stomach. Wellbeloved led his file of five and Corporal Brook, the quill-like Brook of the rimless specs and mental blockages, led the other.

Wellbeloved halted his columns and then ordered them across the road in a line facing the dark bank of men who had fallen still and frightening. Brigg heard the order come out in a voice he did not recognise as Wellbeloved's. He felt his legs walking him into the middle of the line across the road. Christ, I'm scared, he thought. Look at the murderous bastards. Enough to trample us down. No guns though, no guns he could see. They had eight rifles and Wellbeloved and Brook had stens. No, he couldn't see any guns. Just pieces of stone, and batons of wood, and in the centre three men with spiked lengths of iron railing. Christ, he was scared.

Brigg could hear Tasker's teeth chattering although he was a yard away. Why the hell couldn't he clench them? Both the rioters and the soldiers were silent, apart from Tasker's chattering. It was as though the street were empty except for a set of teeth. A dog came out of an alley and dissected the neutral roadway between the groups. Brigg thought the silly thought that Wellbeloved ought to shoot the thing while he had a chance.

'Where's the banner?' said Wellbeloved, taking hold of his voice and getting it out quite firmly. 'Bring up the banner.' Two quaking conscripts from the rear moved forward in a drill practised to perfection on the red shale on innocuous Saturday mornings, carrying with them a banner.

'SHOW THEM THE BANNER,' ordered the Sergeant, and the two privates rolled the supporting poles outward until there was revealed a blank stretch of white canvas.

The rioters made an undercurrent of noise. Wellbeloved turned, meaning to point dramatically to the banner, but his intended words melted in his throat.

'Cunts!' he shuddered. 'Turn it round the right bloody way.'

Embarrassed and confused, the banner bearers padded an awkward circle to reveal the true side of their burden, a message in Malay and Chinese,

163

telling the disturbers that the army was in charge and that they must disperse quietly.

A massive laughing burst from the mob. The mud that the rain inside Brigg's stomach had caused moved around, icy, sticky mud, making his body fearful. They were all shouting and howling now, and Brigg knew it would not be long.

He thought they might rush immediately. But instead one of the three in the centre, one of those with the spiked pieces of railing, stepped out and screamed at the Panglin soldiers.

Wellbeloved said: 'Corporal Brook. Disarm that man.'

Brigg thought he was going to be sick in the road. Tasker dropped his rifle with a terrible clatter and only retrieved it at the third grasp.

Brook, three from the left end of the line, was drained of blood. His eyes swelled under his spectacles. His feet stayed with the same piece of road although his body leaned forward as if it was obeying.

Wellbeloved said again: 'Corporal Brook. Disarm that man.'

'I was just going,' said Brook in a shapeless voice.

He went forward towards the man with the spike. As he walked, Brigg suddenly saw him again on the cricket field, a month before, a white man in a white shirt and shorts, bowling slow, anaemically slow, down the shorn wicket. Brigg saw the batsman strike the ball, hard and red along the ground and realised again that it was coming to him. His hands pulled it up and he re-felt the sharp sensation of it. He saw once more the batsman slip as he ran, and knew the thrill again of his arm going back and the fling of the ball towards Brook at the wicket. It had jumped easily into Brook's long fingers, first bounce, and the batsman was still foundered sixteen feet away. But Brook, clutching the ball, had done nothing more. He had stood there paralysed, with the ball, never moving his hands to take the bails from the stumps. He stood, frozen, while the batsman got up and, unbelievingly, ran safely in.

'He can't do the next thing. He can't do the next thing. He can't think it. He can't think it.' It bleeped through Brigg's head like one of the signallers' running codes.

Brook went forward. The rioters dropped to silence. There was only his unsteady bootsteps on the road. Two yards from the man with the railing spike Brook stopped. He had his sten pointing at the man's lungs. They stood still as though taking part in some military colour ceremony. Nothing. There was nothing. Brigg knew what had happened to Brook. So did the others. He could do nothing. Neither speak, nor take the spike, nor shoot, nor run, nor blink away the tears of fear that were blocking his weak eyes.

The man could see. Just like the batsman, Brigg thought. He pulled back his dreadful railing spike.

'Brooky!' screamed Brigg. 'Brooky!'

But nothing could stop it. The spike hit the thin, white corporal in the lower pelvis and he bent, with only half a scream, on to it, his body snapping in the middle like a thin feather.

Driscoll shot the rioter dead, right in the centre of his face, as he came around the corner with his section at that moment. He loosed a whole magazine of his sten over the heads of the mob, the bullets fracturing a water tank on the roof of a shop. The water cascaded over and, while the rioters fled, it flowed beneath the dead Corporal Brook, diluting his already thin blood on its journey to the monsoon drain.

'Rusty nails!' shouted Driscoll into Wellbeloved's face. 'Remember rusty nails!'

They remained in the city while the riots burst and faded, breaking out in different places a dozen times a day. Gutted cars and lorries lay about the streets like dead men when the vultures have been at them. New fires crackled, more men, innocent and guilty, died in violent ways, no one walked the widest streets alone.

Under their shelter in The Golden World arena, the Panglin men lived the days with the hideous thought of Corporal Brook and the iron spike in his pelvis. Wellbeloved was louder than ever among the silences, talking a lot about the misfortunes of a soldier's life, and the good men *he* had seen go down. They were waiting, all of them, for Driscoll to do something about Wellbeloved.

The patrols, every few hours, took them along the strewn streets. When it rained there was everywhere the damp, charred smell of fire put out by water. People looked from windows and doors and alleyways at them as they trudged by. Sometimes they had to go near the Raffles Hotel and then they felt quite good because the people with money, some of them good looking women and girls, looked out and waved to them encouragingly, knowing only that Britain's army was marching outside and having never known of Corporal Brook, and what a thin man looked like with a railing spike in his middle.

Panglin, they heard, was quiet, but Brigg kept worrying about Lucy. The segment of the city where she lived had been flushed through by fire and fighting on the first couple of days. On the fifth day he found himself in the very street, working in pairs, and asking Lantry, his partner, to wait, he jumped up the stairs leading to the door of her flat.

She opened it as though she had been waiting. He all but fell into the room, stocked as ever with toys and trinkets, with the bed in the corner cool and accommodating, and an iron and an ironing board against the wall, with a lead dropping from the centre light.

Lucy was in a Chinese dressing gown. She caught his hands as though she were saving him from falling. She said nothing at the beginning, but pushed his hands beneath the gown, where she was naked.

'I wait all the time for you, Bigg,' she said. 'We have bed-love now, for I have not been busy for days.'

Her face was pressing against the tough sling of his rifle looped over his shoulder. He took his right hand from her small, lumpy breast, and unhooked the rifle from his shoulder. He leaned it against a big golliwog sitting blindly on a chair.

'We can't now,' he said. He was astonished at his own relief in finding her and the huge luxury there was in feeling her.

'But we must,' she said, backing daintily like a dancer in a Chinese play towards the bed and persuading him with her. 'I am so rested. I can give you many things.'

He moved her on to the bed and hung above her, taking his main weight on his hands, but lying so that their bodies, his encumbered with his uniform and equipment, hers open and vulnerable, were butting all the way down.

He kissed her well, because he had decided that he

loved and needed her. She said: 'Put all yourself on me, Bigg, I am very strong.'

Somehow she got his whole ear in her mouth. Her hands wriggled down urgently between their pressed bodies like white, burrowing ferrets and unbuckled his webbing belt with practised lack of difficulty. When she did something like that it was always like a full stop for him. The way she knew about men, all about them, even taking the whole of their weight because she was strong and accustomed to it, and knowing how to undo army belts, flicking off the brass hook as though she were flicking off a switch.

'I've got to go,' he said getting up from her.

'No, no, no, Bigg,' she said. 'I have learned The Saying. Listen.'

'I'm on duty,' he protested. 'There's a riot on.'

'But I know The Saying. Listen. Stay and listen, Bigg. You must listen, darling.'

'All right.' He smiled at her childishness.

'The Saying,' she said gravely, as though that were the title, and recited it, giving every trite word a full expression. Right down to '. . . But ain't the roses sweet.' He did not want to laugh. She was so proud of what she had learned from the silly words he had written for her. Her gown was open and inside it, half hiding, was her good, white body, a pale shaft between the deep silk.

He touched with one finger the right side of the

gown and slid it outwards so that her breast appeared like the moon from behind a dark sky. He put his mouth to it, bending down to her from his height, and feeling his two shames, his shame for her and his different shame for himself, because he was so ashamed of her.

Lucy adeptly pulled his trousers down, then they did it immediately, standing up, she on tip-toe, each naked foot placed on the laced-up insteps of his solid army boots. He walked her over to the bed like that, she laughing as though she walked on stilts. It was a hell of a sensation, he thought, as they stepped out the paces like Siamese twins. On the counterpane he kicked his trousers clear of his gaiters, then over his boots, and eventually to the floor, without once missing a movement or taking his head from her lovely hair.

He became frantic, as he always did with her, and she bit his cheek at the height of it. When they lay quiet and he began to think how odd he must look, nude from gaiters to backside. She giggled and said: 'You are not a little virgin now, Bigg. It is like trying to hold a storm.'

He edged away from her. 'I'll be in the guard-house if I don't get out.'

'More,' she pouted. 'Just one more. For Lucy.'

'Nothing doing,' he said gravely. 'I've got to shift.'

'For Lucy, Bigg,' she repeated. 'I want so much.'

'No,' he said, picking up his trousers.

She eased herself from the bed. 'I put them on you,' she offered. She took them from him and bent down before him, and began kissing him about the groin. He felt the urge again and pressed her black hair into the top of his legs.

'Bigg, one more,' she whispered.

'No. No,' he said, pushing her gently. 'Give me my pants.'

She made a small motion as though to return them to him, but then, with a child's squeal, she whirled them like a green flag and flung them out of the window.

'Silly cow!' exploded Brigg, quickly at the window. He looked out. The trousers were lying, legs spread out, in the alley below.

'Now you stay! Now you stay!' she cried, running about in short, infantile jumps and dashes.

Brigg strode to the door. 'Lantry!' he howled. 'Lantry!'

There was no answer. A Sikh pedalled majestically by on a high bicycle.

'Lantry!' Brigg called, desperately, hiding his naked legs behind the door. 'Horace, for God's sake.'

Lantry appeared casually and gazed up at him. 'Oh, you've *done*, have you? You've actually finished.'

'For Christ's sake,' appealed Brigg. 'Go and get my trousers, will you?'

Lantry stared at him. 'Where?' he said. 'Where are they?'

'They're down behind this place. In an alley. This silly cow threw them out of the window.'

Lantry laughed unbelievingly. 'She's keen,' he said. He went around the corner of the building and came back. 'They've gone,' he said simply.

'Gone!' cried Brigg, still cut in half by Lucy's door.

'That's right. Somebody's had them.'

'Oh God,' shuddered Brigg, realising the awful enormity of the event. 'I'll be court martialled.'

'Yes, you will,' confirmed Lantry.

He would be court martialled, and the newspapers would be there, because they always were, and people – people! – Joan! – would know that a Chinese whore had thrown his trousers out of her window. And he was on active service too. In a riot.

Brigg jumped back into the room. He caught Lucy by the arms. He shook her like a bully. 'Get me something, quick,' he said. 'Something to put on. Someone's picked them up.'

She became frightened at his anger and sorry, like a little girl. 'I get something,' she said.

In the dark of his mind he had half-hoped that she might have a pair of trousers put away somewhere, a pair that had been left behind by one of her customers. But she did not. They always took them with them.

He flung his arms through her wardrobe, through dresses and silk coats, and an old fur she had never been able to wear but she hoped one day to use in a colder climate.

Then she said behind him: 'I have trousers. Green trousers.'

He turned. But she was holding a pair of green, silk trousers, the pyjama sort worn by Chinese women.

Brigg heard Lantry shout: 'Hurry up then.'

In despair he climbed into the trousers. The wide embroidered bottoms hung halfway up his thin, hairy shins, like flags on flagpoles. 'Oh, Jesus,' he breathed. Then without looking at Lucy he charged out of the door, came back for his belt and his rifle, and tumbled out again. He thought Lantry was going to choke with laughing.

'Shit,' said Brigg to him. 'Come on. We've got to get them.'

They ran down the wet alley. Lucy watched from her window, chastened and sad, seeing nothing funny in Brigg wearing her trousers.

By a miracle they found the garment almost immediately. The Sikh who had cycled past was standing around the corner, his bicycle against a post, measuring the trousers against himself.

'They're mine,' said Brigg, hugely relieved.

The Sikh looked at him with dignity. 'They are

mine,' he corrected deeply, in excellent English. 'I found them.'

'I know,' argued Brigg, making a grab at them. The Sikh snatched them away.

'Then they are mine,' boomed the Sikh.

'Arseholes,' shouted Brigg. 'Why do you think I've got these bleeding things on? New issue or something?'

'I regret,' said the Sikh. 'But I find and I keep. Please understand that.'

He was tall and chesty, so Brigg did not hit him. Instead he pulled out his bayonet, clipped it to his rifle, and stuck it nastily near the Sikh's midriff.

'Give me my trousers,' he said, quietly boiling. 'Or I'll shove this in your fat gut.'

The Indian looked at him with shattering calmness. 'It is important to have the trousers back?' he asked.

'Of course it is, you nut,' said Brigg. 'Give me them. I'll stick you like a pig if you don't, old mate.'

'The point of that implement is hurting me,' said the Sikh, handing over the trousers. 'I will return them. Don't lose them again.'

Brigg snatched them and put them on. 'Thanks,' he said. 'I'll make sure I don't.'

He and Lantry backed out into the alley. They were hautily regarded by the big Indian. As they

turned the corner he said, deeply and loudly: 'God
save the King.'

'Rusty Nails,' said Driscoll.

He said it clearly and carefully. He had walked
across the floor, under the arena seats, to say it. He
said it squatting in front of Wellbeloved. Right into
Wellbeloved's eyes.

The young soldiers were crumpled asleep all
around. Driscoll had waited until now before saying
it right at Wellbeloved. They talked, a yard between
them, with the signallers working at their bleeps and
green lights a few steps away.

'What about him?' said Wellbeloved into Driscoll's eyes.

'Remember, then. You do remember, don't you?'

'If it's the same one, I remember.' Wellbeloved
said it stiffly and moved his eyes quickly over the
sleeping soldiers. 'If it's the same one.'

'There was only one,' smiled Driscoll. 'Nobody
else could be Rusty Nails.'

Wellbeloved said: 'There's no need to spell it out.
You've been on enough about it these last few days.'

'I'm glad you remembered old Rusty,' said
Driscoll.

'Did you know him then?'

Driscoll shook his shadowed head. The bleeps

stopped at the signal point and one of the signallers started pouring out tea in enamel mugs. 'Want some tea, Sergeant?' he called to them.

'No,' said Driscoll.

'No,' said Wellbeloved.

Driscoll said: 'I didn't know him at all. Never heard of him till the other morning. Poor old Rusty.'

'Listen,' said Wellbeloved, swiftly, sharply. 'What's this all about, Sergeant.'

Driscoll said: 'We don't want to wake the lads.' He said it in an acted whisper, and added: 'Why don't we go and talk about it in the big room?'

'In there?' said Wellbeloved, nodding at the door to the arena.

'Yes, in there, Sergeant,' said Driscoll getting up. He walked ahead. They went into the huge dark belly of the place. Inside the door, by them, was a box of switches. Driscoll pulled down one bar and up in the caved roof three pans of light flowered and the white stamens hung down on to the basketball area in the middle. The lined sections, the half circles, the two posts and their nets, suspended like toeless socks. From the edge to high up on the walls behind, the brown seats were banked and piled and terraced. Driscoll and Wellbeloved were the only ones there.

They sat uncomfortably on the thin, hard arms of two seats on opposite sides of their particular gangway. They were ten rows up the hill from the bottom.

Driscoll shook out a cigarette, lit it, and threw one across. Wellbeloved caught it and lit it from Driscoll's. His big head trembled when it bent near Driscoll's hands and the red end of the cigarette. He took the light and retreated and sat on the arm of the seat again.

'Funny,' said Driscoll quietly. 'Funny how after hearing you go on all these months about what you did when the Japs came, and what you did in Changi, that I should hear about Rusty Nails.'

Wellbeloved said: 'Let's hear what you heard.'

'I had a letter, the day after we came down here,' said Driscoll. He took the blue airmail envelope from his tunic pocket.

'Sergeant Grant,' he said, keeping the letter folded. 'Remember Laurie Grant, don't you? Little nutty chap from the pay office.'

'I remember him,' said Wellbeloved.

'Went home six months ago.' Driscoll opened the letter and nosed along it with a small smile. 'Says here, he wouldn't have bothered to write to me without good reason. But this is one.'

He stopped there and a signaller came up out of the door. 'Sure you won't have some tea?' he asked. He looked out on the lit arena. 'Not much of a crowd tonight,' he joked. 'Wrestling nights are best. Charlie Chang and The Dragon.'

Driscoll said: 'I'll have some tea, son, if you like. Bring it through, will you.'

'Sure,' said the signaller. 'How about you, Sarge.'

'No,' said Wellbeloved.

The young man ducked down through the door. Driscoll looked around the hollow building. '"Wrestling nights are best",' he reflected. '"Charlie Chang and The Dragon." Have you been? I think it's great when they have all that mud and oil in the ring and slog around in that.'

'What about Nails?' said Wellbeloved. 'Why don't you get on with it?'

'I'm waiting for the tea,' said Driscoll. 'Once I get warmed up on Rusty, I don't want any interruptions.'

Through the door came the signaller again and Driscoll took the hot mug from him. After his first drink he said: 'Anyway, Sergeant Grant said that not long after he went home he got on a bus in London and when he reached in his pocket to get his fare he took out some Malay cents which he had hanging around.

'The conductor, it turned out, recognised them right away. Because they're square and you don't see many square coins do you?'

He looked from his tea to Wellbeloved.

Wellbeloved agreed: 'No, all right. You don't see many square coins.'

'That's right,' said Driscoll deliberately. He took

some more tea. 'Anyway, they began to talk about Malaya because this conductor had been out here in the war, see. Every now and then he had to go off and collect some fares, and that sort of thing.'

'I know what a conductor does,' said Wellbeloved, impatiently. 'I've been on a bus.'

'Yes, well you'll know then that the conversation was a bit broken up, but Barnwell, who was the conductor . . .'

'Barnwell,' breathed Wellbeloved.

'That's it,' confirmed Driscoll, taking his time. He consulted the letter again. 'Roderick Barnwell, that was his name . . . Funny name. Anyway, it turned out that he was in your mob, here in Singapore in forty-two. He was a sergeant. In fact he was sergeant of the guard when they *had you inside* for desertion when the Japs were coming.'

'Bloody liar!' exploded Wellbeloved. 'Bloody lies. All of it.'

'That's what I thought,' agreed Driscoll amiably. 'As soon as I read that I said to myself: "That's a bloody lie," I said. I thought "That Sergeant Roderick Barnwell is a liar. Fancy telling a yarn like that about Wellbeloved, who was in the jungle and fighting the Japs all on his tod".'

Wellbeloved was glinting at him. He was going to move, but Driscoll went on. 'And then, Barnwell told Laurie Grant about this chap they called Rusty Nails.

I thought it was a funny name, but just yesterday, when we were doing a patrol over at G.H.Q. I went and had a look at the roll of honour, as they call it. And there he was. They didn't have "Rusty". It was just Bombardier William Nails, died in Changi, October 29th, 1943. And do you know what Barnwell said, Wellbeloved?'

'What did he say?'

'He said you killed him, mate. Just like that. He said you killed Rusty Nails. Barnwell said it while he was dinging out tickets on his machine and collecting the tuppences.'

'Cobblers,' said Wellbeloved. 'Nobody can prove it.' He had his nasty look now, and Driscoll knew it wouldn't be long.

'Nobody is going to try,' said Driscoll. 'But this Conductor Barnwell – I mean Sergeant Barnwell – said that you delivered Nails over to the Japs in a parcel, and saved your own skin, over some food stealing. He said that they had to move you out of there after that, or something would have happened to you. Something nasty.'

Wellbeloved was purple-faced. 'I don't have to listen to all this crap,' he rasped. 'I'm sick of you! Sick of you!'

Driscoll swallowed the last of his drinkable tea, swished the thick tea-leaves around in the floor of the cup, then threw them casually into Wellbeloved's face.

180

He put his entire fist through the handle of the mug and punched Wellbeloved in the mouth with it as he was getting up. Wellbeloved fell across the seats. Driscoll leaned over, pulled him out, turned him, and hit him again loudly down the steps and on to the wood of the basketball pitch.

Driscoll followed quietly. One step taken at a time. The other sergeant was lying flung out under the isolated lights, like a boxer. As Driscoll got there, Wellbeloved kicked him from the floor. The blow in the crutch sent him lurching in sickness to the first line of seats. Wellbeloved stumbled at him and hit him with his left, then his right fist, full in the exposed face.

Over the back of the seats went Driscoll. Not one but two rows, which was fortunate because he fell down in the wooden chute between them, and by rolling on his side under the seats themselves he took himself from the reach of another blow from Wellbeloved. He felt his face needed straightening and he put his hands to it. Wellbeloved was savage, leaning over the backs of the two rows trying to hit him with mallet fists. He was all rage and it did not occur to him to climb over after Driscoll.

Driscoll, on his elbows, levered himself along the dusty plank floor, behind a main column running up to the roof. It was ten seconds since he had been hit and he was getting sorted out now. He could hear

Wellbeloved spitting like an orang-utan across the backs of the seats. Just then Driscoll only wanted to keep out of his way because he was not quite ready, and he thought he stood a good chance of being killed. Suddenly he wondered who the man was that Rosalind had married. Strange them being on the bus like that. Perhaps the conductor had been that Sergeant Barnwell! No, couldn't be. It was the wrong town. God, his eye was bleeding from inside. That was nasty. He had enough trouble with his eyes as it was.

Now Wellbeloved was coming over the seats like an overweight hurdler. Driscoll got up in time. He caught the other sergeant in his arms and they danced in the narrow space between the tiers.

Driscoll got his sweating head free, threw it back six inches, and gave Wellbeloved a primitive butt. He caught him on the cheek as he turned away, knocking him sideways into the narrow way again. He was not sure he had not done himself more damage because his head resounded and whirled with the collision and the blood was shooting freely from his eye.

He kicked Wellbeloved in the chest as the other sergeant tried to get up, but found his leg arrested at the top of the movement by metallic hands. He knew what he should have done according to the manual, but there was no moving room. Wellbeloved threw him ten yards and he skidded into the open space on the basketball pitch like a tumbler making an entrance at the circus.

At the top of the gangway, by the door, all the young soldiers stood, roused and wakened by the thundering echoes of the fight, or by the others jerking them to go and see. They grouped up there in the deeper shadow, watching in awe and silence.

The battle was in the clear now. Driscoll got up as Wellbeloved followed him under the lights. They punched it out knee to knee, almost like morris dancers in the precise rhythm of their blows. Driscoll went down on his haunches, but caught Wellbeloved with a scissor kick and felled him. Over the floor they rolled, and blood from both of them running along the wooden blocks like red thread paying out from a reel. They groaned as icebergs groan, they spat, coughed and choked in the dust and their own wet sweat.

Together they got from the floor, still wrestling, rising up leaning face to face, arms grasping, almost comically, like two drunks trying to assist each other. When they were on their feet, Driscoll swung a huge blow at Wellbeloved, a wild blow because he couldn't see properly, and caught him on the side of the neck.

Wellbeloved shuddered back as though the buffer of a shunting engine had hit him. Directly in his path

183

was the wooden basketball post. He collided with it shoulder down, snapping it near the base, and stumbling on with it, borne on his shoulder like a banner.

But it was Driscoll who was drained. He did not see Wellbeloved hit the post. He was in the middle of the basketball area spitting the blood from his mouth and wiping it from his face. He had the feeling that blood was coming from everywhere, like streaming armies answering some bugle call. He could not see very well because there was a compound of blood, perspiration and grit in his eyes, and his brain felt as though someone was pressing a cushion on it.

So he did not know that Wellbeloved was going to hit him with the snapped off post until it was all but too late. Wellbeloved hugged it like a ram under his arms, quivered forward in a mad little run, and swung it like a boom at Driscoll's head as he knelt on both knees. Driscoll heard it but hardly saw it. But he got up far enough for it to catch him behind the legs. It threw him over heavily again, and Wellbeloved, unable to stop, went swaying across the floor, halfway to the far rows of seats.

They were like clowns now, red and funny, with odd walks, runs, grimaces and fallabouts.

Driscoll thought it was time he went. He saw the broadest of the gangways and its steps rising before him like deliverance. Half to his feet, and dangling his arms like an ape, he zig-zagged towards it. Somehow he got up the first flight and the second. He was on the second landing before he realised that Wellbeloved was pursuing him, on his hands and knees. Driscoll was pleased that he was on his hands and knees.

He pulled himself around and inched up the third flight. He thought that if he got here, and managed to get standing up, he could wait and breathe until Wellbeloved was three or four steps under him, and then jump out on him, feet first. He was glad Rosalind and her husband and their baby could not see him now.

Driscoll got to the landing. He pulled himself up by gripping the rim of one of a group of three fat barrels that were standing there. His fingers went over the edge as he did it and were touched the other side by a smooth, thick semi-liquid. He wavered to his feet, looked at Wellbeloved's progress as he came, murderous face looking up, one stair at a movement.

Driscoll had time. He looked down into the steel barrel. He laughed, half a choke, when he saw what it was. 'Charlie Chang versus The Dragon,' he croaked.

Wellbeloved was just starting the third flight of steps, up on the flats of his hands and the flats of his feet, like a bear. Driscoll hobbled around the rear of the barrel of oil and mud, leaned against it, and tried to topple it. It might be good for wrestling in, all spread out in the ring, but it was hard to shift in a barrel. Then he felt it go, pushed at it with every dreg of strength left in him, and got to the apex. He saw it going and shouted 'Rusty Nails!' as it slurped over, spilling, finally splashing down the stairs in a jet river, thick and sticky. It gushed in a wave against Wellbeloved, but the steel barrel that bounded down after it somehow bounced right over him. He pawed and slithered, tried to crawl, and slid back. Driscoll could see his eyes through all the shiny black, like a minstrel.

He went behind the other drum. He could hear the conscript soldiers running and calling in echoes as they came around the top gallery of the arena in his direction.

He pushed against the second barrel. It was only two-thirds full, so it was easier than the first. Wellbeloved saw it coming and began a panic paddling of his legs and arms, skidding, skating, but unable to get out of the way.

As he pushed it over, Driscoll croaked: 'And this one's for Brook, you bastard!' The oil and mud went, so did the barrel, once again missing Wellbeloved. And this time Driscoll followed, unable to stop himself as his weak feet fell away beneath him on the black slide. He tobogganed, head first, down the awful slope, striking Wellbeloved and carrying him with him to the bottom, on to the arena space once more.

At the top of the stairs the young soldiers halted and watched, the streaks in the treacle path running down from them to the two sergeants, pawing about like tired seals. They were smothered in the mess, bulging like bubbles of the tar lake that spread to reach further each second across the woodblocks. On hands and knees they went to each other, flopping and falling, but finally getting there. Both men pulled their hands out of the muck, and raised themselves on to their knees, facing each other close together in anonymous black. While Wellbeloved was clenching his fists, Driscoll butted him once more with his head. His crown smacked into Wellbeloved's forehead and skidded off.

Wellbeloved grovelled forward and remained still like a nun in prayer. The other sergeant was still too, resting on his hands and knees. All the watchers stood soundless.

It was a long time. Then Driscoll, moving like primeval man, just born, got to his feet. The oil and mud, stretched around him, sticky ropes trying to hold him down. The strands broke and fell away.

First he straightened himself and wiped his oily hands across his oiled face. Then he bent, caught Wellbeloved's collar, and pulled him like a sledge across the floor, leaving a cleared road through the black lake, and a black road over the untouched part of the basketball area. The conscripts remained like a frieze high up against the wall. They watched Driscoll pull Wellbeloved to the broken basketball post, lying there, and carefully and painfully push his enemy's head through into the net.

When he had accomplished it he fell back on his bottom and sat looking at Wellbeloved's face and head unconscious in the net. He thought he looked like a squid.

After two minutes there was a movement from the other end of the arena. Major Cusper, the Panglin Adjutant, came through the dark, striding purposefully. His steps, echoing, slowed in disbelief as he focused the dread scene in the full lights of the arena. But he prided himself on never being shaken by anything for long. He walked into the lights, to the edge of the oil and mud lake, and peered at Wellbeloved in the net and the crouching form of Driscoll like a man squinting into a dark hole. Once he had established who they were, he drew himself up, tucked his stick beneath his arm and said: 'Sergeant Driscoll.'

Driscoll seemed to grow out of the ooze. He stood up, almost to attention. He had lost his hat so he did not salute. 'Sir,' he said thickly.

'Driscoll,' said the Major. 'Will you and Sergeant Wellbeloved there jolly the men up a bit. We're going back to Panglin. There's some trouble up there.'

9

The lorries droned up the white road again to Panglin, where the fighting was only beginning. In a preliminary skirmish the garrison troops had machine-gunned one of the legs off the *charpoy* bed owned by the Indian who kept a store within the garrison and who slept on the bed at the front of his harmless shop every afternoon from one until three. The shooting occurred at two-fifteen. It was the first indication to anyone, and especially the Indian, that the battle of Panglin had begun.

Behind sandbags on the barrack blocks, around the bathhouse and armoury, the troops waited after that, in the still disquiet of the bright, hot afternoon. A detachment had been deployed to protect the offices, the Army Laundry which was still loyally operating on piece work, and the family houses on the far side of the wooden bridge. But this split the garrison resources in two. Colonel Bromley Pickering did not like it, any more than he liked his men machine-gunning one leg off an Indian's bed, but the far flank of the ravine had to be protected, and so did the pumping station at the reservoir. He was relieved when he saw the convoy returning from the city with his other men.

Neither Driscoll nor Wellbeloved returned with the troops from Singapore. They were in beds separated by only a locker at the British Military Hospital. Driscoll's eye was still bleeding from the inside and Wellbeloved had a fractured cheekbone. Both suffered from multiple abrasions and were being treated as riot casualties, which is what the hospital understood they were. The doctor who examined them on admission and believed that they had fallen in the tanker dock, joked that they had so much oil on them that they looked like the wrestlers from The Golden World.

At Panglin, Colonel Bromley Pickering had secreted his men behind sandbags, partly because they were a depleted force, partly because of his phobia about having the blood of a national serviceman on his ageing hands, and partly because the soldiers that were left behind were hardly fit to be seen.

The halt and the bent, the lame and the languid, the blinkers and the duffers had remained. All those with disabilities, except for Driscoll, whose lack was secret, and the tragic, spiked, Brook, were manning the sandbag emplacements, afraid and frayed. To them the return of the Panglin force from the riot city was a touching relief.

They were none too soon. Rebel leaders had moved from the main centres and were organising local risings and rumours. At Panglin the trouble was brimming. The returning troops were hardly out of the lorries before the first act of terrorism occurred. There was an explosion and orange smoke from the swimming pool as the rioters blew up the high diving board. The troops stood and saw it bend, sag, and finally topple with grace into the water.

'They've really started now,' said Major Cusper grimly.

Brigg, standing at the truck tailboard, saw little men running through the elephant grass towards the offices and the laundry on the far side of the wooden bridge. He looked anxiously at the houses, Phillipa's house, further up the rising road.

Major Cusper said: 'We're a bit weak over there, aren't we, sir?'

'R.S.M. Raskin, Sergeant Fisher and a dozen men were all I could spare,' said the Colonel.

'Fatty Fisher,' groaned Brigg.

He was startled to hear the Colonel say: 'Some of the people are still in the houses, Cusper. All this has come up a bit suddenly, you know.'

'I'll take a party across,' said Cusper bravely. He wagged his moustache and picked out half a dozen men from the group on the road. Brigg was not pointed at, but he went with them and no one noticed.

Major Cusper, who was quite gallant really, and enjoyed waving his revolver, led the men down the steps to the bridge. They bumped across the slats and went towards the houses. People were white at the windows. Strengthening smoke was rising from the wooden office buildings and someone was shooting. Brigg thought suddenly of all Joan's letters locked away in his desk over there. And his demobilisation chart.

Cusper's party went towards the smoke. Brigg turned the opposite way and went straight to Phillipa's house. He went through the back door. Mrs. Raskin was kneeling on the floor of the living-room weeping and imploring Phillipa to come down from her bedroom.

Phillipa did so as Brigg was lifting her weighty mother from the carpet. She laughed when she saw Brigg. 'Christ, aren't we warlike?' she said. 'What's happening?'

'We're getting out, that's what's happening,' he said, hurt because she wasn't afraid.

'Getting out of the garrison?' she said.

'No. These houses. There's hundreds of them, and they're coming here.'

'Daddy said we had to stay here,' said Phillipa. 'He'll kick up murder if we leave.'

'Sod Daddy,' said Brigg unfeelingly. 'We're going now.'

'Don't be so bloody brave,' laughed Phillipa. 'They can't hurt. You've got guns, haven't you?'

Mrs. Raskin was cooing over the angel fish, making consoling sounds.

Three Chinese appeared in the front garden, shouting and waving their fingers. Brigg fired his rifle from the hip and they ran around the corner. He felt very scared. He let off another bullet which shattered the fish tank, throwing fish, ferns and water in a wave on to the carpet.

'They'll all be drowned!' screamed Mrs. Raskin, picking the little fish up by their shivering tails.

'Quick, quick! Get something!'

Brigg was screaming in her ear to get out quickly. He pushed the suddenly trembling Phillipa towards the back door. Mrs. Raskin was putting the fish in a milk bottle half-filled with water. One by one. Brigg got her out of the door with his rifle butt. Twenty or thirty men were at the corner house. Brigg could hear firing but couldn't see any soldiers.

'Run,' he whispered. 'Run, that way.' He pointed uphill, and the two women began to run and scramble across the little square gardens. The Chinese mob was rushing towards them now. Phillipa and her mother were screaming. Brigg pushed them on, behind some sheets hanging on a

194

line. He ran behind the sheets himself. He was very frightened and he could feel his face all wet and his neck and his eyes were bulging. But he quite deliberately brought his rifle up to his shoulder and fired once between the narrow gap in the washing. He saw the two leading men fall and for a wild moment thought that he had hit both of them. But the others dropped down too, behind the fences, and he knew they were just taking cover. But the rifle felt hot and real and lethal in his hands. A powerful exhilaration flashed through him. He banged another shot over their crouching bodies, then turned quickly and ran after Phillipa and her mother.

The two women were sobbing and breathless, trying to run up the narrow path at the far end of the row of houses. Brigg ran up to them. Suddenly they all stopped and realised that the roadway below, the road for which they were running, was full of Chinese. It was reaching dusk, and Brigg, after the first moment, saw that they hadn't been seen.

Suddenly he heard Wellbeloved's voice, like a ministering angel, a voice from weeks ago, saying: 'I used to go along the pipeline. They never knew how I travelled so fast.'

Brigg whispered: 'The pipeline. We'll get out that way.'

They had all but made it when they were seen.

Phillipa was up on the broad black pipe, twenty feet above the ground. Her mother was trying to climb the supporting struts. Brigg was on the ground pushing her backside with one hand and ridiculously holding the milk bottle of angel fish with the other.

Then the men began to run up the steep bank from the road. It was red shale, wet and crumbling after rain. As they scrambled with their fingers and toes, Brigg got Mrs. Raskin up on to the pipe.

Phillipa had not waited. She was running in her bare feet along the arched back of the pipe, fifty yards away. She had pale brown, well shaped feet, and Brigg had admired them against the black of the pipe when they had walked it together before. Now she was running. Mrs. Raskin, like a dishevelled picnicker charged by a bull, was running. Brigg cut his bootlaces with his bayonet. You couldn't walk along the pipe in boots because they slipped and skidded. He threw his boots towards the men climbing the bank, wishing they had been grenades.

They had virtually the same effect. The first two of the mob, over the lip of the slope got one boot each and began to fight. Those behind joined the tussle. Brigg ran in stockinged feet, padding along the pipeline towards the white shadows that were Phillipa and her mother. After sixty yards, Brigg glanced around to see the white shirt of the leading chaser outlined at the end of the pipe. Others were bobbing behind him, shouting and squabbling and trying to get up the supports. Brigg dropped on his knee and fired two shots at the blurr. He was short and he heard the bullets ricochet off the metal. The white blurr dropped from sight with a howl and he straightened up and ran on.

He was sweating into his eyes, and he was frightened. But he was held up now by Mrs. Raskin, crying as she went along the pipe with a jog, which was all she could manage. She held her angel fish in a milk bottle close to her flopping chest. Brigg had one hand on her waist, his thumb hooked in the top of her hard corset, so that she would not slip and fall.

But the pipe was wide even for her. And no one could chase them only along the pipe, for the jungle twenty feet below was like matted hair and full of ponds, mud and sliding riverlets.

Phillipa was thirty yards to the front. Brigg realised she was laughing; laughing and skipping along the pipe like a child now, believing that the danger had gone.

After fifteen minutes, Mrs. Raskin doubled up on one of the flat junctions where the supports from below met the pipeline. 'I'm puffed, I'm puffed,' she puffed. She was like an old fish-and-chip woman, Brigg thought. He tried to pull her up but he couldn't. '

'Phillipa,' he called into the dark. 'Come back. Your mother's whacked. Come back.'

He was shocked when she called back: 'Leave her. Leave her there.'

'Come back,' he shouted harshly. 'Come here, I tell you.'

He saw her reappearing along the pipe, her bare feet gently smacking it. Her face was sulky.

She looked down at her mother, panting over the milk bottle, held as though it were some holy relic and she a pilgrim.

'Leave her,' she said again. Her mother sobbed but did not look up. Brigg was looking hard at Phillipa. She looked into his indistinct face.

'*Leave* her,' she said again defiantly. 'They don't want her. What will they do with her? They want me.'

Brigg said nothing. He bent and put his arms beneath the heavy woman and pulled her to her feet. 'Come on,' he said softly. 'It's not far now. We'll be on the road soon.'

'It's miles,' said Phillipa. She turned and began to flip along the pipe again. Brigg steadied her mother with both hands now, his rifle slung around his neck, the weapon hanging across his chest. They jogged along painfully, his hands on her hips.

'We're like kids playing choo-choos,' he joked. But she didn't hear or didn't understand him. Then she

198

slipped violently to one side and he was unable to stop her. She went over into the dark like a suicide. Brigg heard her hit the undergrowth and the water down below.

'Phillipa! Phillipa! Come back!' he howled along the pipe. She returned, this time without argument, and stood holding his rifle while he struggled down the metal legs of the pipeline into the dark cave of wood and water.

Brigg found Mrs. Raskin, a bundle of wet old clothes, lying across some trapped driftwood, almost at the centre of a black stream of thick water. He tried to reach her by walking, but the ooze underneath caught his feet and sucked at them. Up on the pipe, Phillipa was whimpering: 'Hurry, hurry. I think they're coming. Hurry up.'

He managed to extract his feet from the muck. Then he launched himself through the thick cocoa water, warm and moving fast, towards the bundle that was Mrs. Raskin. One swimming stroke got him there.

She was clutching the milk bottle and weakly trying to look into it. 'They're gone,' she snivelled. 'They've swum away. I know they have.'

Brigg caught hold of her. 'I'm not going,' she said without looking at him. 'Where are they? I'm not going without them.'

'Oh Jesus,' prayed Brigg desperately. He took the

bottle and pretended to look into it. 'They're all there,' he lied. 'Every single one. Come on, let's get back. We can't have them down here in this muddy old water.'

To his powerful relief she believed him. He got her under the arms and ferried her the few yards to the firmer mud, while she grasped the bottle neck and crooned down into the hole at her imagined fish.

Brigg was very tired. His arms felt as though they were coming out of their slots. He was still very frightened too. He pushed and levered Mrs. Raskin up to the pipe again, using the cross members of the supporting legs as steps.

'Help her then,' he gasped at Phillipa who remained staring back down the pipe

'I can hear them,' Phillipa cried. 'I know they're coming.'

'Help her!' roared Brigg. He choked with the mud and foul water in his throat. But Phillipa moved, bent and pulled her mother up on to the pipe again.

'We've *got* to leave her,' she urged Brigg. 'She'll never get along like this.'

'You sound like you're trying to get rid of your mum,' he observed. She did not reply. He told her to keep still and bent and put his ear to the pipe. There was a soft rhythm coming along them. They were coming all right.

'You run,' he said to Phillipa. 'It's not that far now.'

'What about you?' she said, hurriedly giving him his rifle.

'Your mum's going back down there,' he said.

'Good,' she said with finality. 'You should have left her there anyway.'

'I'm going with her,' he said. 'We'll hide down there till they've gone.'

'No! No!' she said, stamping her wet foot on the pipe. 'You can't leave me. What about me? They'll catch me! They'll hurt me!'

He looked at her steadily. 'Then you'll have to come as well, won't you?' he said.

She went down first and between them they got her mother and the milk bottle down. Mrs. Raskin was all but unconscious now. They could hear the sounds coming clearly and firmly along the pipeline from the dark.

Brigg rolled Mrs. Raskin under the thickest of the roofing jungle. She half sank into a pool of mud but Brigg could not help that. Next he pushed Phillipa at right angles to her mother. He could feel thorny pieces tearing at her dress as he forced her right in. Then he went with her, feeling the dual softnesses of the warm mud and her body pressing on two sides of him. He looked at her and grinned, but she had her eyes closed and was talking quickly to God and Jesus.

Brigg cut short the conversation with his muddy palm across her lips. They were coming now. Running along the pipe in bare feet, chattering among themselves. Brigg hid his face away, resting it next to Phillipa's. He could feel her trembling so hard that he thought the men on the pipe must hear it. They were directly above now. And they stopped.

As he clutched her, Brigg thought he was going to be sick. He prayed that Mrs. Raskin would not start moving or mumbling.

They were on the pipe. There did not sound very many of them. Perhaps a dozen. Brigg slid one hand along towards his rifle. He felt the bolt mechanism covered in mud. He was sure they had been seen. But the men were clearly arguing and suddenly he heard them running again. He followed their voices and realised they were going. He waited, his face nuzzling into Phillipa's breasts. The men did not return.

'They've gone,' she said at last. 'They've gone away.'

At first he thought her mother was dead. But she was still holding on to life and the milk bottle. They had no strength left to move her or themselves.

They lay close together in the mud, half dozing, half awake, the remaining hours of the night, until the ripe dawn arrived and the jungle birds began to caw and croak and the midges began to move on the water.

Then they found they were three hundred yards from the safe end of the pipeline.

As he walked up the road towards the garrison in the hot mid-morning, Brigg was thinking that he might be some kind of hero. The village was being policed by Gurkhas and there was an armoured car loitering outside the Chinese cinema in the street. But most things seemed us usual.

There was a fragile stream of smoke coming from the offices, but all the buildings in sight seemed to be intact. The diving board at the swimming pool peeled over like a stork taking a drink.

Brigg was stained and aching tired, but he was warm inside because he was a soldier and had fired his gun, been in a real action, and had saved two women, one a lovely girl.

Phillipa had ungraciously gone to the hospital with her muddy mother. Brigg had jumped a lift on an R.A.F. truck back to Panglin. On the way he had modestly described his adventure to the driver.

Tall and lean now, he paced the tipped-up road to the garrison. Over the sandbags at the main gate he saw little puddings which he knew were the heads of the soldiers. Fatty Fisher, red and blowing, thumped out into the road to meet him.

Brigg had rehearsed it.

'Reporting back, Sarge,' he said quietly.

'Glad you could come,' said Fisher with no enthusiam. 'The Colonel wants to see you.'

'I thought he might,' said Brigg to himself. 'Shall I get bulled up, first?' he asked aloud.

'No,' said the Sergeant. 'He said as soon as you got in.'

'Right then,' said Brigg quietly. 'Let's go.'

He marched off behind Fisher, watching the fat man's buttocks bounce like boulders, and aware of the soldiers behind the sandbags regarding him with pointed awe.

They got to the Colonel's office. Fisher butted his head in the door and said: 'He's back, sir. Private Brigg.'

The Sergeant pulled his big head out, nodded Brigg to enter, and followed him. Brigg saluted and held the same hand ready in case the Commanding Officer should rush around the desk and seek to shake it. But he remained in his chair. Brigg quickly reasoned that years as a soldier had made him keep his feelings under suppression.

The Colonel blinked his good eye and said: 'Stand at ease, Brigg.'

Brigg opened his feet.

'Brigg,' said the Colonel after a silence. '*Where* have you been?'

'Well, sir, I've . . .'

The Colonel interupted: 'Take your time, son, and let's hear it from the very beginning. It should be worth it. Start from the time when you got out of the lorry out on the road there late yesterday afternoon.'

Brigg swallowed. That was it. They wanted the *words* from him. For the citation!

'Sir,' he said firmly, 'I went across the bridge with Major Cusper's detail just after the diving board was blown up and the rioters began attacking the offices.'

Colonel Bromley Pickering said: 'Were you detailed for that deployment, Brigg?'

'No, sir,' replied Brigg uneasily. 'No, I went on my own initiative, sir.'

'Oh, did you? Yes, go on.'

'I was thinking about the people in the houses, sir. Particularly Sergeant-Major Raskin's wife and daughter sir, they being friends of mine.'

'Friends?'

'Well, sir, Miss Raskin is a special sort of friend.'

The Colonel turned his eye away like a fish moving to swim round the corner of a tank. 'Hmmm,' he said.

'When I got to their house, sir,' continued Brigg, 'the rioters were coming up the road. We could hear them shouting, and then some of them were in the garden. Mrs. Raskin was trying to pick up her tiddlers from the floor . . .'

'Her what?'

'She had some little fish, sir. In a big bowl. She was very fond of them.'

'How did they get on the floor?' asked the Colonel.

'I hit the tank with a bullet,' confessed Brigg. 'There were these rioters in the garden and I fired a shot over their heads, and when I fired a second shot I was a bit off and I sort of shattered the fish bowl.'

'Then what?' said the Colonel. He hid his face behind his hands. Brigg thought he looked tired.

'I got Mrs. Raskin and Phillipa, that's Miss Raskin, sir, out of the house. Mrs. Raskin had her fish in a milk bottle. She was kicking up a fuss and she wouldn't go without them. There was a bit of a panic on, but I managed to get everybody into the back garden. Then I saw all these rioters running over the garden fences towards us. I made the women run on and I hid behind some sheets on a line and fired some shots at the men, but I don't think I killed any of them.

'Then I ran after Phillipa and Mrs. Raskin, meaning to get them down on to the road, but when we got to the bank there were about thirty or forty rioters on the road, shouting and yelling. I thought the best way out would be along the big pipeline, sir, so I got the two women up there and climbed up myself.

'By this time, sir, the mob was climbing up the

bank after us. All screaming. I was a bit frightened, sir, but I stopped about fifty or sixty yards along the pipe and fired at them as they were trying to get up. I heard the bullets fly off the pipe, but I don't think I hit anybody.'

The Colonel said: 'You hit somebody, Brigg.'

Brigg burst. 'I did, sir!'

'Yes, but we'll discuss that in a minute. Go on.'

Brigg began to wonder what was wrong. 'Well, sir,' he continued, 'we had a very hard time on the pipeline. Mrs. Raskin is not young and she kept holding us up. She got very tired and then she fell off.'

'Off the pipeline!' exclaimed the Colonel. 'Good God!'

'Yes, sir. It was very nasty. It was dark and she fell right down into a muddy pond in the undergrowth.'

'Good God,' breathed the Commanding Officer again. 'What did you do, Brigg?'

'I climbed down and managed to get her up again. She wouldn't come at first because the fish had escaped out of the milk bottle.'

'She still had the milk bottle?'

'Oh yes, sir, she wouldn't move without it. Anyway I was very frightened that the mob would be coming along the pipe after us so I kidded her that the fish were in there. With Phillipa I managed to heave her up on to the pipe again but it was a job because she's not very light and she was all muddy and soggy.'

'But you got her up there,' said the Colonel, not looking up from under his hands.

'Yes, sir. Then we had to push her down again.'

'Down again!'

'Yes, sir.'

'Into the mud and stuff.'

'Yes, because we could hear them coming along the pipe. We rolled her under some thick leaves and Phillipa and I wedged ourselves under there too. We sank halfway down in the mud, and Mrs. Raskin had more or less passed out.'

'Oh God,' said the Colonel. Brigg wondered why he kept saying that and why his eye kept opening wide like it did. Fatty Fisher was still standing there staring straight ahead.

'It was very frightening,' admitted Brigg. 'We heard them coming along the pipe and they went by us without spotting us. And we stayed there until it got light.'

'That's all?' said the Colonel.

'Yes, that's all, sir,' answered Brigg.

'Where are the ladies now?'

'Oh, yes. Mrs. Raskin was taken off to hospital and Phillipa went with her.'

'Oh, God,' said the Colonel again.

There was a stretched silence, Brigg and Fisher

standing there and Colonel Bromley Pickering looking down at his desk through the cage of his fingers. When he looked up his patience was lying in distinguishable surface layers across his face. He flapped one hand impotently on the papers lying on the pad. 'Brigg,' he said without raising his voice. 'Brigg, the first thing I want you to realise is that by going across the bridge with Major Cusper's detail in the first place you disobeyed an order.'

He thought for a while then started again: 'No, you did not actually *disobey* an order, because no order was ever given to you. What you did was *obey* an order you should not have *obeyed*.' His voice dropped unsurely. 'If you see what I mean, the order was not *intended* for you. You understand that?'

'Yes, sir,' answered Brigg faultily.

'Why did you go then?'

'Initiative, sir.'

The Colonel nodded hesitantly. 'Initiative?' he wrote on a pad. 'Well, we'll put that down for a start.'

He placed his pencil carefully at the side of his pad. It rolled over and the naked point stared straight at Brigg's stomach.

Colonel Bromley Pickering said: 'Now we come to a more serious matter, Brigg. Didn't you know that, particularly during a civil disturbance, you are not supposed to let off your rifle all over the bloody place, shooting indiscriminately?'

'But it was an emergency, sir,' whispered Brigg. 'They were trying to get us. God knows what they would have done. I mean with Miss Raskin and so on. And I wasn't shooting indiscriminately, sir, I was shooting to kill.'

The Colonel gave a small groan and put his fingers like a window around his eyes again. 'Son,' he said gently. 'Did you have any doubt at all about the men running across the gardens and down in the road being rioters?'

'No, sir,' said Brigg brightly. 'They were rioters all right, sir. They chased us over the fences and when they saw us from the road they all came scrambling up the bank at us. And then they tried to come along the pipeline after us. That's when I fired at them.'

He thought that sounded complete and satisfactory.

Then the Colonel said in a sad, patient voice: 'I have to tell you now, Brigg, that they were not rioters. They were the loyal Chinese from the Army Laundry who were running away from the mob.'

'Oh Jesus,' said Brigg.

Fisher looked at him sharply. The Colonel went on. 'If they were rushing and scrambling up that bank and in Sergeant-Major Raskin's garden, and eventually along the pipeline, then it was because they were frightened and trying to run. And you were shooting at them.'

Brigg opened his mouth, but Colonel Bromley Pickering lifted his palm. 'Don't say any more yet, son. There's more to come. One of your shots on the pipeline ricocheted and took the middle and index fingers clean off one of those Chinese.'

Brigg felt himself shrinking inside his damp uniform.

'Two fingers, sir,' he said.

'Off at the lower knuckle,' added the Colonel. 'The victim was the old man you may have seen outside the laundry every day turning that huge mangle.'

'Yes, sir,' stumbled Brigg. 'I've seen him turning the mangle, sir.'

'Well he's been at it man and boy for fifty years. He even mangled the Japanese shirts. He's looked up to there. Respected. He's the sort of doyen of the laundry. Now, they say, his mangling will be impaired if not terminated altogether. There is a total strike down there, nobody can get so much as a pair of underpants washed, and they are demanding compensation and justice.'

He said it ominously.

'Justice, sir?' asked Brigg.

'Justice,' confirmed the Colonel. 'Their trade union johnnie has been up here this morning kicking up hell. They stayed loyal, he said, when everybody else was rioting, and they washed the shirts and the rotten army drawers cellular, and then they get shot at.'

Brigg listened, stunned. The Colonel paused. 'Actually they were in no danger from the mob yesterday, any more than you were, Brigg. The troublemakers were stopped at the first row of office buildings by Major Cusper's detail, and Sergeant Fisher's detail.'

'Thank you, sir,' said Fisher saluting.

'Assisted by two companies of Gurkhas and three armoured cars which happened to come down over the causeway to help sort things out.'

'Quite, sir,' agreed Fisher, saluting again.

'What about me, sir?' Brigg blinked. 'You said something about justice.'

'Exactly,' replied the Colonel sadly. 'That's what they want. They want you put away for ten years.'

'Oh, God, sir,' said Brigg.

'Quite apart from that,' said the Colonel, 'this is a court martial matter you know, shooting civilian's fingers off.'

'Yes, sir, I understand.'

'But because of the circumstances and because you were acting on initiative, not altogether a bad thing, and because you're a young soldier and made a silly mistake, I'm not going to let General Headquarters know anything about this. And Heaven help anyone else who lets them hear about it. If the Chinese kick up a row we'll have to say we cannot trace the shooting soldier. If they argue further we'll prove it was one of the rioters.'

'Thank you, sir,' breathed Brigg. 'Thank you very, very much.'

'On the other hand we're going to have to pay this wounded chap some compensation. We don't want to make it official, so it will have to come from somewhere else. The amenities fund or something. After all fingers are amenities.'

He laughed shortly, and Brigg tried to laugh, but only a piece of mud came from his mouth.

'You will pay six weeks' pay towards the compensation,' the Colonel said to Brigg. 'It will all be done strictly unofficially. I want you to come in here every Thursday and put your pay down here on my desk. We want nothing written down. I'm not even going to charge you on an Army Form B252 for the obeying-the-order offence.'

'Thank you, sir,' said Brigg. 'I'm very grateful. I'll bring my money right over.'

'Right,' muttered the Colonel. 'I think that's all. Dismiss.'

'Dismiss!' bawled Fisher in his mightiest regimental manner.

Brigg had reached the door when the Colonel stopped him. 'This fellow's got an interesting name,' he commented. 'The chap whose fingers you shot off. I'm told it's a perfectly normal Chinese name, but perhaps you'd like to remember it when you're sitting about for the next six weeks with no pay. It may give you some comfort.'

He beckoned Brigg over. Brigg went to the desk. Fisher was stretching his bison neck near the door. The paper on the desk had the Chinese victim's name written in capitals.

Afterwards Brigg trudged to the barrack room. He lay on his bed, miserably considering the ceiling. Then he mumbled 'How I shot FUK YEW the Chinese Mangler.'

And he began to laugh.

10

At four in the afternoon the heat would often go. The sun would back away over the sea and the island would lie cooler. In the streets the buses and cars and trishaws moved more comfortably; there would be a football match on the Padang, in front of the Supreme Court, with the toothy shadows lying across the moving players and the grass.

Brigg went in on the bus on the Saturday. He had five dollars, the remnant of his final pay packet before his empty weeks.

All the violence and the fire had gone. The smoke had drifted with the wind. There was nothing left of the riot. If it had not been for Brook settling down there in the military cemetery, a very old Chinese with two fingers missing, and a soldier with six weeks' pay missing, it might never had happened.

First he went to the services club and eased himself out on one of the long line of wicker couches; one at the end which was very popular because it had the best view of the Chinese girls in *cheongsams* working in the club shop. He had a pot of tea and some buns and wrote a long letter to Joan. Then he walked in the calm yellow evening, across the putting green to the concrete edge of the ocean.

The wall was six feet tall and the waves running in from the China Sea stunned themselves against it and fell away every thirty seconds. Some palms, stunted like freaks by monsoon winds, hunched along by the sea. Bright, metallic bands lay across the harbour as the sun doused itself. There were steamers, junks and sampans riding it out on the gold.

He was going to see Lucy again that night. But this was the last time. He looked at the sampans and felt again the wooden boards across his buttocks and her thick hair flowing all over his groin.

But there would be no more. He would be going home in two and a half months. No more of this. That same sea would wash the red dust of this place from his feet, the heat and the smell would go, the jabber of the crowds would fade and the close sickly nights, the hot days, the warm violent rain, the steaming roads and barrack square. The demobilisation calendar's squares were nearly all filled in black now. Soon he would be in sweet England with his wistful and waiting Joan. In the meantime he had to think of a way to have it with Phillipa.

216

Brigg had neither seen nor heard of her since they kissed their muddy goodbye at the end of the pipeline that morning and she followed her miserably moaning mother to the ambulance. Colonel Bromley Pickering had a talk with R.S.M. Raskin, and the Sergeant-Major had not accused him of abducting his daughter and attempting to murder his wife, not to mention allowing her angel fish to escape. All he had done was look at him.

But this would be the last time with Lucy. He would not go to her flat right away in case she was busy, so he walked by the sea and the sampans until the harbour was spread with lights. Then he went back to the services club for a dollar supper.

It was still early when he got to the Liberty Club. It was the same as it ever was, except that Lucy was not there. Because it was early the lights were sharper, unclouded by smoke and the girls lolled on their ringside chairs waiting for the customers. The band bent forward over the floor, straining over the rough notes as though each one had been hit in the stomach. There were only three couples on the floor. Lucy's usual chair was empty.

Brigg sat at a table and took his time over a beer, waiting for her. She was sometimes late. The nights he had come here just to dance with her, knowing that he would have to get the final bus back to

Panglin and not sleep with her. He danced and always gave her the tickets, which he thought was right because she earned her living, or some of it, by dancing and being given tickets. So he always paid for dancing with her. They would move close together along the great elephants' feet columns lining the strange place, their toes and the rounds of their feet knowing, in the end, every knot and broken hollow in the floor, their ears attuned to each cough, bleat and straggling of the band. They knew the time of night when it got smoky and where the shadows were, so that he could hold both her breasts in his hands and she could work with her fingers like cool, gentle knives. They were always so close when they danced that they could feel each other's sweat – the damp, warm sweat underneath her linen dress and his white shirt, and the hot, wet sweat that rivered down their faces pressed into each other.

But he always gave her the tickets. And, in the end, many times he would have to go and stand by the door while she made an arrangement with another man. He would loiter there, hoping that the contract would never be struck, and when it was he would get out quickly. Once, only once, he remained by the door. Her customer, an airman with bright orange hair, waited for her while she went to the cloakroom, just as Brigg had waited that first time. She came out, looking at the airman as happily and invitingly as she ever looked at him; or that is how it appeared, and they went by him. She never looked at Brigg at all, and he went home miserably in the last bus, through a lashing tropical storm, hating her and promising that he would never go to her again.

But this, tonight, really was the last time. He would take her when she came in, they would stay in the club a couple of hours, because the manager did not like her leaving right away, and then all night they would lie in the dark kernel of her hot little room. But it would all end there.

He steadily reached the floor of his beer glass. The place was filling and the air was thicker. The band played loud in the smoke, but she did not come. He bought a book of tickets and waited until a new dance started. He stood up and went over to Iron Gerda and asked her to dance because he wanted to ask about Lucy. She looked up at him with blank eyes and shook her head.

'Dance?' he said.

'I'm busy,' she said. She got up and took her big handbag over her arm and went across the floor, her backside swinging like an elephant's. Brigg followed her and saw the manager by the door. He was a Portuguese Asian, thick necked, and with a face jolly and round, although he was never jolly.

'Where's Lucy?' asked Brigg, who did not like him.

'Which Lucy?' He picked up some dirty glasses from a table and placed them on the tray of a waiter going by. 'They all call themselves Lucy some time.'

'Oh come on,' said Brigg. 'You know me. You've seen me here with her plenty of times. She sits on that chair, over there. She always sits there.'

'Sure, sure,' said the manager.

'Well, where is she?' asked Brigg.

The man looked at him for the first time. Straight so their eyes met. 'You don't know she's dead then?' he said.

Brigg laughed. 'No, mister. *Lucy*. The girl I go with.'

'That's right,' the manager said sullenly. 'I know. She's dead.'

A swift panic fell on Brigg. He felt as though a bat were flapping itself in his face. 'No! No, you bloody fool. She's not dead. She's only a young girl,' he stuttered.

He grabbed at the manager's shirt and then found himself held from behind. Hands were enclosing both his wrists. He did not turn his head.

'She's dead,' said the man again, jerking his mouth at Brigg. 'In the riot. And it was your soldiers, soldier. They kicked her to death. Your soldiers. They said she had a disease. You know what I say to you?'

Brigg couldn't see him because he was sobbing great tears. He cried out as he stretched forward to try and pull away from the men who held him. He lashed back at them with his heels. They let him go because the manager nodded to them. Brigg stumbled down the single flight of stairs to the street door, banging first to one wall then the other, and crying: 'No! No! She's not! She's not!'

The manager leaned over and shouted: 'It was your soldiers, soldier.'

Brigg went on. Slithered down into the street. Out into the city. But it was like running through a tunnel. He started to run towards the quarter where she lived, shivering with sweat, along the pavements, banging people and not turning his head, just running on. A taxi came up beside him and he groped for it and got in.

He sat in the back and the Chinese driver said: 'Where to, Johnny?'

'Sarangoon Road,' said Brigg. He could never remember the exact name of the place.

'Which end, Johnny?' asked the driver, going out into the moving lights of the traffic.

'Just go. Go there,' whispered Brigg. 'The middle. About the middle.'

'You got a girl?' asked the taxi driver. 'I know a good girl.'

Brigg thrust his face over the back of the seat. 'Charlie,' he said, 'just go there quick.'

The Chinese nodded and they went off through the city. Brigg tried to stifle all the screams inside him. He suffocated them and sat straight and tense as wire in the back seat. 'No,' he said. 'No. That bastard's giving me the runaround. He's trying it on. She's not. I know she's not.' He made himself smile confidently, then he laughed out loud because it was all so ludicrous.

'Funny, Johnny?' said the driver.

'Sorry, Charlie,' said Brigg. 'I was a bit cockeyed. Somebody's having a big joke, that's all. Just get down there, Charlie. It's all right. Just get down there, quick.'

'Nearly there now,' said the driver. He swung the big taxi around a bend and hit a dog square between the eyes as it turned its startled face into the glare. It howled and Brigg almost stifled with fright. He was trying to keep it down, now. Keep the fear under. But he was losing control again. His body was vibrating and he stiffened his arms and legs and knotted his fists, trying to stop it, so that he was like a man struggling to escape from ropes.

'Please, Almighty God up in Heaven,' he stammered, afraid of the words. 'Please, Father, make it not true. I love her. She mustn't be. God, she mustn't be. If she is, I'll never forgive You.'

The taxi stopped by the gutter. A crouching monkey of a man was cooking treacle juice on a little stove and held up a sweet saucer for Brigg to try and to buy. Brigg did not see him. He ran away from the taxi and as the driver called for his money he took out a dollar note, which was not enough, and threw it over his shoulder so that the air caught it and slithered it along the pavement. The old treacle man picked it up and held it for a moment, then put it into the thin hand of the taxi driver hanging out of the cab window like a feeding bird.

Brigg had to run along the alleyway at the back of the flat. The place where she had thrown his trousers. He was exhausted although he had only run two hundred yards. He turned the corner and saw at once the light in the window of her flat. He stopped and the light wavered in his tears, bending like a flame. 'Oh, thank You,' he said.

He went forward again. Of course she would be there. He'd go back and slaughter that bloody idiot at the club. He would run in and hit him two or three times and then run out again before the bodyguard had a chance to move. He jogged under the window.

'Lucy! Lucy!' he called buoyantly. 'Lucy, I'm here.' A Sikh asleep in the alley stirred like a clock and stopped again, falling back when he saw that it was only a soldier calling. A red jeep from the military police went by on the road at its junction with the alley, but did not falter, and a streak of shadow went across the ceiling of Lucy's room, the part that Brigg could see.

'The little cow,' Brigg breathed happily. 'Working again. She'll have to stop that.'

He was still going up there and if it happened to be a Dutch stoker or a Coldstream Guardsman it was too bad. He went out into the road and around to the front of the building where the wooden stairs went up to the flat. There were swords of light around the badly fitting door. Brigg went up the stairs. At first slowly, one at a step, his face intent on the door. His awful terror for her was still coiled and ready inside him and he could feel it. But it was all right. He knew it would be all right. He half fell on one of the middle steps, and standing up again he suddenly ran madly up the rest and threw open the door in his run.

'I'm sorry,' he began.

A yellow Chinese woman sitting on the bare bed-frame looked up at him. She had Lucy's golliwog in her hand and had been examining its funny black face. Her pointed eyes, from their deep cheese holes, looked straight at Brigg as he stood there. She was the only one in the room. It was empty of everything except her, and the bed frame, the light bulb, the golliwog and a pile of dust and rubbish on the floor.

'Lucy?' said Brigg. 'Lucy?'

The hag got up and shuffled past him, out of the door and went pattering down the steps behind him.

'Lucy!' screeched Brigg. He stood in the middle of the floor, arms out, screeching. 'Lucy! Lucy! Lucy!' There was nowhere to search because there was nowhere to hide. A huge sickness drained all the blood from him, he turned to the bed frame, and fell on his knees by it, crying so much that he choked. He pressed his thin face to the wire springs and felt them cutting a pattern in his cheeks and his ear and one side of his mouth.

She was dead then. Kicked and killed, like the man had described, by soldiers who thought she had the disease. The almighty horror of it whirled around him like a roundabout, making jangling music.

He got up in the end and looked around the hollow room. On his knees he went to the pile of rubbish and pulled it apart. There were squares of paper, dozens on which she had been writing in huge unsteady letters about Eeney, Meeny, Miney, Mo and about the world being a funny place.

He read it through as she had written it. 'Oh, but this world's a funny place, and yet it's hard to beat. With every rose you get a thorn . . .'

He remembered writing it for her. So she could learn it. He remembered Tasker writing. 'Don't it get on your tits?' as a last line.

Brigg got up and walked out.

It did, didn't it?

Then he wondered if she did have the disease.

At the northern hump of Singapore Island, near where the single white finger of the causeway leaned across the straits to Malaya, there was a base ammunition depot.

Brigg was there three nights a week, squatting on a box among the mashed leaves, bored with the bullfrogs, and, when he was not on guard patrol, writing sincere letters, lying and long, to Joan back in England. There had been a new order from General Headquarters detailing men from all camps on the island for guard duty at the ammunition depot. It was a dark place, too near the jungle and the causeway, and the bandits just across the causeway, to be an easy duty. Brigg, who had taken no pay for three weeks, offered to substitute for any Panglin man who was named for guard duty there. He charged three Singapore dollars per night. By arrangement with the orderly room the change was always accomplished without trouble.

But it made him fatigued. He walked the muddy paths around the ammunition stores blinking his eyes at the tireless moon, or whistling back at the night-birds, to keep awake. He would feel his rifle dragging on his shoulder like an invalid, and his boots ploughing through the slough, and he would become startled a fraction too late at every hoot, scramble and urgent noise.

'One thing, though,' he would tell himself. '*I'm clean*. And I'm going home to *her* clean.'

After being in Lucy's room that hour he had gone to the all-night emergency medical centre, where they gave the soldiers paste and contraceptives if they felt the bad urge so much that they couldn't help it. It was, for Brigg, a month or more late for using an emergency sex pack, but there was always a medical officer there to examine the men who had been and had not taken the precaution of having a sex pack with them or had been too embarrassed to use it.

Many young soldiers felt that it was unnecessarily shaming to have to cover vital parts with paste and rubberware while watched by a warm Chinese girl. It spoilt it. So most of them went to the medical centre afterwards.

They gave Brigg a blood test and pronounced him unaffected by any complaint that Lucy was rumoured to have, and for which she died an ugly death. They told Brigg not to do it again and he promised he would not, and he meant the promise too.

So he was clean. Clean but bankrupt. Every pay

day he had presented himself at the pay table, saluted, and received his money which he had immediately borne to the Commanding Officer and added to the amenities fund for the Chinese laundry mangle-man with the strange name.

In the barrack room they suggested having a collection for him each pay day, but this he refused. Instead Tasker lent him an occasional coin to pay for his tea in the morning break, sometimes a beer, and on really hot days a strawberry ice cream with chocolate sprinkling. Until the idea of hiring himself out for guard duties came to him he spent his moping hours lying on his sheets, damp with sweat, watching the high ceiling and the gradual shoots and stems of early evening moons.

There was no more Phillipa. She had been sent abruptly to start a nursing course in the hospital at Kuala Lumpur, two hundred miles north. Brigg had never seen her after their parting at the other end of the pipeline on that morning. He thought he might send him a letter but she did not.

Some men had gone home and new, white-kneed, ingenuous conscripts had arrived, their green uniforms hanging on them like bean leaves. They went through all the familiar sicknesses of asking how far away the bandits were, and whether they ever came across the causeway, how much did indecent women cost in Singapore, and if the ice cream man would let you run up a bill. Brigg smugly showed them his demobilisation calendar, with only the few weeks of empty days left, and they went away and began to make their own calendars covering the next year and a half.

Sinclair wrote a thesis on Malayan railways for an enthusiasts' magazine and was put under close arrest for twenty-four hours for contravening King's Regulations and not submitting it to the Regimental Sergeant-Major for censorship. Gravy Browning lost the all-Asian services table-tennis championships to an Australian wonder stoker who practised his life away in the belly of an aircraft carrier. Browning put away his bat and ball for ever and never played one against the wall with the other again. He spent his nights consuming steak and chips in the village and finally slept with a feline Chinese waitress who had never been known to give herself to anybody before. And for nothing.

Fenwick had stopped poisoning his ears in the pool, and was no longer seeking a medical repatriation through creeping rheumatism. He still owned to having rheumatism, but this was so he could go for physiotherapy treatment at the Military Hospital where he had fallen in love with an earthy Yorkshire nurse who worked with hands like breaths of warm wind. Fenwick began to dread going home.

*

At the ammunition depot there was a small, muddy, permanent detachment of Ordnance Corps soldiers, swelled each night by the twenty men from the other inland units. One of the Ordnance men was a corporal who used to organise bull-frog races for money.

The men who were at the depot all the time, and had very little to do except see that it did not blow up and was not stolen, had their own private bull-frogs which they painted different colours and kept in boxes. They trained them to race and initiated the actual races by flaring a small dash of gunpowder a couple of yards behind them. The races were held along a wide curving concrete gully that ran the length of the depot. It was supposed to be full of water for use if the ammunition caught fire, but the soldiers regularly drained the water away so that they could hold the races. The depot was always sticky with mud and engineers were always searching for a leak or a fault in the gully.

On most nights the bets on the events were small, but on pay nights the stakes would pile. The men who had arrived to guard for a single night had to go and catch their own bull-frogs in the clammy under-growth, but it was not difficult because there were hundreds of them and they made a lot of noise.

But these wild frogs were mostly no threat to the trained frogs. They were given a stripe or two of distinguishing paint, but they rarely reacted to the sizzling of the small pile of gunpowder in the way that the experienced ones did. There were no odds given, only in side bets, the rule being the stake in the kitty and the winner take all.

Brigg had never had a frog because he had no money to put on its back. But the Ordnance man said that since he was there so frequently he ought to get himself one and train it.

He first saw his frog posturing in a patch of cream moonlight. It was the early-hours patrol, when the jungle all around was all screams and whispers. Brigg walked the perimeter path of the depot, the wires of his nerves bending at every swift sound. No matter how many times he did the duty his reactions never softened.

The bull-frog was singing throatily in the middle of the path. It was a bulky and strong-looking frog, but not too fat: the sort that could do well in the longer races. He was facing Brigg, quite impudently, his jelly eyes protruding from his flat black head, and his pale waistcoat thumping and sobbing with the emotion of his elegy.

When Brigg had made up his mind to catch him, and had moved towards him, the frog bounded half-left, flopping on the dead leaves at the fringe of the path. It was a good jump for sideways and Brigg knew by now that the front jump was always half as powerful again.

'Here, boy,' encouraged Brigg, slinking towards him. 'Come on. Good frog.'

The creature gave a short, low leap, and then another. His glowing belly tickled against the leaves as he went.

'*Good,* that *was* good,' Brigg told him. 'You could be a champ, son. Come on, come here.'

The frog spat at him as he went towards it again. He was a fighter too. That was even better. Brigg rushed him and he went heaving along towards the darker places under the trees. Going after him, Brigg knew that if he was ever going to have a frog to race for him it would have to be this one. The animal seemed bent on proving Brigg's choice, because he jumped at right angles again and tumbled into the wide, hard gully where they held the races.

'Now let's see,' whispered Brigg with soft delight. 'Now we'll see how you go.' He chased the bull-frog in an unhurried way, going forward demonstratively every time the thing landed after a leap, thus forcing it into another immediately. They followed the bends and straights of the long gully through well over half its distance. Then the frog sat down still and tame and allowed Brigg to fold it in his beret.

He took it to the guardroom and put it in the empty tea bucket until morning. The tea bucket had a lid to keep the tea warm, so the frog could not escape. He took it out again before the dawn guard went off for the tea.

The Ordnance soldiers thought the frog was a promising one. They agreed to look after it when Brigg was not doing a guard duty and they gave it a big ammunition box, plenty of mud and leaves and some spiders to eat. Brigg chose yellow and white as his racing colours and he painted stripes of these down his frog's back. When he went back to Panglin he sold his camera for twenty dollars and went back on guard at the ammunition depot on the next pay day.

As soon as the duty officer had circled on his inspection tour at ten o'clock that night, the racing started. Nearly all the temporary guards had caught frogs and had money with which to back them.

Brigg collected his frog and inspected it. It seemed a bit thinner than when he had captured it, but this was good.

'You'll have to call it something,' said the Corporal who organised the racing. 'What's it going to be?'

'Lucy,' said Brigg suddenly. 'Juicy Lucy.'

'You can't call a bull-frog Lucy,' said the Corporal doubtfully. 'Can you?'

'I am,' said Brigg.

'All right,' said the Corporal. 'It's a mare then.'

'No, it's a girl,' said Brigg, and the Corporal looked at him oddly.

The first race was a short one over twenty feet, for dollar stakes. Some of the soldiers did not enter their frogs but stood watching by the white sugar light of the depot's flood lamps which had been diverted from the ammunition dumps to the racetrack. They cosseted their frogs in their hats or in boxes, or the ammunition pouches attached to their webbing belts. Some of the frogs made a loud and unhappy noise, but those in the ammunition pouches mostly coughed because of the smell and dust of the blanco.

A muslin net from the cookhouse was used to hold the racers immediately before the start as the powder, emptied from a .303 cartridge, was approached by the small flame biting its way along the short fuse. It sizzled, giving off small explosions, always sharp but not too loud, and the officer in command was dependably in the distant mess by this time. Some of the officers knew about the racing and sometimes turned up to watch. But they only had side bets on other people's frogs because they had none of their own.

Brigg put his frog under the net with the others. The spiteful little flame nibbled down the fuse. When the net was adeptly pulled away just before the big flare-up Brigg's frog was facing the wrong way. He shouted at it. But the gunpowder flamed and the creatures went hopping off crazily. Brigg's frog jumped sideways and straddled the warted back of one of the other entrants so that both were immediately without a hope in the race.

It was a two-dollar race next. Brigg doubtfully dropped his money into the stake-keeper's greasy beret. His frog was throbbing in the cup of his hand, staring out with a black, unbelieving ogle, and croaking as though its heart was breaking.

'This time, Lucy,' said Brigg quietly, 'face the right bleeding way. And jump. Understand? Jump.'

There were more entrants this time. Twelve, fat, uncertain, protesting things, stuffed under the muslin net and giving leaps and groaning jumps beneath it so that it bulged and sagged and quivered as though it were alive itself. Brigg put his frog quite surely facing the right way and joined his anxious face to the ring of lit, concerned, faces around the gully. The charge burned and fanned noisily and away the frogs flew. Sometimes some leapt clear of the gully, and the owners, following wildly along the bank were permitted under the rules to throw them back into the race, but one pace back from the place where they had left the course.

Almost stifled with excitement, Brigg saw his frog leap gracefully into the lead from the start. It went in gliding, bounding arcs, landing straight and confident and seeming to know where it was going and what was expected of it. The race was over fifty feet and Lucy had a ten-length lead when the first and only bend was gained. Brigg ran with the others, slipping and scrambling along the bank, running all of them, with a funny crippled, bending run, their faces down low near their frogs, mouthing curses and encouragement, urging, stumbling and sometimes falling over.

When Brigg's frog was clear of the bend, it sat down. It seemed happy and satisfied with its performance and took on a frozen immobility that none of Brigg's shrieking altered by even a jerk of a muscle.

'Move, you black bastard!' howled Brigg almost on his knees with involuntary pleading and the need to get as near to his animal's ears as he could. But Lucy sat blandly and blindly and allowed the rest of the field to pass. Just as the winning frog crossed the final line in mid-leap, Lucy came alive again and executed a small token jump. Then she sat, full of her private thoughts again, until the stewards announced that the race was run and won and Brigg stepped down to pick her up. Then she really jumped, clean through his pincher arms and down the straight course like a thoroughbred. Brigg ran in pursuit, a hundred feet along the gully and then out into the wet and heavy going of the perimeter road and its collar of bush and brush.

'I'll catch you, you bugger,' promised Brigg as he

ran, sliding down banks, caught by the fingernails of thorny creepers strung from the thicker trees. One of the entrails cut him across the face like a lash, filling his eyes with water and bringing a taste of blood to his mouth. But he never lost the bull-frog. It was always just ahead, sometimes bounding, sometimes slithering, sometimes impudently resting, waiting for him to catch up. Then it surrendered, again without fuss, sitting squatly on a flat leaf and waiting for Brigg to reach and pick it up.

He carried it back. If it had not escaped he might have abandoned it as a racing frog and saved his scarce money. But now he was decided to try once more. Just once. He left it out of the next two races, watching instead the silent capers of the frogs and the rowdy antics of the owners.

The last race was for a ten-dollar stake per man. There were twenty frogs entered. Brigg put his money into the hat with a sad shrug, and placed the curiously dry-wet belly of the frog on the starting area. It was a crowded start, with frogs climbing on other frogs' backs, investigating other frogs' ears and smells, and all finally smothered by the wide white net, held down firmly at each corner by the hands of the stewards.

It was over seventy-five feet around two bends and into a short, straight finish. The strong impersonal floodlights glared down on the grouped soldiers in green, hunched and anxious, waiting for the start.

The gunpowder charge spluttered and suddenly spread and the taut faces flowed into mobility, working and shouting and urging as the frogs launched themselves away from the sudden sound.

Lucy went off like rubber, throwing herself forward from bound to bound and immediately into the first three, the yellow and white stripes on her back wrinkling and stretching like elastic with each free and muscled movement. Because the start was so crowded several frogs were left sprawling in the mud at the line, two were stonily facing the opposite way from the course and one had a seizure and died immediately the starting charge went off.

Others leapt on to the sides of the gully, out of the ruck and rush, only to be flung back into the race by angry owners. On other sides of the gully the soldiers ran hysterically, willing on the slimy racers, their faces transformed by the bright, holy, hopeful light that shines on those consumed by greed and gambling.

Brigg loped along one side of the gully, praying that Lucy would not jump out of the race on the other side. This had finished the chances of several owners who lost every thread of hope in the time it took to run around the gully to reach their stupid champions. Some soldiers threw the frogs forlornly into the fray again, one or two patted them with understanding, put them in their pockets for another night or sent them on their way into the undergrowth. Others threw the frogs aside in hate and disgust and one flung his entrant high and murderously at the shining moon.

After thirty feet there were eight racers left of the twenty. Lucy was contesting the front with a vicious bull who jumped as though he had been promised freedom if he won. Brigg had stopped shouting now, his breath too meagre to form words let alone bawl them. The big bull belonged to a sparse-haired lance-corporal going like an ape along the opposite bank, calling to it in thick Liverpool phrases. The frog had a white skull and crossbones on its broad pimpled back.

Third was a little beetle of a frog, bearing a red cross like some under-nourished Crusader, busily making ground a few inches behind the squared backsides of the two in front. This one was running for a Medical Corps corporal who had shot it with dope behind a secret tree two minutes before the start.

Lucy was a snout ahead at each skimming jump. She was using her low-leap technique, taking off like a hare instead of a frog, barely leaving the ground, but economising on effort with every jump. The big bull was taking a breath at each landing, but every time he pushed out with his steely springers he went in a high parabola, long and powerful, but still not quite matching the neat, straight jumps of Lucy.

At the second bend Lucy stopped, squatted squarely, and emitted a loud honk, a sound loaded with satisfaction. Brigg covered his face with his fingers. He tried to shout, but the words came out noiselessly, like jugged air.

'Please,' he eventually framed. 'Please, for Jesus' sake. Please, frog.'

No reaction came from Lucy. The big skull-and-crossbones bull was bounding ahead and the stimulated beetle-frog with the red cross flew by on a wave of hyper-tension. Others followed and passed.

Tragedy seemed complete for Brigg when Lucy suddenly skimmed forward again, as though she had merely been collecting her breath. But the beetle-frog, at almost the same instant, flopped into the mud and died. As Brigg was urging his frog again into the contest, the big bull belonging to the Liverpool soldier stopped and began groaning and thumping rhythmically two feet from the finishing line.

Its owner cried bleakly and rolled and postulated on the side of the gully begging, threatening and willing his frog to finish the race. The frog stared a deep liquid stare, straight ahead.

Lucy went through the field like a charger. She

leapt on joyously with Brigg at her side. He shouted nothing now, just made little sounds with his mouth and sweated and stumbled as he ambled. She went by the dead beetle-frog and overtook some of the hopefuls who had gone by when she was resting. Then, when she was level with the skull-and-cross-bones frog, she came to another sudden stop and squatted again, completely level with her rival, eight inches to his left. They sat, intent, like two old women watching a love film. The Liverpool youth looked over the gully at Brigg, an uncertain triumph rolling over his face. Brigg looked at him, then got down and began to hiss at Lucy, low spurts of breath that he hoped sounded like a snake.

Both frogs remained motionless perhaps in some secret communication. The stragglers were catching up now. A ghastly red-painted animal was puffing its way up the track in the lead of three others.

Then the big bull jumped three inches and his owner sprang with excitement against the sky. Lucy seemed to consider the move, leaped four inches then another three and finally made a smart and graceful jump across the finishing line.

Brigg shouted and stamped. He leaned over, laughing, and caught his frog in the tender bed of his hands.

'Oh, you beauty,' he giggled. 'Oh you bloody beauty.'

11

Nothing happened. All the way up-country, up through the stalactite length of Malaya, the train went and nothing happened. Brigg, half awake with apprehension, half asleep with fatigue, stretched in his top bunk, the ceiling curving only one hand away.

Everyone knew that the bandits liked shooting through the roofs of trains. They did it every week, lying on the high brush-coated embankments and firing a whole bren magazine through the passing roof of a carriage. They did not even have to move the bren. They merely kept it steady and firmly hooked the trigger, and the running train would do the rest, processing itself through the point of fire. It was like pulling the carriage of a typewriter along and repeatedly stabbing at one middle letter.

All the trains had notices about what should be done in the event of firing from the side of the line, and some experienced soldiers used to make sure, in the day-time, that they sat near a Malay or Chinese or Indian girl so that they could lie with them on the floor, or perhaps even protect them by lying on top of them when the shooting started. Others preferred to get down first, hoping that everyone else would be a little slower. At night, the veterans said, they never slept on the top bunks.

There was a low light in the middle of the sleeping car and Tasker and Langley were sitting with two guardsmen, playing poker. Brigg wondered why they bothered to give you rifles and ten rounds if you had to lie down on the floor when there was shooting. It was a good idea to lie down, because, apart from protecting the Chinese, Indian or Malay girls, you would never be able to see anyone shooting from the jungle anyway. So there was no point in showing yourself and returning the fire.

Sinclair lay on the bunk opposite, studious, even in sleep. He had enjoyed a good day. He had been at Singapore station early so that he could examine the engine, talk to the greasy driver, and photograph the wheel arrangement. He took some pictures too of the little pilot engine and its weighted trucks which ran bravely each night in front of the express in case the rails had been taken up by the bandits.

He had also investigated the armoured truck with its old, mounted Lewis guns, fixed on the rear of the train, until an Irish staff sergeant, in charge of the truck, had told him to go away.

The top three inches of a curtained window projected up one side of Brigg's bunk. He pushed the thick material away from the glass and looked out. Rain was slipping back almost horizontally in the direction from which they had come: strong tropical rain. Brigg was glad to see it. He supposed that bandits did not like getting wet either.

Brigg slept in the end. When it was light they had to leave the train and get on the ferry at Prai. They went by flat ferryboat across the channel to Panang Island as the sun was beginning to burn.

The leave centre was beside the beach; lines of chalets and huts. Brigg lay on his bed, late on the last afternoon of the first week, in from the beach in the cool, the sun coming through the shutters in stripes across his chest and the towel around his middle.

There were four beds, two of them with folded blankets, empty, and the third with a private from the Anglian Brigade asleep in its cavity. He was by himself at the leave centre, and he smoked a lot in the night. Every time Brigg had wakened, he had seen the firefly end of a cigarette in the dark across the room. The private's name was Charlie Waller, and he and Brigg had been put in the same room because Brigg had been a late booking and Waller's friends had been killed just before their leave.

Brigg did not know about them being killed until that afternoon. He lay, enjoying the roughness of the blanket against his cool back, enjoying the cleanness after his shower and all the sandy grit from the beach washed away from his body, all the sweat gone.

Outside some of the soldiers were playing football on a spare piece of ground, shouting like children in a schoolyard. Waller uncoiled and reached for his cigarette case and lighter from the locker.

'What's the time?' he said.

'Nearly five,' answered Brigg. All their conversations had been like this, single sentences, question and answer, trickling comments that had never thickened into any real talk. Waller went off by himself in the day, or slept, or smoked, and at night Brigg had seen him at the Piccadilly Lights, dancing with an old hostess.

Waller was young and he had a long ugly face, like a stovepipe, but his voice was not rough. The sun was filtering through his window too and bruising his hard face with deeper shadows. He began to smoke, and said to Brigg: 'How long have you got to do?'

'A month and a bit after this leave.' Brigg felt the familiar smugness fall over him as he answered. Whenever they asked how long you had been out there, or how long before you went home, you always felt like that. A sense of seniority and achievement. Once, in Singapore, a military policeman had stopped him and Tasker because they were in civilian clothes and wearing beach shirts outside their trousers. They knew he had not been out there very long because his uniform was too new. He asked them how long they had been on overseas service and they told him and he went away without a word.

But Waller took the boast casually.

'How long for you to do?' asked Brigg across the beds.

'A year and fourteen days. Thirteen tomorrow,' said Waller.

Brigg laughed. 'The year's going to be the worst.'

He sensed that Waller was not returning idle talk. He really wanted to know. He did not smile when Brigg laughed, nor was he making a joke when he talked about the fourteen days and the thirteen days. He could have told the total in minutes and hours.

'Been up-country much?' said Waller.

'Not much,' muttered Brigg uncomfortably. 'Just in Johore. Place called Buksing.'

Waller grunted. 'How long was that for?'

'Couple of weeks. Well, two and a bit. It was just a training camp.'

'Oh, yes. I see. In Singapore the rest of the time then?'

'Yes. That's right.'

Waller spurted some smoke from his mouth and it

hung about like a cloud with the sunrays thrusting through it. He watched the cloud disperse. Brigg was just going to get up and go out when Waller stopped him.

'How do you get into a bit of the army where it's nice and safe and you don't get killed, and that sort of thing?' he said. 'How do you do it?'

Brigg felt his own resentment rise in a blob in his chest. 'What d'you mean?' he said, keeping his voice to the same conversational level as Waller's. 'Nobody "gets into" anything, you know that. They just put you where they think they will. If they think you ought to push a pen then you've got to push a bloody pen. Even if you'd rather be using a gun and that sort of thing.'

'You wouldn't,' said Waller. It was a flat statement.

'Wouldn't what?'

'Rather be using a gun and that sort of thing. Not unless you were mental.'

'Some of us would,' asserted Brigg stoutly. 'We're not conscientious objectors or anything. It's just that they've stuck us in an office. Some of the blokes would give anything to get out of the bleeding place, I can tell you.'

Waller snorted a little laugh. Then he said: 'I wondered how you got into a nice safe little bit of the army. So you reckon it's just how they sort you out

248

at the very beginning, taking into account what you were doing before you joined. Whether you were pushing a pen or pushing a milk cart.'

Brigg said: 'I suppose so. I was a clerk before I came into the mob and I'm a clerk now.'

'I wasn't a bloody gamekeeper though,' said Waller in the same voice. 'But they gave me a gun.'

Brigg heard himself laughing weakly. He wanted to get up and put his shorts on and get out.

'Now I know where I went wrong,' said Waller. 'I said the wrong thing when I first went in with my calling-up papers. I was training to be an architect, you know. But the boss kept giving me all the rough jobs to do, all over the building sites, because I was the junior, the apprentice see? I got fed up with clogging around in the mud, and when I took my army papers in I must have been extra bitter because I told them I was a builder's labourer. That's what I reckoned myself as, even though I was training to be an architect. It was only a joke, but they put it down in ink and I got stuck with it. Every time I tried to explain it after that they thought I was trying to give them some yarn so that I could get out of the infantry. Bit of a scream really. But they wouldn't listen. So I got lumbered with this shitty lot.'

'It's rough is it?' said Brigg as though inquiring about a man's pain he could not know himself.

'Rough?' said Waller wryly. 'It's awful. It's so God bloody awful that you can't imagine it. Swamps and stink and prickly heat.'

'We get prickly heat,' claimed Brigg lamely. 'In Singapore.'

'It's like living your life in a sewer,' said Waller. 'And you can't find the manhole to get out. And you spend your life looking for some ginks you can never even see. And while you're looking for them they're looking for you too, to kill you. Only they're better at it than you because they've lived all their lives in the arsehole jungle, and they're good at hiding and killing you when you don't expect it.

'Some of them have been at it for years, you know. They were doing the same to the Japanese. Hiding in the jungle, then popping up and killing them. In those days they were resistance heroes, but now they're Communist bandits. One of them we caught was still getting a pension from the British Government for his time in the resistance. He had his pension book on him when we got him, all stamped up where he had been popping into Ipoh to draw his money and sleep with his wife one night a week.'

He cackled like an old, dry man and lifted his head to the window ledge to see the football game.

'It's nice here,' he said. 'Marvellous. Lying about and seeing the sun in the open instead of buried in the trees. And I've been shagging the oldest whore in Penang, a real dear who can dance an old-fashioned tango. Maybe you've seen her at the Piccadilly Lights?'

'Hmm,' said Brigg. 'I saw you with her a couple of nights ago.'

'She's an old love,' said Waller in his unchanging voice. 'When I first went in there I couldn't believe she was on the game. I thought she was the lavatory attendant. But she's marvellous. She's so grateful for the money and the rest of it. She does every variation in the book, and she doesn't charge hardly anything so I can have lots more.

'When I knew she was on it, I thought, "Well, you're for me, old dear. You're just what I want. Uncomplicated." I don't want complications, nor any trouble, and I don't want to spend my time buttering up some young bitch who's not going to give me the lot in the end. I haven't got time for all that muck. I don't want to have to think about it, nor do I want to have to worry in case somebody else is going to horn in before me. I want it easy. She's rough, I know. My mother looks better. But it's dark in her room.'

Brigg said: 'Why did you come by yourself?'

Waller stretched. 'Well that was half the trouble. Or more than half. Two others were coming with me. Arkley and Houseman, my friends. They were going to be on those two beds. We'd all fixed our leave together and were going to do everything including all the *young* whores.'

'Couldn't they get leave?' asked Brigg.

He half knew the answer before Waller gave it. 'No, they didn't need it. Last Thursday afternoon they both got killed. About three o'clock. Four others too.'

'Christ,' said Brigg.

'Old Houseman was a great bloke,' said Waller. 'Great. Quiet, you know. Nothing very marvellous about him, but a great bloke. And Bill Arkley. There was a randy bastard. He had cheek like you never heard, too. He once got a bloody knob and they sent him to the clinic to get injections and things, and he made a date with the nurse there! Have you ever heard of anyone having nerve like that!'

He laughed, a sound like dead leaves in a drainpipe, and Brigg croaked a sort of laugh too.

'It wasn't just that they got shot,' said Waller. 'It was so stupid.'

He did not seem to intend to go on. So Brigg said, 'How?'

'We had a new lieutenant out from England. Frankling. Knew less than we did, but I suppose he didn't want to let on and make it obvious. He went with a detachment to have a comb through a rubber plantation a few miles away from the camp. Arkley and Houseman went. When they got to the plantation they got a message that a latex truck was burning, so they went over and went straight into an ambush.

'They got into some sort of depression in the ground and tried to hold off his lot. This Frankling, the officer, had a Very pistol with him and was supposed to fire a red flare if they needed assistance and a green one if they were okay. But he only took white flares with him. So a couple of miles back no one knew what was going on. It would have been too late anyway. By the time we got there they were all dead, lying in the bit of sunken ground.'

Waller sat up on his bed. 'It was worse than seeing them dead, really. Just dead, I mean, even though they were my friends. But it was worse, much worse than that.'

Brigg said, 'How?'

'Because the bastard bandits had cut their teeth out and taken them away. Trophies. Like the Red Indians did with scalps.'

Brigg stood up and got out of the door. His towel dropped from him as he began to run. The footballers hooted at him. He ran down the beach and into the sea. He got a mouthful of salt water and as he stood up he was sick all over a little wave.

On most days Sinclair would go into Georgetown, the island town, and then to a bungalow on the further side where a Chinese merchant had built a scale model railway in his garden. The man was a rich shopkeeper, and Sinclair had made contact with him through the Railway Society. The lines of the railway swooped like snakes through the cacti, the bursting shrubs and the bubbling flowers of his tropical garden. When the man's two sons came home from school they would help Sinclair at the control switches, changing points, clicking signals, opening and shutting crossing gates. Later the merchant would drive home in his car and they would have all the eight little trains chasing like animals through the garden.

Three times as well Sinclair took the ferry over to the mainland and spent the hot day in the railway terminus, watching the up-country trains coming in and going. He got permission to go into the sheds and see the cleaning and oiling, and watch the expresses gaining their strength and the small working engines clanking and perspiring. When he came out of the sheds it was like emerging from a gritty oven and the bare sun seemed almost cool on him.

He was content most evenings to return for a meal and a single drink to the leave centre, but sometimes he went out with Brigg and Tasker and Lantry to the town. His mind was usually somewhere else as they walked the streets, with the air spiced and clanging, and the people all moving in the many lights or squatting still in the shadows.

Usually they ended at the Piccadilly Lights where

they had beer and danced with the women. The women were Chinese, Eurasian and Malay, with a few Siamese, who were said to be the best, but Sinclair hardly saw them. He sat, uncomplaining, at the basketwork table, and checked his engine numbers, or memorised wheel arrangements, or dreamed of the steamy excitements of Swindon, while it all went on around him.

The others would bully him mildly, but he returned the remarks with a studious smile and an offer to buy everyone a beer. Sometimes they forced a ticket into his hand and pushed him out to dance, but he did not enjoy it very much.

One of the Eurasian girls was called Little Nell, and she liked Sinclair because of his quietness, his tallness and his glasses. When she was not busy she would sit at the table with all four, and never charge for her time, and was flattered when Sinclair talked to her in his low, earnest manner. He said she had hair the colour of a coalbox.

Tasker remarked: 'She's a lovely shunter, son.' But neither Sinclair nor the girl took any notice. She became very intrigued with his detailed description of the London Underground system, and repeated the names of the station – Earl's Court, Morden, and the difficult Tottenham Court Road – carefully and with obvious enjoyment. Her favourite was the Elephant and Castle. She reminded Brigg painfully of Lucy.

She made it clear that her friendship with Sinclair was a personal thing, but that if the others wanted to engage her professionally she would be willing. They had all danced with her. She was a very close dancer with an adjustable body that seemed to fit any size or shape of man. Most of the hostesses when they danced with a thin man looked as though they were carrying him like a broom, and fat men appeared to propel them on the extremes of their stomachs, like bulldozers pushing mud. But Little Nell was always comfortably a woman.

'I wouldn't mind,' said Tasker, as the soldiers lay on the beach in the afternoon. 'She'd be a marvellous performer, wouldn't she? But it's old Sinclair. It wouldn't seem right.'

'That's the trouble,' agreed Brigg. 'It wouldn't be.'

Lantry sowed the sand through his fingers. 'Oh, I wouldn't say that,' he said. 'I mean she's told us all if any of us fancy it then she's happy. And old Sinclair wouldn't care. It's not as if she's a goods train or anything.'

They laughed. 'I *wouldn't* mind,' repeated Tasker reflectively, slowly.

'Nor me,' said Brigg extravagantly.

'I'd *like* to,' said Lantry. 'Definitely.'

'Well, we can't all at once,' observed Brigg with some relief.

'Different nights,' suggested Tasker.

'Well, I'm first then,' said Lantry rolling over with finality. 'Tonight.'

Sinclair was dancing with her. They had given her a ticket and she had nagged at him until he danced. He was like a giraffe.

'I'll leave it,' decided Tasker, looking at them on the floor. 'One of you two.'

'I don't care,' shrugged Brigg.

'Nor me,' said Lantry. 'I'm getting a bit short on money.'

Tasker changed his mind. 'I'll have her then.'

'No!' exploded Brigg. 'You just said you didn't *want* her. If it's going to be like that, I'll have her.'

'*You* didn't care a minute ago,' said Lantry to Brigg fiercely. 'I'm the one who started this in the beginning. On the beach. It's *me* if it's anyone.'

'You haven't got any money,' Tasker pointed out.

'I'll manage. Look at her, she's lovely.'

They looked.

'Toss then,' said Brigg. 'Come on, toss.'

'Leave it. Leave it,' grunted Tasker. 'If we're going to fall out over it, I'd sooner leave it.'

They were silent and ashamed. They drank from their glasses.

'All right,' sighed Lantry. 'Let's drop it. She's

probably hellish expensive anyway. I can't *really* afford it.'

'Why argue then?' said Brigg. 'Let's forget it. I've not got much money either. Just about enough to last the leave.'

'I'm the same,' admitted Tasker. 'No sense really, falling out over her when we can't pay, none of us.'

They looked across the floor and saw her laughing at Sinclair's seriousness. The free musical sound came over to them.

'We could always borrow from each other,' suggested Lantry.

'Borrow!'

'Borrow! How d'you mean?'

'Well, the one that goes with her borrows five dollars each from the other two. That should be plenty.'

'Christ,' said Tasker. 'I'll come and lift you on and off if you like. Bloody nerve.'

Lantry looked annoyed. 'I didn't say me. Necessarily.'

'But you *meant* you,' said Brigg.

'No I didn't.'

'Let's have your money then,' said Tasker aggressively.

Lantry said: 'We've got to toss for it, or something like that. And the winner takes all. The girl and the money. But he pays the money back when we're in Singapore again.'

'Right enough,' nodded Tasker. 'We'll toss.' He felt for a coin.

'I've got a better idea,' said Lantry.

'I thought you might have,' returned Brigg.

'We'll have a race.'

'Oh no,' said Tasker. 'I'm not running. Why don't we have an erection contest, you're good at that.'

'Racing is out,' said Brigg. 'We'd be fit for nothing after that.'

Lantry leaned over the table. 'Not running, I mean we could have a race in trishaws. Down to the jetty and back. And the winner gets the cash from the other two. And Little Nell, as well.'

Outside, along the gutter, were the trishaws, the evolution of the rickshaw, a bicycle and a sidecar with the coolie pedalling. The bicycle men beckoned and called to them as soon as they came out of the lit door. They selected one each.

'How's your English, George?' asked Brigg as he climbed in.

'Fine day,' said the coolie. 'Lovely fine day.'

'Very good,' sighed Brigg. 'Now my mates and I are going to have a race. See?' He pointed towards Lantry and Tasker getting into their trishaws, and explaining to their bicycle men. They were going to race down the main street, to the quay, through a whorehouse garden, and back again to the Piccadilly Lights. Inside himself Brigg was doubtful. He did not really want to win. Not really. Because there was only the few weeks now, and he didn't want another girl, because he was going home to Joan and he was clean. He wanted to stay clean.

'Race. Understand!' he said to the coolie, hoping that he wouldn't.

'Fine,' said the coolie. 'Fuck the sergeant-major.'

Brigg looked across to Lantry and Tasker. He did not know whether their explanations had been successful. But their trishaws were now moving slowly out from the gutter, into the street, and his coolie bent his head and went out too.

Then Tasker, when they were roughly abreast, shouted: 'They're off!' It was a loud shout and people turned in the crowds. Tasker and Lantry urged on their pedallers and Brigg shouted too. Or half shouted. The three coolies understood at once. They were old rivals and they flew along the road, heads out like horses, muscled legs jumping on the short steel rods.

Tasker had decided he did not want to win either. It was going to break him, even if the others lent him five dollars each. Suppose it cost twenty dollars. It would mean four miserable, mean days, and he would not have any money to have 'Love and Duty' and a dolphin tattooed on his forearm: something he wanted very much.

'Steady, son,' he cautioned his coolie, speaking like a bad ventriloquist, through gritted teeth. 'Not so fast.'

'Go easy, John,' whispered Brigg to his man. 'Not that much of a rush. Easy.'

Lantry watched the lights and the faces fly by like escaping balloons. Street wanderers jumped when they saw his trishaw speeding in front of the others, hiccoughing over the cobbles and scattering dogs and innocent sleepy children. Lantry was sorry he had suggested the race, now. He did not want to win. It was Sinclair who worried him. He liked Sinclair. What would it be like to just walk up and take his girl and walk off with her? He wouldn't be able to do it. Anyway she might have something nasty. They did, didn't they? And he was going to get married when he got home – probably, anyway – and it wouldn't do to have something nasty.

Besides which, even with the money the others would contribute, it would be stretching his means a bit. And he had promised himself to have 'Faith and Love', and a dagger tattooed on his bicep before he went back to Singapore. He did not want to win. Not truly.

'Slower, Charlie,' he told the enthusiastic boy. 'You'll have me out in a minute.'

But Lantry was winning: by a little, with the others careering behind, their front wheels spinning alongside his rear wheel. The three coolies raced full out, and nothing was going to slow them now. Stiffened by the dangers whirling by, and by the knowledge that he was in the lead, Lantry hung on to the side of his little box carriage and put his hand flat across the top of the small, naked lantern hooked on the frame. He hooted in agony as he burned, wrung his hands and twisted his face. Creasing up in the seat, with his hand wrapped deep down near his stomach, he cried out again.

His coolie had reached the quay now, hesitated, and had seen Tasker's coolie, miserably but inevitably directed by Tasker, take the wide turning into the whorehouse garden. Lantry's man had overshot the opening, and mistook Lantry's furious cries for anger at having missed the corner. He turned his bicycle and its attachment almost on its side as he strove to rectify the error and get to the gate before Brigg's advancing trishaw.

They went in together, scraping wheel to wheel in the gateway. Brigg and Lantry exchanged frightened, false grins when they were level. Tasker's man was plunging ahead, up the drive, under the dark, sweet hanging trees and perfumed plants.

The girls of the house were all sitting in the garden, in accustomed manner, gracefully elongated in wicker chairs, beside the curving path, beneath the bending trees. They were the usual racial mixture, with the addition of one Indian girl, of whom the house was very proud, and who lounged on a basketwork couch instead of the chairs of the other girls. But they were all known for their finesse and composure. There was no rushing, either in the bedrooms or outside. Charm was the speciality of the establishment.

Tasker's trishaw came around the moon of the drive in a chariot cloud of red dust. It ran over the painted big toe of the first girl in the line, a Siamese, who made a habit of sprawling elegantly from her low seat in the path of every frothing customer who arrived. The girl squealed as though stuck, but the alarm had hardly died before Brigg's following carriage mounted the grass verge and knocked two further harlots from their chairs.

Lantry's coolie shouted through his sweat, his thrashing wheels showered red earth and stones, and the young girls scattered, screamed, and fell over each other and their garden furniture in their panicked withdrawal. Lantry was still bent, as in prayer, over his burned hands.

From the exit gate the vehicles shot. Each passenger was hanging on, sick and silent now. The race was between the bicycle men. Brigg screwed his eyes into his lids as they spurted by other trishaws, aimlessly driven lorries, and wandering cars. Tasker's trishaw hit a fish stall as it jumped traffic lights, spilled the fish, and limped on with a buckled wheel, the stall owner running after it, and the coolie now pedalling with fear, not sport.

Brigg's coolie had a length lead on Lantry's. Seeing Tasker's misfortune, he leaped ahead, swerving and skidding, and finally arriving back at the Piccadilly Lights with Lantry twenty yards in the rear and Tasker walking, having jumped out and let his coolie fight it out with the fish-man. Brigg had won.

Solemnly they gave him their five dollar notes. Heavily he led the way back to the music and the smoke, looking for Sinclair and Little Nell, who was now going to be his, clean or unclean.

But they could not find them. Sinclair and Little Nell had gone.

It was very dark when Sinclair left Little Nell. He walked from her flat, down some concrete steps to the beach and then along the sand towards the place where big waves were coming white over the rocks like sporting ghosts. Sinclair felt sick.

Why was it always such an obsession with them? Now he was further than ever away from the answer. He didn't mind, he wasn't objecting or anything, but they always had sex in their talk and their minds, and in their dreams too from what they said some mornings in the barrack room. Each one took it about with him like a dog on a lead. Every soldier, or everybody for that matter, or nearly everybody, had their dog: leading it around and picking it up and fondling it when they felt like it, which was often, as far as he could see.

The sand was sidling in his shoes, so he took them off, and his socks. He was walking at the waterline and the sea was going out and the sand felt cool around his feet. He didn't mind, as he had just said. But they considered he was mad because his hobby was railways. Sex, he had always thought, when he *did* think about it, would come along one day in its own good time, or his, as naturally as death, and when it came he would see what it was all about. But he had been quite willing to wait, and he had anticipated waiting until his wedding night. It had nothing to do with morals, or God, or even health, which was all the others seemed to be frightened about. It was just that there was no hurry, was there?

But he had allowed himself to be led to it. By popular demand, that was the right phrase. By popular opinion and demand. Brigg and Tasker and Lantry, and the others back at Panglin, going on – 'Why don't you try it? You'll like it' – on Saturday nights. And finally the girl who had seemed interesting and as nice a partner as you could wish for during the initial experience.

But it had not been right: not at all right. In fact it had been thoroughly bad. It was expensive for a start, and the money made it seem false and he did not like that. But he paid because he felt that he had to go through with it. Nothing went really as it should have gone. It was like asking a chess player to turn out at rugby football. He was pleased with that thought. It had *not* been his game.

She had rained some terrifying perfume on herself in the flat, and that was enough to ruin it. He had kept rearing away from her and she had become very upset and gone and sulked for a long time in her tiny lavatory. When eventually he had allowed the sex to happen, just to please her, he had looked up and out of the open window, across the straits to the mainland and had seen the little yellow beans that were the lights of the midnight express steaming for Butterworth.

Anyway it had not been any good. For him or her. He admitted that much without shame for himself or sorrow for her, or anger for his friends who had made him take their randy dogs for an outing. He just did not care.

On this beach the waves came up noisily, banging their fists on the shore and trying to grip the shingle with their fingers as the parent sea pulled them away again.

Sinclair looked at his watch. He noted the time

with excitement. He might just do it. There was a night ferry at one o'clock.

He threw up the sand behind him as he ran. At the end of the beach he stretched his long legs up four steps at a time on the concrete stairway. Along the quay he chased and bounded aboard the ferry as it was stretching itself to leave. He sat down and wiped the sand from his feet with his handkerchief and put his shoes and socks on once more.

On the other shore he went quickly away from the jetty, doubled behind the warehouses and into the railway yard. Then he reached the cave door, the wide and high entrance to the main locomotive shed. A place full of red shaded steam and flowering orange glows, hissing and banging and a gritty smell. And heat that hit you in the chest as soon as you stood at the door.

Sinclair smiled.

They had a canoe at the leave centre: an outrigger. On the last but one day Brigg was driving it through the blue spray two hundred yards off-shore when he saw Phillipa, in a white dress, standing on the beach.

At first he thought it was just a girl. A browned girl in a white dress. The beach was empty because it was lunchtime, but Brigg had not felt like eating. He saw her and paddled the canoe closer to look at her properly. Then he saw that it was Phillipa and she was waiting for him.

He sent the shell skimming towards the sand like a shark. He rolled it too, to show off.

'You're showing off,' she called as he came in.

'Of course,' he shouted back, nosing the boat through the lacework of spray. 'Of course I'm showing off. Watch this.'

He leaned over heavily and lifted one paw of the craft out of the boiling water, then fell the other way and brought the other paw clear. Bringing the balance right he ran the canoe up the beach and stepped easily out.

Brigg walked up to her and kissed her. The heavy warmness of her breasts under the clean, soft dress pressed against his hard, dark body. The same linen ran all down his raw thigh until their naked knees prodded each other. They broke and considered each other, sharply surprised at first. Then they smiled.

'How d'you get here?' said Brigg, standing in front of her and holding her finger tips. 'I thought you were a nurse in Kuala Lumpur or something.'

'Not yet,' she said. 'I've got years of training to do. Absolutely years. But I transferred up here, to the hospital in Georgetown. How long have you got here?'

'Until tomorrow,' answered Brigg.

'Tomorrow! Oh no.'

'Oh yes.'

'Oh Christ.'

She looked over his shoulder then. 'Your boat's floating away, mister.'

He turned and saw the canoe quietly sneaking away on its own, heading out towards the adventure of the big waves. He ran a few steps, threw himself into the water and went in a furrow after it, capturing it by one of its arms and towing it back to the beach. Phillipa helped him tie the painter around a big turtle-shaped stone.

'I've been here nearly two weeks,' he said. 'My leave's finished, just about, and I'm going back to England in a month.'

She threw some sand up with the toe of her sandal. 'I've been in Penang ten days,' she said. 'I didn't know you were here until a fellow called Waller came over to the hospital yesterday. He told me there were some Panglin people here and I asked him if he knew their names. He only knew yours.'

Brigg said: 'He shares a room with me. What was he at the hospital for?'

'He gets pains in his kidneys, I think,' she said. 'Something like that.'

'Oh, yes,' said Brigg understanding.

'Never mind about him, anyway,' said Phillipa, sitting on the sand, and pulling him down. They sat and didn't say anything for some time.

'Was your old man wild about that night?' said Brigg eventually.

She laughed. 'He wanted to kill you, but the Colonel wouldn't let him. I mean you *did* almost kill my mother. Pushing her off that pipe into the swamp.'

'I didn't push her,' protested Brigg. 'She fell. She slipped and over she went. And it was her fault, messing about with those silly bloody fish of hers.'

Phillipa rolled back in the sand and laughed. 'Wasn't it marvellous! And you shooting that Chinese man's fingers off! I'll never forget it!'

He caught her hands. 'It cost me six weeks' pay,' he said. 'I only came up here because I won some money.'

'And we were lying down in all that muck and mud, frightened stiff to move, and poor old mother was groaning and we thought she was dying.' She laughed straight at the sky again. Brigg rolled over on top of her. He pressed her hair back into the sand with the weight of his mouth on hers. He could feel himself growing. She began to struggle.

'No. No,' she stuttered. 'You're wetting my dress.'

'Am I?' he said surprised, rolling off. 'Oh, I was too. I'm not dry yet. My body isn't dry, I mean.'

'I know,' she said looking at him. 'That's what I meant.'

'I'll get dressed,' he said getting up.

She said: 'Yes, I'll wait.'

He walked over to his room. It was just the same, wasn't it? She was fine until she got frightened, or whatever it was, and then that was the end. All right until she knew you *meant* it. That's how it had always been with them. She was beautiful to look at, but he was glad he was getting out and going home. They'd only start the same old tasteless thing again, and he didn't want all that. Ah, well, he was going home to Joan. There wouldn't be any of this freezing-up rubbish with her. He didn't think so, anyway. No, there wouldn't be. Of course there wouldn't. He'd just get the next day over, and then the next few weeks and that would be that. He'd spend today with Phillipa, if she wanted to. Just one day, and if nothing happened – and it wouldn't, he could bet on that – then it was just too bloody bad.

In the afternoon they went up the thicker, emerald country in the hilly centre, up to a temple with a golden pagoda, and a pool full of turtles. They walked along the corridors of shadows around the temple courtyard, looking across the bright, hot tiles outside in the sun, and the hanging flowers that glistened on the walls.

They stood, holding hands, and peered into the

pool and the crowds of turtles there swimming with their big wooden feet, banging their shells together in the crush, and laughing with their soundless ugly mouths. An old man came across the courtyard and squatted by the pool and told them that the people brought turtles there as an offering in the hope that their lives would be as long as the turtles' lives.

Then Phillipa and Brigg went further up the hill and road to where a slender waterfall tipped over a shelf like a green glass pipe inserted into the body of a brimming pool. It was cold in the water when they swam, much colder than the sea, and deep too with green dungeons to explore and strange pool furniture made of rock upholstered with soft weed and slime. There were no fish, only shadows, and the central column of the waterfall always roaring down, smooth like treacle, and breaking up down in the stomach of the pool and digested into its round body.

Brigg came out of the water and lay like a sacrifice on a flat rock, feeling it burning into his shoulder blades, his backside, and the flesh of his legs. The cold water almost steamed off him, the sun drying it from his face and hair, and the rock skimming it from his back. Phillipa levered herself out and sat on a ledge just below him, throwing her hair about to get the wet from it. Brigg turned his head to her. She was looking out across the tumbling jungle that cluttered the lower hills to the sea glistening like steel where it slotted into the sky far away.

She did not turn to Brigg and he was able to study the line of her sweet face and her neck and the running of the clean line that was etched from her throat to down between her breasts. She was wearing a black swimsuit and her nipples pricked through its drying surface, clear as buttons. The upper flesh of her breasts was tender brown and the hidden parts bulky and full. If he had wanted to do it then, Brigg could have reached out and torn the front of the swimsuit away. He wanted to. Badly. But he knew it would never be any good like that. Or any way. He would never be able to feel her and love her like that because she wouldn't understand and she would scream almighty rape. And he did not want trouble because he was going home.

They said nothing, but sat and let the sun bake them dry. She hardly moved her head and he turned his away from her again because he could hardly bear to look at her. He did not even want to kiss her because that was not enough. It only made him feel worse. He moved his head away and watched a lizard panting on a rock two feet away. Its tongue moved in and out and its eyes were heavy as though with desire. Brigg knew how it felt.

Phillipa stood up after a long time and walked over to where she had left her dress and shoes. She stepped into the white dress and slid it up her legs and body like a flower. He watched her wriggle to feel herself in it, and saw her take an age over every button from navel to the crease of her breasts. He stood up too and pulled his trousers and shirt on, then slipped on his canvas shoes and took her hand.

They got a bus from the foot of the hill into Georgetown, arriving when the shadows were probing everywhere, and the sun was drifting away on its evening journey. The streets were cooler and they walked to the place where she lived.

It was a residential hostel spread out on one floor, well planned about a terrace and a small swimming pool. Each room had a door facing into the pool and the terrace stones, damp as though someone had been recently swimming. Each had a rattan blind over the window and another at the door. Phillipa walked into her room and Brigg stood at the door, until she turned and called him.

'There's no need to be so proper,' she said. 'You've been the perfect gentleman all the afternoon.'

'I thought that was how you wanted me to be,' said Brigg, walking in. It was a big, shady room with a primrose counterpane over the bed, some chairs, a bookcase, a dressing table and a wardrobe. Phillipa's suitcases were in one corner, the dressing table was untidy with her cosmetics, and a satin slip was climbing over the back of a chair. A door led off to what he guessed would be the bathroom.

'Who told you so?' she said.

'You've never said so, but you've made it pretty clear otherwise,' he said. She went into the bathroom. 'Can I sit down?' he said.

'Yes. Sit on the bed. The chairs are a bit wooden.' She came back into the room.

'It wasn't much of a success, was it?' she said.

'I wouldn't say that.' He looked at her steadily. 'Not at all. We had some time together and we had a swim and, what else? Oh yes, we saw the old turtles. It was all right.'

She walked to the window and pulled apart two strips of the blind and looked out.

'Did your mother ever get any more fish?' he asked.

'More fish?' she slowly said, not turning around. 'Oh, no. My father said he would get her something else instead, but I don't know whether he has yet. I haven't been home.'

Brigg said morosely: 'I thought we might send her half a dozen of those turtles. That ought to last her.'

She began to laugh and turned around. She walked over to him and bent down and kissed him like a friend on his forehead. He thrust out his arms and encircled her legs and pulled her funnelled thighs to his cheek. The dress felt as fine as dust against his face and the flesh, shaped and warm beneath.

'No,' she said softly. 'No, darling.'

'No! No! No!' shouted Brigg jumping up. 'You're always bloody no!' He hit her with the palm of his hand, not hard because he pulled it at the last second, but with enough force to send her staggering to the wall.

'You're the great No Girl, that's what you are!' bawled Brigg. He straightened up and stumbled towards the door. But he couldn't go out. He leaned his tall body against the wall and hid his eyes in his hands. He was shivering with tears. She said nothing. But he could feel her looking at him.

'How do you think I've felt?' he whispered. 'You're there and yet there's not a bloody thing I can do about it. I'm stark mad crazy about you. I don't want to hold hands. Understand, Phillipa, I don't *want* to hold hands.'

He realised he was hoarse and silly like a protesting child. He stayed where he was, his eyes hard against his knuckles, his knuckles thrust into his tears. He was going to get out. Get out for good, and forget it. He was going now. He put one hand down towards the handle of the door. He found it and, still shaking, but not turning, he made half a step towards it.

'Look at me,' he heard her say.

Brigg turned obediently. She was standing on the other side of the room. She was naked with her dress and her bathing suit curled up on the floor like pets asleep.

Brigg was stunned by the sight of her. Then he walked forward, slowly at first and then quicker, not quite straight, like a blind man who can suddenly see. His hands felt out before him and she stood still and lovely while his fingers, at full distance, touched the centre of her breasts. He stood that far away, throwing the tears from his face, sending his ecstatic fingers scooping around the convex walls of her bosom, stroking each silken place with a boyish wonder and pounding excitement.

They still stood at arms' length and Phillipa had not moved. He moved half a pace towards her, his eyes full of power, hers calm and waiting. Now his palms ran down the smooth meadow of her back, up and down again and finally resting on the hollows of her waist.

He stopped there, trying to remain still, but quivering in every muscle and cell.

Phillipa said: 'My turn.' She smiled, and quietly, deftly began to unbutton his shirt at the top. Her fingers played down until she had opened every button to his belt. Still not moving her body, only her hands, she slipped the buckle of his belt free and continued with the buttons on his trousers. She opened them like a skin, and sent both soft messenger hands straight to his centre.

Brigg went mad, clutching her wildly to him, trying to wrap his arms and steely legs around her and into the pillows of her body. Her mouth was on his neck and her teeth gnawing him. He stumbled on his trousers, lying on the floor, they staggered together in a comical dance, stepped backwards, and at the last moment collapsed on to the bed.

He kept calling her his darling and at the same time was frantically trying to hook the heel of one of his canvas shoes with the toe of the other. Everything was going right. The shoes slid off without trouble. She almost tore the shirt from his back.

Phillipa cradled him in her brown arms, pale honey against the darkness of his skin. His first impatience went and he nuzzled his face into her breasts, first one side then the other, and they flowed about and back again as though eager to play with him too.

'Your back is like leather,' said Phillipa, running her arms up both sides of him. 'You're very brown, darling.'

He moved suddenly so that he fell between the isthmus of her legs. 'And big,' she breathed. 'So big too.'

Brigg was not going to rush. Lucy, dear Lucy, had taught him that. He was not going to frighten her by rushing. After all she did not know.

Strange though, because she lay unashamed and breathing deeply, with her eyes slits, savouring the iron feel of him. Strange for an apprentice.

He held her left breast captive and put his mouth to it. His whole body was straining now, screaming to go. His hands made another journey down her until he turned them inwards like a seal's flippers, resting them firmly on the twin grooves between her thighs and her soft navel, one each side. Tiny hairs curled like springs about each of his little fingers, the flats of his hands rested on velvet and the utmost tips of his long middle fingers were in the hot dark.

'I won't hurt you, darling Phillipa,' he promised. 'I'll never hurt you, darling. Never.'

She smiled her answer and he sent pressure to his hands to open her legs like the two parts of a padded door. He crawled up her in trembling urgency and arrived fully, deep inside, wondering what the hell had happened to her virginity.

With her it was like turning the switch of an electric motor. She began to move smoothly but with great power, slowly still, and he complemented the movement, the eyes of both of them closed as they voyaged in the dark.

He tried to forget her hymen, but the question bit at his slothful brain, like a wasp around a pink blancmange.

So strange she should have lost it. He doubted if she had ever been over a vaulting horse in her life.

But she kept tugging him back to the luxurious present reality, her rippling movements getting faster, with his, until the sweat rolled from him and joined with hers. She was perspiring so much he could hardly hold her, and he began slipping first one way then the other as he tried to correct the fault. His face was wet and his hair was stuck flat in a fringe. Then abruptly she stiffened as though her limbs and her trunk had become metal. She threw back her head and made a little cawing noise like a bird. Brigg was two seconds behind her. Then they lay and cooled in the dim room.

Brigg slept an hour, crouched on the bed. When he woke she was just coming out of the shower. He showered and they dressed and went into the town to eat. By ten o'clock they were back in the dark room, making love again.

Then they went under the shower together, washing each other with clouds of lather, then standing lip to lip, breast to breast, knee to knee, as the clean water fell on to them with its sharp points.

They went into a far sleep then, both of them, wandering half the night, until Brigg awoke and felt the marvellous feel of her, and smelt her soft breathing, and studied her face a few inches from his own. Now who, he wondered, had been responsible for her strayed virginity. He could not imagine.

But she was beautiful. He kissed her motionless lips. She opened an eye like a still pool and smiled. 'Goodnight, sergeant, darling,' she whispered.

Brigg never saw her again. It was light when he roused, with the sounds of children playing at the school across the road filtering through the window with the strong sun.

Phillipa was gone. He called her, but there was no answer. Hooked on to the cistern in the bathroom was a note which read: 'On early duty. Sleep well.'

He looked at his watch and panicked. In an hour he was due to be on the ferry. He pulled on his clothes, ran out of the building and caught a taxi in the street. The others at the leave centre were packed and ready. He loaded everything into his case and ran out in time to jump aboard the waiting truck.

On the ferryboat they stood on the deck while it grunted its journey to the mainland, sidling by big ships waiting in the roads, and labouring sampans and junks. The water was glistening with oil and sunlight.

Brigg stood and waited, and watched Penang going away, and wondered.

Sergeant?

12

They had to wait all day for the train. There had been shooting from the lineside and trouble with the bandits in places spaced widely between Kuala Lumpur and the north.

There was Brigg, Tasker, Lantry, Sinclair, and Waller, the infantryman who was going to get off the train half-way down the country to go back to his unit. At the station they sat until the columns of sunlight standing from openings in the roof to the floors, had banked and gradually become rafters of the same roof. Tasker went to sleep curled up on two suitcases. Sinclair took Lantry to see the engines.

Waller said to Brigg: 'I went to hospital in Penang.'

Brigg said: 'I know. About your kidneys or something.'

'The nurse, the girl you know, told you? You saw her?'

'That's right,' said Brigg.

'She's lovely,' said Waller. 'Is that where you were all night?'

'Yes,' said Brigg smugly. 'All night. Thanks for telling her.'

'I went to see the doctor,' said Waller. 'I thought if I could start building up a medical case I might work my ticket, or get down to Singapore, or somewhere else where I didn't have to have my teeth chopped out.'

'What did they say?' asked Brigg.

'Mumbled about, as usual. If you told them you were going to have triplets they'd not disbelieve you. And I thought it would *look* better if I reported it when I was on leave because it's not the time anyone would normally try to pull a fast one, is it? They'd think you were too busy enjoying yourself and if you went to hospital then it must be genuine.'

'What do you do next?' asked Brigg.

'I've got to tell my own M.O. I've got a note,' said Waller. 'And I'll take half a dozen salt tablets, the ones they give us up here because of the salt we lose sweating. That'll make me spew like mad and they'll think there is something really wrong. I'll be down there pushing a pen yet.'

It was dark before the train went out. The small pilot engine probed bravely before the express, searchlight out in front, down through the black, jungled country, with nothing to see only the poor peeping lights of villages every ten or twelve miles.

Brigg lay, on the bottom bunk this time, which was better, jolting with the track, staring up at the middle bunk low over his forehead. It was hot, and sometimes Tasker, who was above him, passed down a bottle of pale beer.

Sinclair, by counting the rhythm beats of the train, could tell each mile as it went by. Brigg listened to the hasty talking of the wheels too. When he was a child he remembered listening like that as they went to the seaside and saying to himself: 'Soon-be-there. Soon-be-there. Soon-be-there.' He did it now, but moved his wet lips without sound to 'Soon-be-home. Soon-be-home. Soon-be-home.'

That's all he wanted now. Not even Phillipa, because she was running away from him with every roll of the wheels. He knew that was how she had intended it. To give him one night, a night of plenty and love, which was fine, except that she called him sergeant.

Now he must not consider her any more. Or Lucy, sweet Lucy, who had taught him love in return for rhymes. Now there would be Joan and home. Joan-and-home. Joan-and-home. Joan-and-home.

The first bullet came through the roof and went like a drilling wasp through the toe of his boot standing on the floor by his bed. He frowned at it, for he could not see the ceiling, and the buzz from his boot and the hole suddenly in it made him think stupidly that something was trying to get out from inside it, forcing its way through. Once at Panglin he had stamped through a parade with a crushed and suffocated beetle, the size of a small mouse, imprisoned in his boot, in the channel under his toes. Now he thought there was another in it and was boring through to the surface.

Then Tasker and Lantry fell from above him like rocks.

'Shots!' croaked Tasker. 'They're shooting!'

Another bullet sawed through the side of the compartment and blew the nozzle from a fire extinguisher on the wall, sending a soda fountain of spray all up and around.

Brigg found himself on his hands and knees on the floor. The long alleyway was full of crouching, colliding figures, like animals in a pen. Brigg put on one boot, but took it off again and left them lying there. He had both hands gripping the stock of his rifle. Somebody was moaning: 'Oh Christ. Oh Christ.' From the front of the express came a great heave as though the engine itself were throwing up.

They were all tipped forward on their faces in the gangway. All the voices were frightened, mixed, and then drowned by a vivid bang from the front of the train and a drumming din that shook the carriages as though the express were rubbing its skin against the jungle trees. The men were rolled and spilled about, then levelled out and left hugging the floor and each other as the train made a final hit, and bent itself off the track, back on, and then off again the other side like a crumpled straw.

It stopped and it was like the inside of a drum in Brigg's compartment. The air was full of dust and darkness, and the fire extinguisher was still gurgling. No one moved. They were piled on each other as though they were dead and in a mass grave. From the darkness came coughs and sobs. Then a stream of machine-gun bullets did a savage trepanning of the front part of the carriage, opening up the roof like a lid.

'Get out!' howled someone. 'They'll be chucking grenades in.'

They scrambled and escaped in a panic from the coach and into the next one. This was lying tilted, screwed upwards with the windows facing the tree-tops. It was full of civilians, all thrown and lying in the deepest trough. Brigg could not see them but he could hear them moaning and sense them moving. He heard the sound of breaking canes and he realised it was the bullets coming back.

'Down,' he shouted in a voice that surprised him for its clearness. He felt the soldiers fling themselves on their stomachs around him. Somehow he landed on his back and tried to wriggle over as the bullets bit overhead and the glass in the windows exploded. He realised how illogical it was as he did it, but there was something awful about lying face up to bullets.

When the volley had gone by there was a slow silence as though it had killed everyone. But Brigg could feel the men on either side of him panting. Then, down in the trough where the civilians were, someone struck a match and held its light trembling to the face of a young Chinese girl who stared in death with such horror that it seemed as though she had seen the bullet coming to her. It had struck her through the cheek, and blood was covering the bottom of her face and her neck like a clean, fresh garment.

'Put it out!' shouted Tasker. 'Put the match out.' Brigg saw him fling himself forward and slide down the inclined floor to punch the match away from someone's fingers. The person began to scream and then they all started, sounding like an awful wind.

A grenade rattled along the far end of the corridor, bouncing and sounding like a ball on the floor. A train steward scrambled along the aisle, away from it, like a playful monkey, but it blew up too soon and turned him in a dead somersault. The blast flew over Brigg's head like the beating of wings.

The firing was not continuous. The bandits seemed to be waiting and picking out targets. Brigg cursed the Lewis gunners on the armoured truck because they weren't returning the fire.

It was Waller who got up. 'Come on,' he said. 'They'll bloody slaughter us here. Get out and on the ground.'

They went with him because they knew he knew best. They stumbled along the corridor, over the sickening bundle of the steward, and followed Waller through the gap that the grenade had made in the side of the carriage. Close and quick they dropped on to the wet grass by the line, and slithered around behind the rearing wheels of the wrecked train.

Even from there they could see how thorough the ambush had been. There was steam and smoke and glowing fire coming from places as far as they could see along the broken back of the express. Only a few feet from them, in the ditch by the lineside, was a dead airman, and on the other side a woman was sobbing over someone lying in the grass.

By a soldier's instinct most had not known they possessed, each man was still armed. Waller had a sten and the others rifles. They were still frightened.

They took the signal from young Waller and crept along, spider-fashion, towards the head of the train. They had to slide across the airman just as they had the steward, and his body was still rubbery and warm.

Brigg realised he was still without his boots. The

heavy wetness of the grass was making his socks soggy. They dodged along in single file until they reached the front of the train. All they could hear was the hiss and puff of steam and the sharp eating noise of fire.

At the front of the train, by the first staggering coach were some soldiers and airmen crouching against the wreckage. Waller called softly to them, preventing them shooting them down for enemies.

Up there they could see what had happened. The little pilot engine was lying crumpled some way down the track, outlined in the orange fire which cradled it. The express was hanging half off the track, gasping, with its head resting against a clump of strong trees. They looked like a buffalo and calf hunted and gunned. Brigg instinctively glanced at Sinclair. Sinclair said: 'Good engines too. Both good.'

There had been unusually few servicemen on the train. No one had taken charge. A sergeant from the Dental Corps was in the group at the front, but he said he couldn't do anything because he had smashed his false teeth. It made him sound like a comedian. Someone said that the armoured truck at the back was off the lines. The Dental Corps sergeant said that he had seen some Gurkhas on the train. But he did not know what had happened to them.

Waller took charge. He was trying to sort them out behind the wreckage when another stream of bullets rattled like rain along the coaches and they all rolled down into the ditch at the side of the track.

'They're not all that close,' whispered Waller to Brigg when they were down there. 'They can't be sure how strong we are, and they're keeping a bit of distance. Otherwise they'd be all over us by now. Every now and then they send somebody up to chuck a grenade. We'll get the next bastard.'

Brigg felt himself steadied by Waller. If he was as frightened as they were, he didn't show it. He moved around among the fifteen men and sent them sliding on their bellies over the sleepers, under the coaches.

Moving along twenty yards over the flints between the track, Brigg flattened himself behind a big metal wheel of the leading coach that was still flush to the railway line. It gave him good cover and there was a loophole for his rifle and another for him to see. He began to feel less cold with fear. He waited.

Suddenly a scampering shadow rose up only a few feet ahead of him, resolving from the anonymous black of the scrub. Brigg shot him down like a cowboy shooting from behind a wagon wheel.

He even remembered the safety catch, thumbed it forward, felt the trigger around his finger like a metal worm, and then the firm jolt and bang as the weapon went off. The man reached up as though trying to catch something in the sky, then fell stiffly on to his face.

'Ha!' shouted Brigg. 'Ha! Ha! Ha! Ha!' He was almost hysterical with the excitement of killing his first human being. 'Ha! Ha!'

'Wrap up,' snorted Waller. 'Shut your mouth, will you.'

A patch of darkness which had been standing motionless moved quickly and became men running at the train. They screamed as they ran. Everybody began firing then, shooting from the tracks, from the shelter of wheels and the piled wreckage. Brigg loosed off half his magazine before he realised that the sparks coming from the running men were guns that they were firing too. He felt the earth shudder under him like someone shaking a carpet and saw the dirt spray and bounce two feet away. A man was rolling on the track near Brigg and screaming. Waller, lying with his snub sten to his shoulder, pushed another flat magazine into its side and processed it through like a chocolate bar as he sprayed the ground ahead.

Brigg was shooting like a madman now. At least they couldn't say this lot were from the arseholing Chinese laundry. The bitter smoke was thick all around, and the noise numbing. His ears were senseless from the explosions of his own rifle, and his cheekbone bruised with its kick against his face.

The attackers fell back, on the ground and crawling away through the trees. Waller told everyone to stop firing. They did, and saw red darts towards the middle of the train, and heard the clapping bangs.

'Those Gurkhas must be up there,' said Waller. 'We'll shift up towards them, I think. The closer we get the better.'

They left two dead men: the Dental Corps sergeant, apologetic without his teeth, was one, lying on the track. None of the Panglin soldiers had been hurt. Brigg saw Tasker's face near to him, round with excitement, and with no fear. Sinclair was wiping his glasses carefully and Lantry slotting a fresh magazine into his rifle. Brigg felt warm and heroic.

'I got one for sure,' said Brigg.

'I know,' agreed Lantry. 'The first one. I saw you get him.'

'Shut up,' said Waller again. He led them at the back of the track behind its slightly humped back.

The Gurkhas were grouped around one of the centre wagons. A warrant officer was with them and they had got a lot of the people out of the exposed coaches and had them lying down behind the embankment. They had driven off a sharp attack, and now everything was quiet and waiting.

There was no change in the expressions of the

dark men as the British soldiers joined them. They were all small and the warrant officer was like a little boy. He looked them over.

'Any jungle soldiers?' he asked briefly. He caught Brigg's arm and turned his sleeve around, but seeing the yellow lion, the Singapore garrison flash, he released him. He did the same to Sinclair and released him.

'No jungle soldiers?' he said.

'I am, sir,' said Waller. He turned his shoulder to show the Malaya district insignia. The Gurkha nodded. 'East Anglia brigade, sir,' said Waller.

'Good,' nodded the Gurkha. 'So far they come only from front. Over there.' He nodded towards the frontal shadows. 'But soon all around. Over us everywhere. You take your men up at the back and cover from there. Except one. We need one.'

Waller nodded at Sinclair. 'You stay then,' he said.

Sinclair blinked behind his glasses. 'Yes. What do I do?'

He was sent with one of the Gurkha riflemen to the end of the train where the armoured truck had come off the line. Two men were already there, lying watch across the tracks, and another was altering the Lewis gun stand so the guns could be brought down horizontally even though the truck was tipped upwards. At the Gurkha's signal Sinclair climbed up on to the turret, behind the twin guns. They had them fixed now, so that the arc of fire could sweep the ground all along the side of the train. There was a small searchlight positioned alongside the gun. They pointed to that and made it clear that Sinclair had to operate it.

He stood behind the unlit light and found the switch and the swivel operator and smiled in his studious manner at the Gurkha, who nodded back. The Gurkha who had walked along the track with him now stretched himself across the lines with the other two. The little man who had been fixing the gun, crouched behind it and swung it experimentally. Sinclair trod on something soft and looked down to see it was the hand of one of the original crew, who was sitting dead alongside his cold partner down inside the armoured car.

The rest of the Panglin men, and the other oddment soldiers, and airmen, were strung out on the embankment now waiting for the attack from the rear.

Brigg felt his heart punching the ground. 'Surely all the noise, all the shooting, would have made someone realise we're in trouble,' he said to Waller.

'Who's someone?' asked Waller, still squinting across the brief patch of open grass ahead to the wall of trees.

'Well, anyone,' said Brigg. 'Isn't there anyone

around here at all?'

'You realise in this country,' said Waller softly, 'that there is *never* anyone around. It's a good bet that the nearest army unit is twenty or thirty miles away. So they're out even if the boys in the armoured truck sent out a radio message. And twenty miles through all this muck is as good as a hundred unless they can get to the railway. The last town on the line with a road going to it was miles back. You can bet on that too. That's why they picked this spot. They're not daft, you know. I told you the other day they've been in the jungle for years. They know all about it.'

'But surely there's a village nearer than that?' whispered Brigg.

Waller still did not move his face. 'There might be,' he agreed, 'and when they heard all the banging going on, d'you know what they did? They stuck their bloody heads under their pillows, or their wives, or something, and tried not to listen. Because they have to live with this, mate, all the time. And they're terrified. Just like we are now.'

They stared. Then Brigg said: 'The only hope is if another train comes along. The overnight leave trains always cross somewhere.'

'The timetable is all out,' said Waller. 'We were hours late starting. I shouldn't count on that. Besides which they might have taken the track up further downline too.'

'Sinclair could tell us,' whispered Brigg hopefully. 'He'd know to the minute. He knows all the times. Shall I go and ask him?'

Waller laid his hand heavily on Brigg's forearm and tightened it. Brigg looked where Waller was looking and saw the shadows moving from the trees. In another second it was happening again.

From both sides they ran. Just as the Gurkha warrant-officer had said. There were shots from the front first and at once Sinclair's searchlight threw itself across the scene, fanning over the grass and the fluted trees and lighting up the yellow faces as the bandits ran.

'Fire at will,' ordered Waller softly. Brigg glanced at him, as though he had said something theatrical, unreal. But Waller was stern and bent across the short length of his sten, using it from the shoulder as he lay against the climbing ground. He began firing it in vicious, short bursts. Brigg returned to his rifle, suddenly conscious again of the danger, yet still shocked by the calmness and authority of the infantryman who had once confessed how frightened he was.

But there was no time to think. They came at the crippled train and the soldiers firing into them brought some to their knees, and others thudding like stones on to the ground. But it was a big bandit gang. The Lewis guns on the askew armoured truck were throwing bullets in a wide curve following the track of Sinclair's searchlight.

Sinclair stood upright, turning the searchlight with a mechanical coolness back and fro across the banks on both sides. As the beam swooped over the back of the train and flew over the attackers in front of Waller's men, Brigg realised how many enemy there were. They lay flat as the light came across, and charged again as it went by. But Sinclair flicked it back immediately, beautifully, catching them stark in the beam. Their many faces were fixed by it.

'Christ,' breathed Waller. 'They're like a football crowd.'

He began firing steadily again. One of the airmen at the end of the rank stiffened and stood up, before flopping over like a clown. But the attack was held. In the front the Gurkhas were holding too. Then the battle vanished into the darkness as the bandits went back to the trees.

'How many did we get, d'you think?' Brigg asked Waller. He felt jubilant at remaining alive, and yet having killed.

'Why don't you go out and count them,' suggested Waller without rancour. 'One thing's certain: they'll be back in a minute. They're going to sort us out.'

'Perhaps they *won't* come back,' said Brigg, afraid of Waller's certainty.

Waller did not answer for two minutes. Then he

said quietly: 'Here they are now.' And louder: 'Ready. Fire at will.'

This time there was no way to stop them. They shattered the searchlight with an immediate burst of fire. It flew around in Sinclair's hands like a toy drum. The Lewis-gunner fell across his guns immediately, and began to swing on them in death like a man lounging across a gate. One of the Gurkhas below the armoured truck jumped the side like an ape, but they were waiting for him too and they shot him as he reached the top, curling him over so that he dropped and jammed in the already crowded hatch.

Next two bullets hit Sinclair, striking him in the lower chest and pitching him silently out of the armoured truck and into the ditch beside the railway.

Brigg did not see it. He was terrified now. They came on with such force that nothing could stem them. While Waller was alive he stuck his ground, firing from the hip. But Waller died with a surprised start, falling over his hot gun and slewing sideways.

Brigg ran sideways along the ditch. A sort of comedian's exit trot, tripping over bodies and guns and mud, and shouting apologetically all around, to friend and foe: 'Going for help! I'm going for help!'

The bandits had almost overrun the train from both sides now, with some of the Gurkhas holding out from inside one far coach. The shots were fewer, grunts and sobs and bodies falling were all sounding in the darkness. From it all, Brigg with almost juvenile ease slipped away, jabbering in terror, and running straight through the trees from which the bandits had emerged to make their rear attack. He was going for help. Where he was going he did not know. But he was going.

Sinclair regained a little life in the ditch, stirring in the mud made muddier by his leaking blood. The shooting was all done, it seemed, but he could hear rapid movements and voices and someone crying.

The crying was very near. On one elbow he pushed himself into a sitting position, although it was very painful.

The train was fiercely on fire now. Twenty yards from his ditch he could see the girl who was crying. She was a Malay teenager, plump like a puppy. One of the Chinese was standing in front of her, one hand carelessly holding a sub-machine gun and the other pulling open the front of the girl's dress. She stood still and weeping, unable to move for fright, while he casually tore the linen away from her body.

Sinclair watched while the bandit unbuckled his belt and threw open the buttons on his trousers. The girl's body reflected the fire; it glowed on her fatty breasts and her young neck. She put her hands to her face, but still did not move away from the man. The bandit pushed out his free hand and quite gently threw her backwards on to the ground.

There was a dead man in the ditch with Sinclair. Near his sightless head was a sten gun. 'Dirty little dogs on leads,' thought Sinclair. 'They were all the same.'

He positioned the sten on the bank of the ditch and manoeuvred it carefully, in bitter pain with each movement and feeling the blood leaving him in quicker flow. He pulled the trigger and tried to get a curving action on the weapon as he did so.

The effect was astonishing. The streaking line of bullets almost cut the bandit in half at the waist. He tore apart like one of the sacks they used to use for bayonet practice at Panglin on Saturday mornings.

Sinclair fell back into the ditch. He could think as lucidly as ever, and he could actually feel the lumps of the two bullets working about inside him like indigestion. He thought of praying, or quite seriously of trying to sing the chorus of a childhood hymn. But it had, frankly, been so long since he had imposed on God at all, that it seemed a bit unreasonable to bother Him.

He made himself more comfortable and thought of Mr. and Mrs. Boot at Royal Oak, feeling the platform quake as the Paddington expresses

300

steamed by. He mentally ticked off the names of the Battle of Britain class locomotives and was pleased that he was well enough to remember them all. Then he thought about his place on the embankment back home, by the gradient climbing to Rugby. Those good, cold nights, watching the big ones working along the steel. Oh, what a damn shame.

He heard the steam and a train whistle drifting through his haze. It brought him sharply back. That was a real whistle, no death dream. With all his strength he listened and heard it again and the shouts. In agony he twisted his wrist around and looked at the luminous dial on his watch.

'Hah,' he noted with satisfaction. 'The one-ten from Kuala Lumpur.'

It was 5.29 a.m. by his watch. By five-thirty he was dead.

When Brigg ran through the trees he was still in his stockinged feet. The stockings were holed and soaked in water and blood from other people and from the cuts on his feet. He went puffing through the tall trees and the skirted undergrowth, looking behind to see if they were following, and imagining that they were flitting through the standing trucks. He could see the glow of the train and hear the occasional fighting, and he kept running, telling himself that he had to go and get help.

There was a small river and some swamp to get through. He jumped clumsily, feet first, into the river, thinking that because it was narrow it was shallow too. But it was narrow and deep. His whole body went under into a thick, green, slow and putrid flow, and he dropped his rifle, which he had carried without being conscious of it, into the carpet of mud that lined it. He came up, comically, like a weedy ghost, and threw himself chest first at the other bank. It was too narrow to swim and too deep to walk. He foundered and rolled and spat and eventually pulled himself free of the water. Then he staggered blindly through the swamp, black to the knees and being frightened by frightened swamp creatures. Getting through it, he looked back again. There was no noise from the battle now. The sky through the trees was a pleasant rosy colour. Brigg ran on.

The ground hardened, and then the trees thinned. He ran up a saucer of grass and came out once more on to the railway track. The lines bent away to both sides and he knew he must have travelled a good way because the fighting and the glow were out of sight and hearing. He turned away from the direction in which he realised the ambushed train must be, and walked along the sleepers, sick with the thoughts of his friends. He had been going about twenty minutes when he saw the lights of an engine approaching.

Standing away from the track he waved his arms like a semaphore signaller, shouting in a voice he could not recognise for its thickness. The engine was the pilot running before the express from Kuala Lumpur. Its searchlight went like a lance down the track in front of it and picked out the frantic arms of Brigg. It was not going fast and it braked and steadied as it came level with him. Two minutes behind it the express, slowed by the signals, heaved up gently. One of the military guards from the pilot engine took Brigg back to see the commanding officer of the express.

Soldiers, garrison soldiers from Singapore, on their way to leave on Penang, fumbled out of their bunks when they heard the shouting up from the track and watched Brigg come up the steps and through the corridors. They stared like schoolboys, fresh and frightened, at Brigg. He walked by them like a veteran.

There were a lot of troops on the train. The Commanding Officer was a major in the Engineers. Brigg told him of the ambush and he became very excited, whirling the chamber of his revolver like a cowboy, and shouting. Three other officers, two of them in pyjamas and the third in vest and pants, came along to the compartment, and three sergeants. One of the sergeants was Driscoll.

Long after, years, when Brigg split it all up again, dissecting each moment and every motive – and he often did – he remembered the train, with the pilot engine ahead, running around the bend and coming upon the place of the ambush.

The broken express was gutted at the front, blazing great flames in the middle, but sheltering in its straggling tail the surviving civilians and soldiers. The bandits had gone. As soon as the arriving train slowed, a hundred soldiers jumped from the boards and ran forward. Driscoll's huge voice alone prevented them mowing down the passengers who bounded towards them with joy, and who they imagined were bandits. None of them had ever seen a bandit.

Tasker and Lantry were sitting, sharing a cigarette, against the lavatory door of the coach. They were black faced and red eyed, their uniforms scorched, and their rifles only now cooling. Their fear and their excitement in the battle was evaporating into a trembling exhaustion so that as one passed the butt of the cigarette to the other they had to synchronise the quivering of their fingers.

Even when Brigg appeared they could not speak to him.

Tasker put his hand up and grasped Brigg by his wrist and pulled him down to squat in front of them. Lantry half waved at him in greeting, as though he were a hundred yards away instead of almost face against face. Involuntarily Brigg stretched out his hands and clasped both of them, at their shoulders, and then around their ears, and hugged them to him.

Tasker croaked: 'Still fancy me then?' and grinned like a sweep. Someone was coming along with beer and the two young soldiers pawed out to get some. Brigg refused his and went off towards the back to look for Sinclair.

Two Medical Corps men were just lifting Sinclair's body from the ditch. Brigg ran, and then stopped and walked the last few steps. He put his arms gently below Sinclair, and one of the others held the boy's lolling head. They rested him on the scorched grass and Brigg knelt by him, looking with tears from the two bullet holes in his trunk up to the face, white, but still amiable. The two orderlies walked away.

On slow nights, all through his life, Brigg re-made it, from the first shot to finding Sinclair like that, building the picture again and again to try and get it right. But it never fitted.

Sinclair had died, so had Waller, always a true

soldier, and Tasker and Lantry had become soldiers at last.

And what had he done? He had *run*. But for help, that was why. 'After all,' he would shout at himself in the dark. 'After all, it was *me* who found the train!'

At first Phillipa thought that Driscoll would not come after all. He had said he would be there when she woke up, but there was nobody. Only the first sun on the glassy swimming pool, and the shadows, and the Chinese servants sweeping and moving about. She stood at the door of her room in her nightdress for a long time and then realised he was not coming after all, and went in.

She had moved to Penang because Driscoll was being posted to the small-arms school at Butterworth, across on the mainland, a ferryboat away. There he was to instruct Malay policemen in the ambidextrous firing of the Colt revolver. He would be home to her every night.

By the afternoon the radio was giving news of the ambush. But she was not worried about him. She went to bed early and re-read his letters.

In the morning she went to the door at the same time, when the sun was early. Against the wood of the door she stood, in her cool nightdress. On the side of the swimming pool were Driscoll's bulky leather cases, and his clothes in a pile.

'Sergeant,' she whispered to herself.

And Driscoll, laughing, was swimming with big strokes from one end of the pool to the other.

13

On the last morning at Panglin they were ready half an hour before the lorry arrived to take them to the docks. Brigg, Tasker, Lantry, Gravy Browning, and Sandy Jacobs were all going home with their time finished. Sinclair would have been with them. Sidney Villiers also, but he had signed on as a Regular soldier because Patsy Foster, who was a Regular, still had another year to do in Singapore.

'But when Patsy has done his year you'll have two years more to do out here,' Lantry pointed out.

'Then *I'll* sign on for another tour of duty,' said Patsy loyally.

'That's three more years.'

'That's right.'

'But Sidney will only have two years to do.'

'Then *I'll* sign on again,' declared Sidney stoutly.

'But there'll always be the same difference,' said Lantry.

'We'll keep signing on,' said Sidney.

'That's love,' shrugged Lantry.

Some of the new conscripts who had arrived on the most recent draft came up to the barrack room and carted away the lockers of those who were leaving, because they were wood, not metal like the new ones, and their demobilisation calendars could be more easily fixed to them. The beds were half-naked to their springs, the mattresses, the sheets and the mosquito nets folded for the last time.

On the floor were the kitbags and the suitcases all stencilled proudly with their ranks and names and numbers and in big white letters: 'Malaya to United Kingdom.' So that when they got home the people on trains and when they carried their kit along the platforms and streets, would know where they had been.

All the others went on to the parade ground. The barrack room echoed like a cave. There was nothing more to do.

They all went to the rail of the balcony, leaning in a strangely forlorn line, looking out on to the barrack square, white with sun and lined with green uniforms. It did not look so bad. The ranks were straight enough and a lot of the crocked and crooked had gone home. Colonel Bromley Pickering had finished his tour of duty a month earlier and had returned to his hilltop near Basingstoke. His replacement was a small officer with a blowing moustache who strode about with his hands caught near his backside and a voice that bristled threats of getting them to look like soldiers yet. No more was there sleeping on guard, and Wellbeloved had been promoted to sergeant-major.

With Driscoll giving his ambidextrous pistol lessons in the far north, and a new, pale breed of conscripts coming off every boat, there was nothing to stop Wellbeloved.

He was taking the morning parade, with the Colonel and the other officers lining the far flank of the square. Wellbeloved's explosive commands flew over the soldiers, and squad by squad they stiffened and strode away in firm formation towards the main gate. These days there was no easy jogging across the bridge to the offices. The parade marched down through the village and up the road on the other side of the ravine to get to their daily desks. Also the ice cream man had been barred from the garrison as a security risk.

The tail of the column swung away and they were left looking out over the flat emptiness of the square, washed completely by the sun now. The palms by the top barrack blocks were without movement in the heat, and the buzzing of the day was loud from the grass and the flowering trees. A garrison general-duties man walked on to the square and began to mend a hole in the net of the hockey goalposts. Two yellow dogs squatted on the concrete and scratched.

Without saying anything, each soldier went away

from the balcony. They heard the lorry arrive outside and took up their kit and their cases and humped them downstairs for loading. Then they climbed aboard. Fenwick, whose ears were completely healed now, and who was going for daily treatment for a dislocated shoulder to the hospital where he was in love with the nurse, waved to them as they went. He should have been with them but he had signed on as a Regular the previous day.

No one said anything as they drove away. Each one looked at the middle balcony of the barrack block, and was silent as the truck took the top road and went down the opposite arm, past the house that was once Phillipa's, and past the industrious offices. Someone was pinning the notice of a football match on the notice-board.

Then the lorry went down the hill.

As it rolled by the Army Laundry Brigg looked up and saw the old man who mangled the clothes, turning his ancient wheel patiently as ever in the sun.

'Fuk Yew!' shouted Brigg exultantly.

The mangler looked up and grinned with a mouthful of gold teeth. They shouted and laughed back and gave him the V-sign.

Laughing still, he returned the insult, extending to them the small stubs of two fingers as the young soldiers went away.